Praise for Jon Talton

The David Mapstone Mysteries
Concrete Desert
"More intelligent and rewarding than most contemporary mysteries."

—*Washington Post*

"Talton looks at his hometown with just the right combination of love, melancholy, and understanding."

—*Rocky Mountain News*

Cactus Heart
"Tightly plotted, smartly paced, and enlivened by dollops of enthusiastic sex...purple-proof. Talton's best yet."

—*Kirkus Reviews*

Camelback Falls
"The story is twisty and crafty, and a large part of the book's charm comes from Mapstone's ambivalent feelings about his Arizona hometown."

—*Chicago Tribune*

Dry Heat
Winner of *Arizona Highways'* 2005 Best Fiction Award

"Taut prose helps tighten the screws, and the winning, sensitive portrayal of the Mapstones—both of them a relief after too many hard-nosed PIs who are all gristle and no brain—lends credibility to the noirish narrative."

—*Publishers Weekly*

Arizona Dreams

"Talton crisply evokes Phoenix's New West ambience and keeps readers guessing with unexpected plot twists."

—*Publishers Weekly*

"As engaging as its predecessors. Talton weaves a couple of primary plot threads with parallel personal narratives, and the resulting synergy produces a more suspenseful tale and a satisfyingly multidimensional protagonist. Make this your Arizona series of choice."

—*Booklist*

South Phoenix Rules

"A haunting noir story vividly rendered by Talton's white-hot prose…original…impressively unyielding."

—*New York Journal of Books*

"Gripping…tough but vulnerable Mapstone will keep you hooked."

—*Kirkus Reviews*

"A profound, heart-rending crime tale."

—*Publishers Weekly*

The Night Detectives

"Tight prose and plotting and a pair of complex and fallible protagonists whose character development continues in a series that just keeps getting better."

—*Booklist*, Starred Review

"Succinct, wry descriptions run alongside the fast-paced plot… The journey is thoroughly satisfying."

—*Publishers Weekly*

Also by Jon Talton

CITY

OF DARK

CORNERS

CITY

OF DARK

CORNERS

JON TALTON

Poisoned Pen

PRESS

Published by Poisoned Pen Press, an imprint of Sourcebooks
P.O. Box 4410, Naperville, Illinois 60567-4410
(630) 961-3900
sourcebooks.com

Library of Congress Cataloging-in-Publication Data

Names: Talton, Jon, author.
Title: City of dark corners / Jon Talton.
Description: Naperville, Illinois : Poisoned Pen Press, [2021]
Identifiers: LCCN 2020036126 | (trade paperback) | (epub)
Subjects: GSAFD: Mystery fiction.
Classification: LCC PS3620.A58 C58 2021 | DDC 813/.6--dc23
LC record available at https://lccn.loc.gov/2020036126

Printed and bound in the United States of America.
SB 10 9 8 7 6 5 4 3 2 1

For Susan

A NOTE ON LANGUAGE

This novel is set in America of nearly a century ago. I have generally used the vernacular of that era. But readers should be aware that this included commonly employed racial epithets that would be highly offensive today. Even polite references to ethnicity or gender in this era would sound hurtful or disrespectful to twenty-first-century ears and sensibilities.

—Jon Talton

One

Night folded in early during the winter.

It was only half past six, the neon of the auto courts and curio shops on Van Buren Street giving way to the emptiness of the Tempe Road, indigo pushing against my headlights as I drove east. Only a few other cars were about.

Cars were fewer in general than they had been only a few years ago and seemed to fit the new times: fewer jobs, fewer businesses, fewer people getting by.

Just after crossing the bridge over the Grand Canal, I parked, shut off the Ford's purring V8, and stepped out. I pulled down my fedora close to my eyes, a habit I kept from my police days on the Hat Squad, stuck a Chesterfield in my mouth, and lit it with the Dunhill lighter brought back from London years ago. I buttoned my suit coat against the desert chill and walked toward the cottonwoods to the south, which loomed like storm clouds on a moonless night.

After walking beyond the trees, I was suddenly inside the camp. It held perhaps fifty denizens. Okies. Workers laid off from the closed copper mines. A miscellany of hoboes. It was outside the city limits and away from the attention of the cops. One of several Hoovervilles that had sprung up during the past three years. Hoover himself seemed ever more isolated and powerless, even though he'd be in office until March. Calvin Coolidge just died. Hoover, the "Great Engineer" who was so popular when he won in '28, might have wished it were him instead. Now he was reviled and rejected.

In the camp, people kept to their clans. The Okies drawn and clad in tattered clothing, the miners with beaten-down faces and muscular bodies in canvas pants, they clustered around campfires and next to cars on their last miles.

Charity wasn't to be much found in Phoenix now; everyone from the county to the churches, Kiwanis and Rotary clubs was tapped out. The Municipal Woodyard to provide help to the "worthy local unemployed" was struggling. Businesses continued to close and lay people off. The lettuce harvest and shipping were complete. Only pink grapefruits were being picked, boxed, and shipped now through March. Any new work in the fields and groves was months away. Maybe some of the travelers would make it to California, the promised land, by road or freight train.

Even with the nighttime cold, the weather was better now than back east. It would be different come summer, and the population of the hobo jungles would plummet.

The campfires glared at gaunt faces. Beyond the next stand of trees, a Southern Pacific freight train trundled past eastbound, shaking the ground, the smoke of its locomotive rising into the night sky. I saw a young man watch it as if it was the fanciest passenger train, only awaiting his presence in the parlor car.

And me? I had a photograph and a hunch and a pocket of dimes. It was my job.

"Hey, buddy, you look too well dressed to be here."

He came out of the shadows and had friends. He was almost my height and had a face that looked like a dry desert river: brown, pocked, and creased by lines that shifted as he spoke.

"Well, here I am," I said, handing him a dime and showing him the photo. He kept staring at me, and I noticed what looked like silver rings on every finger of his right hand. But I knew better and unbuttoned my coat.

"Who dares not stir by day must walk by night."

This came from a rail of a man at his right. He held out his arms as if to fly, then bowed. A thespian.

I ignored him and focused on the big man. His eyes were as barren as an abandoned house. I nodded toward the photograph. "Have you seen this fellow here?"

"We don't truck with cops or cinder dicks." His lips barely moved as the words came out. "You're in the wrong place. Wrong time."

His right hand came up fast. Brass knuckles wrapped around a fist headed my way. But I was faster, slashing my sap against his left temple. Training and experience had taught me how to swing the leather-covered piece of lead just enough to stop a man without killing him. It was all in the wrist.

I was in no mood to have my jaw rearranged or my brains scrambled. Experience had also made me especially wary of brass knucks; some of my former colleagues would have shot him for merely possessing them. His eyes rolled back, and he dropped straight down as if a trapdoor had suddenly opened beneath him. The others backed up.

I assessed them for a few seconds, the black come-along still dangling from my hand. "I'm not a cop or a railroad bull. This face. You seen him?" I showed the pic again and this time the men studied it.

"No need to get sore," the thespian offered. "He's about fifty yards that way, beyond the Okie truck with the piano in the bed. Give him a bottle, and he'll tell you his life story. Claims he was a businessman, if you can believe that."

I slid the sap back inside my belt, gave him a dime, and walked. I took a drag on the cigarette, which had survived the altercation, letting the tobacco settle my nerves. Sure enough, a Model T truck with wooden slats and an antique upright piano was parked beside a campfire. A raggedy family huddled next to it eating beans out of cans. Ten feet beyond, a man sat on his haunches, watching me.

I knelt down. He looked about my age with oily dark hair and a tattered muslin shirt, an army surplus blanket around his shoulders. His eyes took a moment to focus on me.

"Samuel Dorsey?"

"Sam. Who wants to know? I ain't done nothing."

"This is your lucky day, Sam," I said. "Your family paid me to find you."

"You a cop?"

"Private detective."

"Well, gumshoe, I've got nothing for you or for them." He used both hands to rub his face hard, as if he could rearrange his features into a different man. He was several days past a shave. "Lost my job when the plant closed and took to the rails. No greater shame than when a man can't provide for his family."

"Things change. Your wife wired me and said she's come into an inheritance. She wants you to come home."

He eyed me suspiciously, processing my words. Finally: "Her Uncle Chester. He was pushing ninety, and he was a rich man. Never did a thing for us."

"Now he has." I held out a wad of cash.

He reached for the bills, but I pulled them away.

"No, it doesn't work that way. I'll take you to Union Station and put you on the late train to Chicago. Back home."

I'd be damned if he was going to use it on booze, whores, and gambling, ending up back here. Or being robbed by Mister Knuckleduster, once he got over the headache I'd given him.

He looked at me and started sobbing. "How can they want me now? After I walked out?"

"Maybe they love you." I handed him a nail and lit it. He took a deep drag.

He didn't think long. "Okay," he shrugged. "I want to go home. You got a drink?" I shook my head. He hesitated, then stood, leaving the blanket on the ground.

Many people went missing in the Great Depression. Hardly any of it was as grotesque or glamorous as the Lindbergh kidnapping. Men lost their jobs and left their families. Sons and daughters disappeared. Bonus marchers were scattered and lost.

Looking for them was a big part of my business. It often started with a wire from Chicago or Cincinnati or Buffalo, then, if I thought I could help, a photo in the mail. I charged $25 to begin an investigation, another $25 if I found some usable information, and an even hundred if I found the person and could get them home. Money was tight all over, and happy endings were rare.

I walked him out of the camp and back up to the road.

"That's a sweet flivver," he said, indicating my red Ford Deluxe Coupe ragtop.

Opening the passenger door, I let him slide inside to admire it.

Then headlights caught me from behind, and a pickup slid in ahead of me to stop, throwing gravel like a hailstorm. "Stay here." I closed the door.

Half a dozen tough mugs piled out of the truck bed. They were carrying baseball bats and cans of gasoline.

"Gene Hammons." My name came from the driver walking toward me. I could have enjoyed an evening or a lifetime without seeing Kemper Marley.

"It's dark for a ballgame, Kemper," I said. "In fact, I don't even see a baseball."

"You always make me laugh, Hammons," he said, unsmiling.

Kemper Marley was only twenty-six, but he looked older, with thin straight lips and a challenging glare in his eyes. In this light, one could see the old man he would turn into, if he lived that long. He had the posture and personality of a ball-peen hammer but decked out in a new Vic Hanny suit, bolo tie, and a gleaming Stetson, giving the lie to movie Westerns in which good guys wore white hats.

I folded my arms. "What are you going to do when Prohibition is repealed?"

"What Prohibition?" It was the answer I expected. Marley was the leading bootlegger in Phoenix.

His posse shifted restlessly behind him.

I said, "So what's this?"

"We're going to clear out this bunch," he said. "Communists aren't welcome in Phoenix. This country is on the brink."

"And you're going to roll back Bolshevism by burning out a bunch of poor Okies doing the best they can? There's no Reds down there."

He patted me on the shoulder, about as affectionately as a swipe from a mountain lion. "You were always naive, Hammons. Always. Sentimental."

"Sentimental enough to know your thugs should leave those people alone. They've lost their farms and jobs. Mines have closed or are mothballed all over the state. Even the railroads have cut employees."

He spat in the dirt. "I'm not a political man, Hammons, but this country's in big trouble."

"True, but maybe Roosevelt can turn things around."

"Maybe," he said. "But he doesn't take office until March. If it even happens, I'm not sure I trust the man. You know, he's a cripple. I saw him when he campaigned here in '31 with Carl Hayden and Governor Hunt."

"He had polio."

Marley shook his head. "He's a damned cripple, Hammons. People see that handsome head in the newspapers. They hear his voice on the radio. But they don't see how he has the braces on his legs and needs to lean on someone or the podium to stand. I don't trust a man like that."

I stared at him.

He said, "Did you know that only about 20,000 Bolsheviks took over Russia, a country of more than a hundred million people?" His eyes blazed like a blast furnace of paranoia. "It can happen here. Look at Germany. Brownshirts and Reds fighting in the streets. This Hitler will put a stop to that if Hindenburg names him chancellor this month. Mussolini got it right in Italy."

"I don't care for dictators." I lit another cigarette.

"Those are very bad for your health." For a bootlegger, Marley could be quite a prig. He waved the smoke away. "Maybe we need a dictator. I'll tell you this: No Reds are going to take away my property. No Huey Long, either."

"Nobody in the camp down there wants your property," I said.

"Well, I'm not taking chances, and we need that rabble gone. Sends a message. We have to stop these people from bumming their way from town to town. Gas moochers. Our help should only go to local taxpaying citizens."

"It's hard to pay taxes when you've lost your job," I said.

"Look, there's the worthy unemployed and the others."

I couldn't resist blowing smoke in his face. "And you're the one to make that determination?"

He made a face and waved it away. "I agree with President Hoover, no federal relief for individuals. It will sap the American spirit. There's plenty of work for a man who wants to show some gumption. This Depression, they call it, is only a passing incident. That's what President Hoover says, and he's right." He tried to push me aside, but I didn't move. "You want to stop me? Oh, I forgot, you're not a policeman any longer." His thin lips turned up.

I briefly considered shooting the SOB but thought better of it. I'd killed tougher men than him during the war. But I didn't need the distraction tonight.

Reading my thoughts, he said, "I would have fought over there if I'd been old enough. Don't think I wouldn't have."

Marley would have lasted about a day against the Huns. He's the kind of idiot who would have stuck his head above the trench and had it turned to pudding. Or be badly wounded and end up a cripple himself, without Roosevelt's leonine head, fine voice, and first-rate temperament. I let that pleasing thought go and stepped aside.

"Who's that in your car?"

I spoke over my shoulder. "A lost soul I'm putting on the train back to Chicago."

Marley shook his head. "I'll never figure you out, boy. Come by and see me tomorrow. I have some work for you."

I felt bile coming up my throat and walked back to the Ford. By the time I had made the U-turn to head for town, Marley and his gang had disappeared toward the tree line. Me, letting it happen.

Two

At Phoenix's impressive new Union Station, I put Sam Dorsey on the eastbound *Golden State Limited*, escorting him to the Pullman berth I had purchased and slipping a ten and my business card to the porter to keep an eye on him. The train seemed only about half-full, another casualty of our "passing incident." I stepped off as the locomotive signaled highball with two bursts of its whistle and its bell ringing like Sunday morning church.

As the train departed, huffing and clanking, I gave Dorsey a fifty-fifty chance of getting home—he might slip off somewhere along the way. It was the best that could be done. I stopped at the Western Union desk in the depot and sent a telegram to his family, telling them he was on the way and when the train was scheduled to arrive.

This part of the job was much easier than it would have been eight years ago. Until then, Phoenix was only connected to mainline railroads by branches, south to Maricopa on the Southern Pacific and north to Ash Fork on the Santa Fe main. I would have had to ride with him to those junctions. My dad was a conductor on the "Ess-pee." I wished he could have lived to see this.

Now, with the Southern Pacific's main line coming through

Phoenix, we had a wealth of trains from which to choose, even in the Depression: west to Los Angeles, San Diego, and San Francisco, east to New Orleans, Texas, and Chicago. This railroad had so far avoided the fate of so many others, going into bankruptcy.

Then, out of an impulse that was too delinquent to be called noble, I drove back to the camp.

Marley and his men were gone, but a snazzy 1928 Nash Advanced Six Coupe was sitting beside the road, green, two doors and a rumble seat. I looked toward the hobo jungle, which was now visibly on fire. The smell of ashes and gasoline mingled with the pungent scent of the Tovrea Stockyards. The wind had shifted and was coming from the east.

I leaned against the Nash watching low-level lightning strikes from the direction of the camp. In ten minutes, a young woman in tan trousers marched up the grade. Her lush mane of black hair was tied in a ponytail, and she was lugging a Speed Graphic camera along with a smaller, elegant Leica dangling from around her elegant neck, and a heavy bag of other gear on her shoulder. Her large, dark eyes complemented high cheekbones.

"Hello, tall, blond, and handsome. What brings you here?"

I tipped my hat. Victoria Vasquez was a news photographer, a freelancer who sold her images to the Phoenix papers, the Associated Press, and the United Press. The *Republic* and *Gazette* were tiptoeing into using photographs, but the wire services were more likely to send her images nationwide. The caption below her photos carried the name "V. Vasquez" and "Special to the *Republic*" or "Special to the AP."

She also worked for the police and went on some of the most lurid crime scenes. She was the first photographer at the Winnie Ruth Judd murders, and told me how the uniforms had allowed neighbors and reporters inside, contaminating the integrity of the crime scene, before I arrived as the first detective.

"What happened down there, Eugene?" she said. "It looks like a marauding army came through."

"Kemper Marley and his goons, running out the commies, or so he said."

"Oh, bullshit." She took the nail I offered and I lit us both.

She exhaled. "That little punk thinks he's the king of Phoenix."

"Maybe he is," I said, "or he will be. All the land he's buying, plus the liquor business. It gives him a lot of cash to grease the politicians and the cops."

"Speaking of liquor." I pulled out my hip flask, and she took a sip. I toasted her and let the white stuff burn my throat and insides. No way was I going to give Sam Dorsey a toot of this.

She repositioned my hat to a jaunty angle and put a warm hand on my cheek. "You should show off those sad blue eyes, Eugene."

"If you say so." Only my mother and Victoria had ever used my full name.

She smiled. "Have to run. Midnight deadline for the wire services, chance to make the West Coast papers. Girl's got to make a living."

After the Nash swung around on the dark highway and headed west, I walked down toward the fire.

Considering the baseball bats, I was surprised not to find dead or injured bodies. Of course, the gorillas might have taken them in the truck to drop them off in the desert. Marley's pull with the cops might not extend to overlooking cold-blooded murder here, out in the open.

The remains of the camp were without a human soul. Blood pooled in several spots on the ground as if a biblical plague had come through. A left-behind dog wandered, a frightened look in its eyes, barking and whimpering. Most of the cars were gone.

But two were ablaze, along with piles of belongings and several busted-up shanties. Clothes, books, furniture, precious belongings turned to kindling. Sparks flew in the manure-perfumed wind. The piano had made it out, as far as I could tell.

No, the flames shifted and I saw it smashed against a cottonwood, its keys hanging askew as if a giant had been slugged in the mouth.

The only touch missing was salting the earth.

Through the dry air, the vault of the Milky Way looked down on us in judgment.

Then the toe of my shoe tapped against something substantial. Thanks to the blaze, it glimmered in the dirt. Bending down, I picked up a pocket watch. It had a gold case and white face with large numbers. I compared it with my wristwatch and it was keeping perfect time. I slipped it in my pocket and walked back to the Tempe Road.

———

The next morning, after breakfast at the Saratoga Restaurant at Washington and Central, I walked into Isaac Rosenzweig & Sons jewelry store on north First Avenue. Sometimes I acted as a guard for diamond couriers, escorting them from the train station to the store and back. Rosenzweig had also been good enough to allow me to place a small stack of my business cards on the counter after I started my PI business. The old man wasn't there, but his son, Harry, was behind the counter talking to Barry Goldwater. They both greeted me.

"How's the shamus business, Gene?" Barry was strikingly good looking with a shock of wavy dark hair, a healthy tan, and an easy grin. He wore a scraggly full beard that nearly obscured his blue bow tie.

"Probably about as good as the department-store business. What's that wild animal attached to your face?"

Barry's eyes twinkled and even standing still he radiated vitality like a dynamo waiting to be unleashed. It was easy to see why so many women fell for him.

"He's been up in the High Country camping and taking photos," Harry said. "And he's on his way to Otis Kenilworth's shop to get it shaved off, right Barry?"

Goldwater shrugged. "I rather like it. Peggy likes it. But I suppose so."

Otis Kenilworth's real name was William Jones, and he had opened his Kenilworth Barbershop in the Gold Spot Market Center at Third Avenue and Roosevelt Street in 1925. I didn't claim to know why he took the new name, but he was one of the few Negro business owners serving a white clientele and gave the best haircuts and shaves in town.

Barry said, "I'm trying to settle into my duties. My dad's been gone for three years now, so the family is pushing me to take over managing the store. Can't say I love that. It's not in my blood like it was for my dad and grandfather."

"Big Mike" Goldwater, his grandfather, was a legend. He emigrated from the Polish part of the Russian Empire, and after time in Paris, London, and California, made his way to Arizona Territory. Stories say he ran a bordello and saloon in California before turning to dry goods. It's also true he took an Apache arrow driving his wagon through an ambush. Big Mike hit better times with a store in Prescott—he served as mayor there, too—and a Phoenix location opened for good in 1896. His son Baron, Barry's father, trained at Philadelphia's famous Wanamaker's Department Store.

Barry turned and scrutinized my suit. "That's wearing out, Gene. Time for you to come over and buy a new one. Times are tough, but maybe I could barter, give you work chasing shoplifters."

Harry Rosenzweig tut-tutted and came around the counter.

"Watch and learn, my friend." He faced me, half a head shorter, with a high forehead and a big smile. It said I was the most important person in his world, I was iron filings and he was the magnet. "Mr. Hammons, it's so good to see you again. I love this navy-blue suit." He straightened the fabric on my shoulders with expert hands and gently tugged the coat down. "We have a sale at Goldwater's on a gray ensemble that would perfectly complement it. A new fedora would top it off. You'll be togged to the bricks! Remember our motto, 'The best, always.' Come by this afternoon, and I'll personally show you the variety we have."

"I'd love to," I said, playing along.

"You see?" He turned to Barry. "We'll make a merchant prince out of you yet!"

Goldwater shook his head, unconvinced.

Rosenzweig went back around the counter. "So, what can I do for you, Gene? Nice Longines Flagship Heritage wristwatch on special."

"The detective business isn't that good." I gently set the pocket watch I'd found in the dirt last night on the glass of the counter.

"Oh, my friend, please don't tell me you need to sell your father's watch."

I shook my head. I still had Pop's railroad watch, which, unlike this one, had a hunter case which snapped over the face and a gold chain.

"No, I found it."

"Well, let's have a look." He placed it on a felt-covered tray and brought a loupe to his right eye.

"Oh, my goodness." And that was all he said for a few minutes. He took out a cloth, gave it a good polishing, and examined it further. Then: "It's a Hamilton with a Ferguson dial. Double-sunk special railroad variety. The outer Arabic numbers, five to sixty, are enameled black, and the inner numbers, one to twelve in red. Spade pointer hands. Inner hand for seconds. Fancy damaskeening pattern."

He turned it over and, pulling out some tools, slipped off the back. He continued his inventory of the inside works. Sapphire pellets, compensated balance, lever-set, Breguet hairspring, gold screw-down jewel settings, 21 jewel whiplash micrometer regulator, stem-wind lever set... It was all Greek to me, but his tone was that of a dazzled Howard Carter making an inventory of King Tut's tomb.

Barry slipped on his glasses and leaned in until Rosenzweig swatted him away. Goldwater was more to the point. "It's beautiful."

Slipping off the loupe, Harry said, "This is a very rare watch, Gene. I've only seen two like it. Where did you get it?"

When I told them, both men let out sighs. "What are we going to do about Kemper?" Barry said to nobody in particular. When nothing more was said, my mind wandered badly.

In late May of 1918, in the Third Battle of the Aisne, we first encountered German Stosstruppen—stormtroopers employing revolutionary tactics. *Hutier* infiltration tactics. We didn't realize they were among us until it was too late, or nearly so. It was an ugly jolt, not least for us inexperienced Yanks. Our front didn't break, but it was a near-run thing, a bloody education.

"Are you with us, Hammons?"

I snapped to. "Sure, I had a long night."

But behind my lie was uneasiness. I didn't like surprises. I wondered anew about the devil's spell of young Marley over this town, even over these two young men from respectable pioneer families, members of the chamber of commerce, and in the case of Harry at least, a budding politico. I felt guilty about suspecting my friends, but there it was.

Rosenzweig went back to the watch: "It's hard to see how a man would let it go, even in times like these. But I might be able to give you a few clues about the owner."

Three

The next night, Wednesday, I went to choir practice at Central Methodist Church. I sing tenor, although I'm actually a baritone with a wide range. But the chancel choir is always short of tenors. We practiced Isaac Watts's "I Sing the Mighty Power of God" for this Sunday's anthem. We had sung it before, of course, but not every week could offer up a complex new choral work. I loved it nonetheless, the soaring and confident harmonies, the sentiment of the lyrics.

> *I sing the goodness of the Lord,*
> *Who filled the earth with food,*
> *Who formed the creatures through the Word,*
> *And then pronounced them good.*

I set aside reconciling this with the injustice and violence I had witnessed two nights before. The music made me happy, kept me sane. Not many things moved my heart now, but the music still did. On Sunday, we would be backed by the new pipe organ and facing several hundred worshippers. Tonight, we made do with the Steinway grand piano in the choir room.

As we concluded the last run-through, I heard clapping off to the side and saw my brother. All the comfort and inspiration drained out of me.

Don Hammons was tall and broad-shouldered like me, but he had Mother's dark-brown hair and eyes. It was like looking at myself through a distorted mirror. A trench coat was draped over his arm as he brought his hands together. But even his applause sounded cynical. This didn't stop my fellow choir members, especially the women, from surrounding him. Of the two Hammons brothers, Don was definitely the charmer. And the dresser: a soft cream glen-plaid cashmere jacket, tangerine patterned necktie, coral pocket square with a leaf pattern, dark woolen trousers, and wingtip oxford shoes in stone and dark tan.

We walked outside in silence and sat on the steps of the imposing new church building. The nearby Hotel Westward Ho, the tallest building between El Paso and Los Angeles, looked about half full. Like the Hotel San Carlos, Luhrs Tower, and other dramatic projects—the Professional, Title and Trust, Security, and City-County buildings—it was one of the gifts of the Roaring Twenties that gave Phoenix a skyline. We were hardly New York City or any of the big cities I came through on my way to and from the war. But it swept away the remnants of Phoenix as a frontier town. The central school we attended was demolished. The shady Town Ditch where we swam as kids in summertime was paved over.

Those boom years now seemed like a lifetime away, only the elegant art deco structures and inviting neon remaining. The globes of the streetlights resembled collections of full moons orbiting hidden planets. A light rain had fallen, and the pavement reflected the luminescence. The unique pleasing smell of wet desert was in the air.

"Remember when we went to church in the little brick building down at Monroe?" Don said. "Now it's gone, and they're talking about merging our M.E. South with the northern church. Our Confederate forebears wouldn't be pleased."

He pulled out a Lucky Strike and offered me one. He lit us both.

"I can't believe you're still singing there," he mused. "You have a beautiful voice and all, but how could you believe in God after all we saw in Europe, and then the flu? Millions and millions dead. What kind of God would let that happen? No God I'd want anything to do with."

I tried to conceal my sigh. "Humans caused the war, not God, who gave us free will. And the good guys won the war." I was instantly sorry I had taken his bait.

"You think so?" he said. "The Versailles Treaty that forced the Germans to accept total responsibility for starting the Great War? You can count on this, little brother, it only set up a twenty-year armistice, and another war will come. My boys could be fighting the Germans again. Wait and see. I sure as hell hope not. We should have stayed neutral in the big one, and we should stay neutral next time. These are Europe's quarrels. Let them sort it out. How did Wilson's grand plans as savior of the world turn out? Badly. What an arrogant asshole."

He said all this in a lazy Western drawl that dampened the anger behind the words. It helped Don get away with plenty of abuse. His voice was part of his charisma, and a dangerous weapon when he was a detective interrogating a suspect.

"How's Mary?"

He let out a long plume of blue smoke. "Bigger bitch than ever. Bad marriage getting worse."

"She's a nice woman, and things might get better if you tried. You have two young sons to think about, Don. If you didn't go to Chinatown for the dream wax..."

Don smiled. "Clean Gene, Clean Gene, Clean Gene Hammons," he singsonged. "Not very Christian of you to be so judgmental."

"I care about you."

"Spare me. You just have different vices. Anyway, I'm not using opium anymore."

I raised an eyebrow.

He broke a wide smile. "Cocaine is better." He held up a hand. "Gene, I need it because I hurt, and use it only occasionally, you bastard. I was wounded, shrapnel's still inside me. I'm no hophead. And, by the way, I'm still on the police force, while you're trying to make ends meet as a peeper, sneaking around to catch cheating husbands. And in the middle of the Great Depression. What a shit job, Mr. Perfect."

I didn't take those kinds of cases. But I said, "Then I'm not so perfect, am I?"

But he wouldn't let up. "Going to church doesn't give you a right to judge me, Clean Gene."

"I'm not judging you." But I was starting to get sore.

He tossed the nail away and watched it roll like a sparkler across the wet sidewalk. "I'll never figure you out. You were the best detective we had." That was an astonishing admission by my brother.

He continued: "You rose quick and caught the University Park Strangler. Hell, you could have become chief someday. McGrath loved you..." That would be chief of detectives John J. McGrath, officially a captain. "But you fell in love with Winnie Ruth Judd when you and the sheriff brought her back from Los Angeles. You should have stuck with Amelia Earhart."

"I didn't fall in love with her. The brass shoved a shoddy conclusion on us and withheld evidence."

"So pure, Clean Gene. You pulled the pin to save your precious integrity. You think she was innocent?"

"The evidence was consistent with her claim of self-defense. And there's no way she had the strength to dismember two women, put them in trunks, and take them to the train station. She's five-five and a hundred-ten pounds. 'Happy Jack' Halloran helped her. You know that. But the evidence that would have implicated him was never introduced."

"Just an innocent woman with those gorgeous blue eyes and auburn hair."

"I don't know if she was innocent. But the evidence— remember evidence, Don?—the evidence was not consistent with premeditated murder or her acting alone. My best guess is that she's a little crazy, she was pressured into a hasty confession, and Halloran has powerful friends."

"He was indicted. His trial is coming up."

"You know the fix is in."

"And your testimony wasn't introduced in Ruth's trial. Poor Clean Gene."

I felt my face flush. "I wasn't allowed to testify, Dirty Don, even though I was the first detective on the scene. And I didn't pull the pin. I was laid off, remember? Budget cuts, they said. Four patrolmen and one detective were cut loose."

He smiled, unflappable. "You wouldn't have been the one detective if you'd been willing to go along. McGrath really tried to save you."

A couple walked by, arm in arm. After they passed, Don said, "You were always stubborn. The first rule of life is to get along you have to go along."

"Spare me the philosophy."

Of course, he wouldn't.

"All you had to do was keep your head down, do the job your bosses asked you to do, and you'd still be on the Hat Squad," Don said. "Now you're out of a steady job making a hundred-ten dollars a month, and they're going to hang her. Wonder if Ruth will end up doing an Eva Dugan?"

Eva Dugan, a housekeeper, was convicted in Pinal County for murdering her employer and apparent pimp. The whole thing was sordid as Caligula's Rome without the grand buildings. Don and I were sent by the Phoenix Police as witnesses to the execution, even though the crime occurred in an adjacent county.

Don chuckled. "I'll never forget when that long drop decapitated her. Eva's head rolled right up to our feet. Five of the witnesses fainted. Same thing is coming for your girlfriend. Pop goes the head!"

"She's not my girlfriend!"

Don was Dr. Jekyll with most people. He was Mr. Hyde with me, always trying to goad me or worse. I should have been used to it, but I was seething, not least because after talking to him I couldn't walk home with Isaac Watts in my ears.

I stood to leave.

"Hang on there, Clean Gene. We've got work to do."

I reared on him. "Since when is there a 'we'?"

"There's cold meat down by the railroad tracks, and I need your assistance."

"Are you paying? Because, as you keep reminding me, I don't carry a buzzer anymore."

He stood and stretched. "Fucker." He dug a sawbuck from his wallet and handed it over.

———

We drove south in his 1930 black Chevy sedan, then turned east on Van Buren Street, passing gas stations and on the north side, the stately new buildings of Phoenix Union High School.

"Are we collecting tonight?"

Don laughed. "The protection money from those whore-houses and gambling dens prop up the City of Phoenix treasury, especially at a time like this. You know that."

"And the detectives who collect and protect them get a piece of the action, too."

"Don't act like you never played. Anyway, I'm not handling much vice anymore. A convenient opening came up to take the lead in homicide cases. Thanks, little brother." He clapped me on the leg, then stared straight ahead as if he was alone in the car. I was happy to let the silence accompany us.

At Sixteenth Street, he turned south past Eastlake Park until we were at the mouth of the Southern Pacific railroad yard, then he wheeled east again along a dirt road north of the tracks. A switch engine huffed past us, the headlight offering momentary artificial daylight for what lay ahead. I dug my fingers into the seat as the locomotive came close.

Two of the new Phoenix Police radio-equipped cars were parked beside the railroad, their spotlights aimed at the ground. About twenty feet north, I could see the blood seeping through a white sheet that looked like a madman's abstract art.

"What the hell?"

"I'm paying for your consultation."

Stepping out, I pulled my fedora to eye level, not the jaunty look Victoria preferred. I lit another cigarette and took a deep pull. The last thing I wanted was to see any of my former colleagues, to have them see me. My job loss humiliated me, but I could put on a mask, never let them see. We walked past a police ambulance along the cinder-strewn dirt toward the scene. I took one more drag and stomped out the nail.

As we got closer, I saw the white sheet had siblings: three more laid separately a few feet away in geometric precision.

It started to sprinkle again, and I slid on my own trench coat, tightened my tie, armoring up. Just in time. "What the hell is he doing here?" I heard a whisper from a uniformed sergeant meant to be heard and ignored it.

"Railroad bull found this earlier tonight," Don said. "Unfortunately, it's in the city limits. Barely."

The uniforms had tramped around so much that any chance of identifying suspect footprints in the moist soil was lost. Typical. I looked at Don and he nodded. Back in the saddle again.

Lifting the first sheet, I found the torso of a woman. The only reason I knew this was that she was busty and wearing a smart pink suit. Besides decapitation, her arms had been removed halfway between the elbow and shoulder. Her legs had been taken off in a similar fashion. Without a ruler, I guessed the spot was five inches below the pelvis. That would have meant cutting into the femoral artery, a real bleeder. But the suit was only lightly stained.

The limbs were nearby, as if an angry child had disassembled a doll.

Another sheet concealed two legs in nylons and pink pumps. The arms were beneath yet another sheet; her hands were delicate, her fingers lacking any rings, including a wedding ring. I felt like a stagehand ringing up the act curtains on a ghastly play. Finally, another sheet was raised in a dome shape. Don shone his flashlight on the head that had belonged to a woman in her twenties, with blond bobbed hair, bright lipstick, and blue eyes frozen open. The same was true of her mouth, caught in a scream when she was cut apart. Alive, she would have been a looker. I let the sheet drop and stood.

"The bull said she fell from a train. The westbound *Sunset Limited* came through about six, running late."

I rolled my head, trying to unstiffen my neck and shoulders.

"That's all wrong," I said. "The body parts are a good twenty feet from the tracks. And train fatalities typically lose an arm or leg or get mangled. If it's an amputation, the cut is usually clean from the flanges of the train-car wheels. This woman was completely dismembered. But it was done so purposefully. Check the marks. Her head, arms, and legs were hacked off. Like with an axe or a saw. No defensive wounds on her hands or arms. And it looks like she was arranged."

Maybe it was my imagination, but Don seemed to suppress a shiver.

"Give me your flashlight."

He handed it over, and I walked up to the ballasted roadbed where two sets of tracks ran east-to-west; a quarter mile to my right, they opened into the mouth of the railroad yard. No trains were coming, so I walked fifty feet in each direction, Don trailing behind me.

"Impressions?" he asked.

"No blood on the rails or ties, no body parts up here," I said. "She definitely didn't fall or jump from a train—I've seen what that looks like. She was killed somewhere else and brought here. The dismemberment would have left a lot of blood, more than what's down there." I nodded toward the crime scene.

"Maybe." He retrieved his light and we walked back.

"No maybe," I said. "It's a homicide. Maybe Ruth Judd broke out of Florence and did it."

He snorted.

"What about a purse, or was that on the train?"

Don pointed the light to the base of a mesquite ten feet to the north. The handbag was small and pink, with a gold border on the rounded top. "We found it neatly propped against that tree. Uniforms waited for me to open it. No identification. Two tubes of lipstick, compact, handkerchief, rosary, Sheaffer's fountain pen.

Fifty dollars neatly folded, two twenties, two fives. Fifty cents in coins. And this..."

He held up a piece of paper. It was one of my business cards. Now it was my turn to suppress a shiver.

He put a hand on my chest. "Do you know this woman?"

"No," I said. "I have no idea how she got my card."

"Take this."

I hesitated.

"That's evidence, Don."

"You want to end up as a suspect and in jail?"

I shook my head, held the card by the edges, and let it fall into my pocket.

I said, "This was a very personal killing."

"Aren't they all?"

"No. Sometimes people murder for money and don't know the victim. But this girl's purse is full of cash. Sometimes people murder on the spur of the moment. But our guy planned this with great care. He killed and cut her up somewhere else. Then he brought her here, displayed her in new clothes, and moved her just inside the city limits. Then he placed my business card in her purse. He's sending a message."

"You're a smart one," Don said.

Then a fist suddenly connected to my stomach. It wasn't a hard punch, and from our many fights, I knew he could hit much harder. He leaned in and whispered. "Bend over like you feel it."

"Ugh...you bastard!" Under my breath, I told him to get Victoria Vasquez out here to get good photographs of the scene, including close-ups, with copies for me. He nodded, then he pushed me away.

"Get the hell out of here, Gene," he yelled. "You're not a cop anymore. Quit tagging after me."

The others watched in amusement as I pretended to stagger

off. Out of sight, my gait turned normal and took me north to Washington Street, where I caught the trolley back to town. I felt punched in the gut all right, but not by my brother's fist.

———

The rain had stopped by the time I reached my second-story apartment in a newer building called La Paloma. It faced the slender, block-long park encased by one lane in each direction of Portland Street between Central and Third avenues.

I hung my trench coat on the coat hanger just inside the door to dry, but not before carefully removing the business card Don had given me and slipping it into an envelope. Without my access to the police lab, I didn't know how I would check it for fingerprints. But that was a problem for tomorrow.

I loosened my tie and poured a glass of fine Canadian whiskey. It was part of the stash from my days with the cops—when we would confiscate liquor per the Volstead Act. We were supposed to pour it down the sewer, and we did sometimes, with newspaper photographers shooting. But we always kept a few bottles of the best stuff for ourselves.

So much for Clean Gene.

Prohibition. It was one of the dumbest things ever tried in the United States. Both Don and I had been part of the occupation troops in the Rhineland after the war, then had spent time in Paris and London deciding what to do with our lives when we received word that both Mother and Father had died in the influenza pandemic.

Neither of us was going to take up the miserable work of farming or work for the railroad. *How ya going to keep them down on the farm, after they've seen Paree!* But after being discharged, we drifted back to Phoenix and became police officers.

Honestly, it was hard to tell hooch was against the law here, even though the state had outlawed it in 1915. The stuff was abundant in a Southwestern town far from the Treasury Department. People such as Kemper Marley kept every place from the speakeasies to the best hotels well supplied. Al Capone built a bloody empire back in Chicago thanks to appetites that couldn't be outlawed. I wouldn't be sorry to see Prohibition repealed.

Pouring a second glass, I was well beyond humming any hymns, I put a Bennie Moten band record on my RCA Victor phonograph and fell into the sofa. Moten had a hot, young pianist named Basie who put stomp into the Kansas City Stomp style.

All I lacked was a dance partner and some energy.

This was not supposed to be my job anymore, but I was in the middle of a murder again and not protected by a badge. Don giving me the business card didn't sit well, but he was right. If anyone else knew it was in the victim's purse, I would be the prime suspect.

The memory of the woman's severed head lingered through the second pour. Alive, she would have turned heads, with that Norma Shearer face and Marlene Dietrich fair hair. Hollywood stars liked to come to Phoenix in winter, stay at the San Carlos or even at the rentals on my street or one block north on the Moreland parkway. I saw Clark Gable and Carole Lombard a couple of times.

Three times I worked as a bodyguard for George Raft. It wasn't what it seemed. George could take care of himself, and sober he was a good guy, tipped well, paid me generously. But he was a brawler, and my job was to keep him out of trouble. Maybe the stars knew the identity of my dismembered problem.

The phonograph was scratching and otherwise silent when a knock at the door startled me awake.

Victoria stepped in, holding a manila envelope.

"I figured you'd want this sooner than later." She brought her lips up to mine, her coat fell to the floor, I met her kiss and pulled her inside, tossing the envelope of photographs on a table. They could wait.

I was glad once again that the landlord didn't live in the building.

Four

The new office buildings were struggling to find tenants. Several building and loan institutions had failed, and even the biggest banks were teetering. The good news was that rents were low; the bad news was that nobody had much money.

When I set up my private detective agency, I got a great deal on the top floor of the three-story Monihon Building at First Avenue and Washington. This, a pre-statehood structure with a mansard roof, sat in the same block as Newberry's, Kress, and J.C. Penney. Neon signs proclaimed Boehmer Drug Store and Funk Jewelry ("Confidential Credit") on the first floor and Dr. Mapstone's dental practice on the second. It lacked the art deco grandeur of the new Luhrs Tower with its uniformed elevator operators, but I could afford it.

The rain was gone and the sun bright. The sky was cobalt blue and the mountains, miles away, looked as if you could reach out and touch them. Awnings were down in the fronts of the buildings to shade the stream of pedestrians while cars jockeyed for parking spaces and streetcars clanged past. A couple of sidewalk elevators by stores were open and workers loading merchandise for the trip into the basement. My shoes stepped over the heavy glass embedded in the sidewalk to bring light into those underground spaces.

Even in the twenties, you'd still see horse-drawn wagons, but they were gone from downtown now. The stream of humanity was a mixture of businessmen, ladies shopping, and workmen from the produce sheds and warehouses to the south. It was almost as if a Depression wasn't happening.

On Washington, the main commercial drag of Phoenix, the signs were more subtle: The man against the wall with "Brother, can you spare a dime" written on a scrap of paper, desperate faces and furtive eyes darting from business to business like dying flies, seeking jobs that weren't there. Uniformed cops moved along hoboes who had wandered up from the railroad tracks. The sound of Rudy Vallee singing "As Time Goes By" wafted out a doorway. Walk around downtown and you'd see permanently closed doors from the places that had been forced out of business, a third of the city's banks and thrifts closed, much of the music gone.

After paying for an *Arizona Republic* at the newsstand out front, I took the stairs to the third floor.

I shared a secretary with an accountant in the adjoining office. Gladys Johnson had a strained face that reminded me of my child-hating fourth-grade teacher. She oddly favored the flapper clothes and hairstyle that were already anachronisms in this more austere decade. Presiding over the outer office, she wore an out-of-fashion cloche hat and a sequined dress. It was like having a silent movie or paper shirt collar as my reluctant assistant.

She was machine-gunning the Remington typewriter when I came in, but looked up and nodded toward my door, where "Gene Hammons, Private Investigator" was etched in the frosted glass.

"You have a client waiting."

She said it as if such a thing never happened.

I paused to open the newspaper. All caps across the top of the front page: FIVE ESCAPE COUNTY JAIL. So much for the lockup on the top floor of the nearly new county courthouse. The prisoners walked out at five in the afternoon, blending with the crowd.

Otherwise, it looked like the Japs and Russians might go to war. The City Commission was in turmoil again. Will Rogers had a quick unfunny take about banks and Japan taking more of China. Down at Fort Huachuca, the Army was investigating whether voodoo caused a colored private to kill two captains and their wives. On page four, I scanned "Little Stories of Phoenix Daily Life" in search of potential clients, but none revealed themselves.

Quickly paging through, I finally found a three-paragraph story deep inside, bottom of the page: "Woman killed in fall from train." I read it slowly, saw nothing remarkable, and stuck the paper under my arm.

Stepping inside my office and tossing my fedora on the coat-rack, I saw Kemper Marley seated in one of the secondhand chairs facing my secondhand desk. He turned his unsmiling face to me.

"You're late."

"I didn't know we had an appointment."

"I told you to come see me."

I eased myself into my swivel chair.

Marley was wearing a Western shirt, dusty jeans, and cowboy boots, as if he had been riding the range rather than supervising a beat-down in the hobo jungle. His legs were spread wide beneath the Stetson on his lap.

He regarded me with coffee-colored marsupial eyes. "I want you to find some information on a man named Gus Greenbaum."

"Can't say I've heard the name."

"You never heard the name? I thought you'd been a cop."

When I didn't respond, he continued. "Well, the sign says private investigator. I assume you can investigate and keep it private."

I asked him why I would want to do that.

He smirked. "When Prohibition is repealed, I'm going to get the first state license to distribute liquor. And it will be the best brands, thanks to Sam Bronfman. Seagram, you know."

"But without Al Capone." I smirked, too.

"Times change," Marley said. "My distributorship will be totally legal. More than three hundred bars have already applied for liquor licenses since the state repealed its law last year, and I'll be supplying them when the stupid Eighteenth Amendment is gone this year."

"And why would the State of Arizona grant you this? You're just a kid."

He struggled to hide his irritation. "Because important people patronize the disorderly house I own on the east side. And they wouldn't want their wives to know about it, especially about the pretty colored girls they consort with. I have photographs."

He let out a high-pitched laugh like a girl's, a sound I never wanted to hear coming from him again.

"I see."

"And it will be in your interest to have me as a friend and client."

I didn't think Marley had any more friends than a Gila monster. The difference was that the big lizard was prettier and shy. Having him for a client seemed freighted with corruption and complications. When I said nothing, he pulled a wad from his jeans pocket and peeled off five C notes, slapping them on my blotter. I hated to admit it, but now he was talking more persuasively.

"Consider it a retainer."

My considerations were these: Marley was a punk, a thug, maybe a killer. I saw that in action when his bully boys took baseball bats and gasoline to the Okies. On the other hand, I didn't need him as an enemy, especially not with a dismembered blonde carrying my business card hanging over me. What if one of the clients of Marley's "disorderly house," as he called it, was the county prosecutor? I might end up hanging like Ruth Judd. That could disorder my life in a hurry.

Also, clients were sparse now that I had the wire that Samuel Dorsey had reached Chicago. I still needed to pay seven bucks a week for my share of Gladys's resentful time, fifteen a month for the office, another twenty for rent at my apartment, plus some walking-around money for haircuts and shaves, shoeshines and newspapers, and taking Victoria dancing.

The bills were new and crisp. Benjamin Franklin regarded me distantly, offering no wisdom. I felt like Eve in the Garden of Eden with the snake in cowboy boots.

"I have faith in you, Hammons," the snake said.

"That makes me feel peachy."

He dug in his pocket and produced a coin, slapping it on the desk. "Just so you know I'm serious in these hard times."

It was a shiny twenty-dollar gold piece, Lady Liberty beckoning me. I was always a sucker for a woman in a robe.

Pulling out a pad and pencil, I wrote "Gus Greenbaum" at the top and underlined it. In fact, I'd heard the name when I was a cop, not much beyond that. I asked him to tell me more.

Marley said, "Greenbaum runs a gambling wire for the Chicago Outfit that serves the entire Southwest."

"I thought you were tight with the Outfit thanks to Capone and the liquor business."

"Smart guy," Marley said, his lips barely moving. "That's the point. Times change, and I want a piece of Greenbaum's action."

"So, ask your friends in Chicago."

He broke his glare and looked into his lap, suddenly appearing younger.

I said, "They refused?"

"Looks that way." When he looked up again his face was hard again, full of pride. "That's why I need some leverage to get my way."

When I didn't respond, he continued.

"That where you come in, Hammons. This is my town!" He paused. "This is our town, I mean. Phoenix had forty-eight thousand people in the 1930 Census, a hundred fifty-one thousand in the county. That's more than double where we stood in 1920. Way past Tucson now. We've got thousands of acres under cultivation—we help feed the country. This city is going places, provided Roosevelt can save the country as his supporters believe. We've been losing population in the Depression, but that's not going to last. Someday this will be a metropolis!"

I didn't believe it. "I rather like it as it is."

"Of course, you do. But change is inevitable and better to be on the right side of it. That's why I don't want some hood from Chicago to control our future."

I didn't want a local hood, either. Nor did I have anything against Chicago. Dwight Heard was from Chicago, although born in Massachusetts, and he had been one of our leading citizens. His death in 1929 was a calamity, seeming to presage the hard times to come. The Wrigleys were building a mansion on a knoll north of town. Everybody likes chewing gum.

"So, will you help me, Hammons? I can open doors for you."

Suppressing a sigh, I pulled over the currency and wrote Marley a receipt.

"Plus expenses," I said. "Of course, you'll get a refund if I can't get decent information. And this is a one-off. Don't expect me to swing a baseball bat for you."

"Of course not. You're a gentleman. You have ethics. I respect that."

I doubted that he did.

"You ever been hit with a horsewhip, Hammons?"

"Can't say that I have."

"My father used one on me, you know. Sometimes he'd give me a beating in the morning, say it was for what I was going to do, not what I did."

"He sounds deranged."

"Not at all." Marley drew himself up, the son of the father. "He was a fine man. Made me tough. Gave me what I needed in this world."

"If you say so."

We sat for another half an hour, Marley philosophizing about his visions for Phoenix as I tried to steer the conversation back to Gus Greenbaum. I was desperate for a cigarette. When he was gone, I lit up but also wanted to take a shower. Instead, I told Gladys that I didn't want to be disturbed and went back inside my office. I locked Marley's money in the safe I had inherited from the previous tenant—banks weren't trustworthy now.

I called a former colleague, Detective Turk Muldoon, and asked him about Gus Greenbaum.

"Gustave, his given name," Muldoon said. "He came up under the wing of Meyer Lansky in New York, then he started working for the Chicago Outfit. Showed up here in '28 running a wire news service."

"Why am I only now learning about this?"

Turk, given name Liam, immigrated from Ireland and still spoke with a brogue.

"You were the hotshot homicide dick, lad," he said. "You had better things to do than us lowly vice cops. Anyway, he's kept his nose clean in the city. Running the news service isn't illegal. The other thing is, Greenbaum has made friends with some respectable locals."

"So, he's turned over a new leaf?"

"I seriously doubt that. He spreads money around to the city commissioners, so there's no incentive for us to give him a good look. Why are you asking?"

"I have a client who's asking."

"Well, tread carefully, lad. He has friends, and he has the Outfit connections. I'd hate to find you with a bullet in the brain."

I thanked him for that pleasant thought and rang off.

Then I lit another Chesterfield and spread out the murder photos that Victoria had taken.

She said it was the worst she'd ever seen, and Victoria had seen plenty. In addition to her work taking news photos, quinceañeras, weddings, and portraits, the police department paid her to shoot crime scenes. That was her biggest source of income.

She was at the murder house where Winnie Ruth Judd allegedly single-handedly killed Anne LeRoy and Sammy Samuelson. But it was only bloody—the bodies were gone, to be unpacked from trunks in Los Angeles. The photos before me now showed a dead woman in pieces, no trunks. They were among the worst I had seen, too—at least since the war—and my old job had shown me plenty of ways that humans can put an end to each other.

I pulled out the magnifying glass from my middle drawer and scrutinized the images.

The ones of the head showed that disfiguring scream mouth. No bruises were visible on the neck, which would indicate strangulation. But it was hard to tell, given the severed tissue. Her eyes weren't bloodshot, a sign she had been suffocated with a pillow or a hand. The alternative was chilling: the girl had been tied down, gagged, and cut apart. Maybe he started with an arm or a leg, letting her bleed out while he watched.

I spread out other photos. Her limbs didn't show signs of a tourniquet, which might indicate this path, where the killer amputated a limb but controlled the blood flow to keep her alive—and awake.

That left the possibility that the victim was restrained and killed by beheading. The sharp instrument had done the killing as she watched the preparations, then felt the first incision until the loss of blood caused her to pass out and die. The result was too rough to be a surgical bone saw or even a machete. Those left clean marks. I'd investigated a case of a hophead doctor who killed his wife in a fight, then used a bone saw to decapitate her, claiming some fiend had broken into their home. He might have gotten away with it if we hadn't found the saw. Another time, a bar fight in the Deuce saw one participant pull a machete and whack the arm off his antagonist. Again, nice clean cut.

Not this time. It had to be an axe, but a sharp one. Her eyes were wide open, although the black-and-white picture didn't capture their blue, or hair the color of a wheat field. The first blow happened here, severing her head from her body, I'd bet.

But that axe would have to be damned sharp.

More memories informed my thinking.

Back in '24, when I was still a uniform, I caught a call to a house on Lincoln Street, south of the tracks. It was barely more than an adobe hovel, and the neighbor who called was inarticulate with horror. I drew my pistol and knocked, standing to the side of the entrance for safety's sake. You never knew when somebody would shoot through the door.

When nothing happened, I turned the knob, announced myself as police, and stepped inside. I found a colored boy, maybe fifteen years old, holding a hatchet. He was beside a man who had been hacked to death. The boy dropped the hatchet and let me handcuff him. "He made me do it," the teenager said over and over, trance-like. And that was pretty likely, given that neighbors told us the father mercilessly beat his son every day with a horsewhip.

The kid could have run away. But who knows how you'll react in the moment? A Maricopa County jury, not given to going easy on Negroes, let the kid off with a manslaughter conviction.

The point was that my dismembered beauty didn't look like the father on Lincoln Street, either. His wounds were random, wider gashes to flesh, deep but still not fully detaching bones. That was a crime of passion, in the moment, sure. This was obviously calculated. But I had to consider that other tools were used. Unless the cops had found something after Don ran me off, the killer still had the murder weapons with him or had disposed of them elsewhere.

Next I examined the arms and the legs, severed at the middle of the upper arms and near the hips. Like the beheading, this must have produced huge sprays of blood, but little was visible where the body was found.

Her nylons were undisturbed and garters neatly disconnected. I would bet the killer murdered her while she was nude, or wearing other clothes, then wiped her clean with towels. Next, he would have dressed her, the stylish pink suit meant to button up to the neck and the pink shoes. All were nearly spotless. Then he drove her to be found by the railroad tracks and displayed her. It was hard to tell, but it didn't appear that rigor had set in when we were there, so it was three or four hours from the killing.

I ran the magnifying glass across photos of her garments. Victoria took a close-up of a label on the suit: J.W. Robinson's. That was a Los Angeles department store. Maybe she was from L.A. But plenty of Phoenicians took the train to California to shop. It wasn't definitive, but Don ought to check with LAPD about missing persons or similar killings there.

Then I lingered on her face again. I had never seen this young woman before. She had no identification, no address book, no jewelry. Yet she had my card.

Five

I walked three blocks west, crossed Washington with its twin streetcar lines, and headed south. The Spanish mission–style Union Station stood at the foot of Fourth Avenue four blocks away, the roof adorned with red tiles. This route allowed me to avoid passing police headquarters on the southeast corner of the new City-County building, an imposing all-in-one civic structure that also housed the Maricopa County Courthouse and Phoenix City Hall.

Until '29, headquarters was in the basement of the firetrap that was old City Hall. That was when prisoners were photographed in front of the town fountain as part of booking, and nobody bothered asking whether their frequent bruises and other injuries happened during the arrest and interrogation or beforehand.

Now headquarters was modern, spacious, and much more useful, including a first-floor section for the fifteen detectives and a soundproof interview room in the basement. That room also had a window for lineups, with an adjoining space where victims could sit in the dark and safely identify suspects. Stairs and an elevator led up to the male and female jails on the fourth floor. Nice digs. Too bad I had so few years to enjoy them.

Today's route allowed me to tamp down whatever regret or bitterness I felt from leaving the department. A little, at least. Those feelings were never far beneath the surface. Don was probably right: I should have testified as my bosses wanted. But I was sore. And proud. Now it was too late. Don was the kind of man who could effortlessly do such a thing. He turned pages easily. Me, not so much.

As the sidewalk passed under my shoes, I couldn't push away another feeling. It said I was being framed. The business card in the dead girl's purse was a setup.

But by whom and why? I was a nobody now. Ruth Judd was set to hang and, after a sham of a trial, Happy Jack would be in the clear. I was no threat—the justice system, if you wanted to call it that, had spoken. The exculpatory evidence I had was of no value.

Who else would want me in a frame-up? It's not as if I hadn't made enemies as a police detective, but most of them were in Florence on ice. And it seemed like an elaborate piece of bloody theater to nail me for a murder.

The only other option was that the dead woman was on her way to see me and never made it. So, who referred her to a private dick in Phoenix?

Mail and Railway Express Agency trucks were backed to the loading docks on the west end of the long depot, with arches over the doors to the express section matching the architectural signature that marked every entrance to the building. Two cabs sat in front, drivers leaning against their bumpers trading gossip with redcaps. The double doors to the passenger entrance were open, and the waiting room was nearly empty, smelling of tobacco and dust.

Hat Squad detectives liked to hang out at the depot. We looked for single shady characters getting off the train. If they didn't have a local address, job, or money, we told them to get back on board and leave town. It was a reputation the department cultivated: We solved crimes and captured criminals. Stay away. If the newcomer refused to get back on the train, we drove him to the city limits and applied rough persuasion to keep moving.

Today no cops were in evidence. A janitor with a mop was slowly making a dent in the dust, permanently stooped as if a sculptor had created him. I was happy that no detectives were hanging around looking for unsavory characters—I would qualify for that now. No trains were due for hours, and out the south doors a small locomotive huffed back and forth, switching mail and express cars. I got a shoeshine and considered my approach. Then I climbed to the second floor and found the SP railroad police office.

"Gene Hammons!" Jimmy Darrow, a railroad special agent, stood and came around his desk to shake my hand. "It's been too long." That was true. He was a veteran like me, and I hadn't been to the Frank Luke American Legion Post Number One in at least a year.

Darrow was about my age, with dark hair and poor posture. At least part of that stance was from a bad wound he had sustained in France. It caused his left shoulder to permanently sag. He turned off the radio while Jack Williams was reading the news on KOY.

"What brings you to bull territory?"

He offered me a nail and lit us both from a table lighter embossed with the railroad's sunset logo.

"It's about the dead woman found east of the yard the other night."

He went into a coughing fit. Darrow had been gassed by the Germans and the last thing he probably needed was a cigarette. Then: "Aren't you gone from the police?"

"I am. But I'm private now and have a client who has an interest in the case." That was somewhat true, if I considered my brother as the client. Maybe the real client was my skin that was on the line.

He sat on the edge of his desk and regarded me with momentary suspicion, but the look faded.

"I guess it's okay to talk to you. I gave a statement to your brother."

"So, you discovered the body."

He nodded. "I was checking for bums when I found her. Assumed she fell off the *Sunset*, or maybe committed suicide. Both things happen. Plenty of people have been killing themselves thanks to the Depression. I only wish they didn't use the railroad for it."

"Did you touch the body?"

"God, no." He flinched and walked behind the desk, sitting. "She looked plenty dead. No reason to even check a pulse, her head being severed and all. What a mess."

I asked him if, in his experience, he's ever seen a train create as well arranged a mess as that. He admitted that he hadn't.

"Then you called for the cops."

"I ran back to the yard office and called."

"See anyone else around?"

He shook his head. But he hesitated. He was lying.

I let the silence gather; sometimes that's the best way to get the truth, make the person you're questioning feel more uncomfortable. It's one of the most important lessons you learn as a police detective. Silence topped a beating with a phonebook any day for extracting honest information.

"Look, Gene, I'm a railroad bull." This came after a full five minutes, with his cigarette turning to a long string of ash that finally tumbled into the glass tray on his desk. "I'm used to running bums and bindle punks off railroad property and looking for theft from freight cars. I'm no homicide detective. And this was…awful."

"I understand. But what makes you think she fell from the *Sunset Limited*?"

"How else would that much damage be done to a person?"

"She didn't have a ticket in her purse."

He leaned back and forth in his chair, his hands out as if expecting some answer to fall from the ceiling. None did, for this or when I asked if he had questioned railroad personnel as to whether they had seen anything. I remembered that switch engine working the east end of the yard as we arrived. Did the engineer and fireman notice the body on the north side of the tracks? What about the conductor and Pullman porters on the *Sunset*—did a passenger go missing? Was anyone waiting here for a woman who didn't arrive? I tried to keep my questions calm and conversational, but he became more and more agitated, lighting one cigarette after another, using the dying butt to start another. Each time, his answer was "No."

"I walked those tracks, Jimmy. They were clean. If she'd been sliced up by the train, there would have been blood."

More smoke blew toward the ceiling. "You know how many railroads are in receivership, how many railroad men are out of jobs? It's a miracle the SP isn't one of them. I'm lucky to have a job."

"Did you walk those rails, Jimmy?"

He shook his head, and I tamped down my frustration.

"Maybe you'd do me a favor?"

"Sure, Gene," he said, sounding relieved.

"Maybe you could get the word out across the railroad to other special agents, find out if they have encountered anything like this?"

He promised that he would. But I could see he didn't like it.

Afterward, I walked down the marble stairs to the main waiting room thinking it would be a while before he would seek out my company at the Legion hall.

———

Wing Ong stood at the ticket counter, and I waited until he completed his business. He greeted me with a broad smile. He wore a blue sweater-vest under his sports jacket.

"I thought you'd left for China," I said.

"I did," he said. "It was a mistake. I thought I'd find a country on its way up, finally. But things are in chaos. Warlords and communists are fighting the Nationalist government, and I'm not sure Chiang Kai-shek is up to the task of unifying the nation. He's no Sun Yat-sen."

When he sensed I was interested, he continued: "Sun died too soon. Then there's Japan. They've taken Manchuria, and it's only a matter of time before there's full-on war with China. So, I came back home last year. Even though I was born in China, I'm an American."

"I'm surprised you didn't stay in California, Los Angeles or San Francisco."

He shook his head. "California has a bad history with the Chinese. And in the Chinatowns, it's very clannish. Phoenix is home."

I thought about the reasoning that brought me back here after the war.

"I bought a ticket for my sister to take the *Sunset Limited* to Los Angeles tomorrow," he said. "I didn't want to risk the train being full."

"I'm not sure the railroad has that problem now," I said as we walked out the east doors to the outdoor waiting room, shaded by the extended red-tile roof and open in three directions through open arches. We settled on a bench.

"True," he said, "but this is the railroad's flagship train, the most glamorous. So now she's set with a Pullman ticket. Going to visit our aunt, but she's not staying. Things are better for the Chinese here in Phoenix. Chinese children get to attend public schools with the whites. It's not like with the Negroes, who have to go to colored schools and can't get service at so many stores, restaurants, and hotels. Better for them than in the Deep South. At least that's what they tell me. No lynchings. No 'whites only' waiting room here."

He was right. Phoenix had been settled by many ex-Confederates, so it had the feel of both a Southern and a Western town. In the war, I had seen the 369th Infantry Regiment—the "Harlem Hellfighters"—in combat. That cured me of any notion that Negroes were inferior.

Mexicans, like the Negroes, couldn't buy property north of Van Buren Street, but they didn't face the worst of the color line. Some Mexican American families, such as Victoria's, had been here for generations. She was part of Phoenix's small Mexican American middle class. Most Mexicans lived in barrios south of the tracks or farmed outside the city limits. Nobody liked or trusted the small enclave of Japanese farmers—I suspected some of this was jealousy because they had succeeded in places where Anglo farmers had failed. The Alien Land Law kept them from owning property in the state, so they cultivated farms nominally owned by sympathetic Anglos.

Ong paused as the switcher, a squat black locomotive, rumbled past with two mail cars, its engine laboring, the sounds measured and distinct, as if angry steam monsters were chained to its insides and exhaling black curses. I braced myself, put my hands in the pockets of my slacks, ahead of what was coming. Out of sight, they coupled to more cars with a metallic boom. A pleasant breeze filled the space. I hardly flinched at all. After the two birds that were my hands stopped fluttering, I pulled them out and lit a cigarette. I was pretty good at concealing the little bag of shell shock I had brought home from France. Thunderstorms, car backfires, unexpected sharp noises—that was where I had to be careful. No one who has survived an artillery barrage can adequately explain it to a civilian—not only the sounds but the way it tears men to bits or buries them alive in shell holes. And the terrible helplessness.

My companion didn't notice. "Chinese people here who built the railroads are spreading out from Chinatown. We own grocery stores and restaurants all over the city. That's not to say things are perfect. Any time the city fathers want to please the chamber of commerce, they raid the opium and gambling houses in Chinatown. They don't touch the east side, where the action is controlled by the whites, city commissioners, so-called respectable businessmen. Even though those Chinese owners pay off the cops like everybody else." He shook his head. "Then things go back to normal, because there's demand. Who comes to Chinatown to gamble, smoke opium, buy cocaine? The whites."

I couldn't argue with that. Don Hammons was probably the perfect example, especially when he worked vice. You can't pick your family, but you can pick your friends. Wing Ong was one of the smartest people I knew. If he wasn't a Chinaman, there was no telling how high he might rise.

"Sorry to go off on a tirade," he said. "There's corruption every-where. One hand washes the other. And I didn't mean to imply anything about you. You were always very fair with Chinese people."

I waved it away. "I have plenty of tirades in me, too. And just so you know, I left the police department last year."

"You're kidding."

"I've got better jokes than that," I said, and explained my new private eye business without hanging out the dirty laundry that had caused me to lose my badge.

"I like the freedom of being on my own," I lied. It was time to change the subject. "You have a new store?"

"The Golden Gate Grocery, Eleventh Street and Van Buren. Come by."

I promised him that I would. He was about to leave when I said, "Speaking of gambling, have you ever heard of a man named Gus Greenbaum?"

Six

The locomotive huffed away to the east, to the SP yard to find fuel oil and water, blowing its whistle as it crossed Third Avenue. Beyond the yard was the dumping ground of my cut-up blonde. I liked blondes who were cutups, but not this way. The silence was so pronounced we could hear songbirds from the tall oleander hedges to the north, separating Union Station from the Warehouse District.

"If you go to Chinatown or the places on the east side, you can gamble," Ong said. "But it's small stuff. Craps, poker, slot machines. Sic bo or dominoes in Chinatown. Or you can go in the back room of a cigar store or a poolroom or a bar and place a bet with a white or colored bookie. Again, small-time and local compared to what Gus Greenbaum has going. I'm surprised you don't know about him."

I explained that my time handling vice cases was mostly over by '28, when Greenbaum arrived.

"Just as well," he said. "Gus is Chicago mob, sent to oversee the Southwest branch of their national wire network, the Trans-America News Service. Don't be fooled by the name. It's the latest thing and is going to put the old operations out of business.

The idea is to use Western Union to get an edge, so the network instantly transmits the results of horse races around the country. It gives the gangsters a monopoly. It's a vertically integrated business, same as General Motors. At the bottom is the average bookie, who once worked for himself or was part of local organized crime. They depended on the newspaper or radio for results on a race, a game, or a prizefight."

"Now they work for the Outfit."

"Indeed."

"What if the local bookie doesn't want to?"

"They pay him a friendly visit and tell him he can make more money as part of the national syndicate. If he refuses, the next visit isn't so friendly. Broken arm. Burned-down shop. Stuck in a mine shaft out by Squaw Peak with a bullet in his head as an incentive for his compadres to understand things have changed."

"Nice people." I smashed my cigarette butt in the ashtray beside the bench.

Ong offered his shiny wide smile, like a sunny Phoenix day. It didn't last. He shook his head. "On the other hand, the bookie who goes along gets protection from shakedowns."

"How does Greenbaum's racket work?"

"Trans-America News Service. Sounds like the Associated Press, right? Officially, it transmits sporting news by telegraph. Except the only news it actually carries is racing, especially the results. It doesn't deal directly with the bookmakers but uses a distribution network. Trans-America's news is the complete information on every race: the horses set to run that day, the jockey, weight of the horse, odds, all of it. The morning of the race, it wires out the track conditions and if anything in the lineup has changed. Have the odds changed? Has a horse been scratched? It wires the positions of the horses once the race starts, at the quarter and in the final stretch, then the finish."

"The sport of kings," I said.

"And the vice of commoners," he said. "Now, the basic race information is available to the AP, United Press, and International News Service—they'll send it to the *Republic* and the *Gazette*, the radio stations. But Trans-America is faster. At a lot of tracks, maybe half, it pays for the exclusive rights to use a direct wire from the press box. Other tracks, they have a spotter with a telescope or a wigwag artist who can signal the racing results to someone on a telephone. Whatever way they get it, Trans-America has exclusive Western Union circuits leased. The distributors are given what they call a drop—a receiving station with a high-speed ticker. The radio might carry an individual race. The syndicate covers them all, coast to coast, two dozen major tracks."

"I get the speed," I said. "But where's the money made, aside from the truth that the house always wins?"

Ong leaned in. "For one thing, it lets a bookmaker keep taking bets as if he doesn't know the race results. The AP hasn't reported them yet, follow me? So when the bookie already knows a horse has lost, he'll take the bets anyway. Or say it's too late to bet if the customer wants to wager on the winner. Before the hour of the races, when customers line up, the early bettors don't get the full information that the bookmaker has—so they don't know, say, track conditions, things like that, and the bookie sure isn't going to tell them. Easy money, even though most of it flows up to the syndicate. Local bookies have to pay a percentage of net daily receipts, plus a fixed weekly fee to receive the results."

"You know a lot about this."

"I've learned it. This is having a big effect on the older Chinese community, the one that depended on gambling. And I intend to become a lawyer."

"You'll make a good one."

I asked why the cops couldn't stop the operation, knowing it was a naive inquiry.

"This is technically illegal in most states," Ong said. "But so what? The police are bribed. No offense, Gene. And the syndicate contributes to politicians. It's hard to find the big racing rooms anyway. It's not illegal to sell the telephone and telegraph equipment. Western Union has fought every effort to shut the big gambling wire services down."

———

After Ong left, I scribbled his background information in the notebook I kept in my suit coat pocket. Then I walked through the east arches of the depot and past the garden with its immaculate grass, hedges, and flowers to welcome travelers. Phoenix was always in bloom.

To the east, most of the produce houses were dormant or working short-staffed. The big harvests began in the spring. I walked around boxcars spotted at warehouses and wholesale outfits along Jackson Street, making sure they weren't attached to a locomotive and likely to move, with deadly consequences.

Ong's information was useful, but I knew the story went deeper. Chinatown gambling was hardly benign. It was controlled by the Hop Sing Association, one of the most powerful of the tongs that had set up chapters in cities around the country. The tongs presented themselves as benevolent associations to protect their people against anti-Chinese prejudice, and we had plenty of that to go around. But they were also organized-crime gangs that controlled rackets in Chinatowns. The bloody tong wars of the early century were over. But the gangs persisted, although much diminished.

They had been especially quiet lately, after three tong soldiers were found dumped in the riverbed outside the city. This was around the time I was laid off from the cops last year. Each one had been tapped three times in the head. At the time, we wondered if it was retaliation from a Paris Alley gunfight in '31 where the Suey Sing tong from L.A. tried to muscle in. We worried the assassinations could be a revival of the old tong wars. Now, especially given the manner of the latest killings, I wondered if they had been a message from the Chicago Outfit and Greenbaum, instead.

The landscape became grimmer, especially when I crossed Second Street and entered the Deuce, our city's skid row. Paris Alley, between Jefferson and Madison streets, was a dense collection of barely concealed bars and gambling houses.

When I was a cop, it was a nightly cockfight, only with guns and knives, every hood a rooster until he was assuming room temperature on the cobblestones. The metal call box sitting at head level on a telephone pole, labeled POLICE TELEGRAPH and below it THE GAMEWELL CO. NEW YORK, made me feel strangely nostalgic. Every cop carried a key so he could open it and call headquarters for backup or a paddy wagon.

In an emergency, a blue light on a pole above headquarters lit up, and a horn sounded. You were supposed to drop everything to reach the nearest call box, open it with the distinctive Gamewell key next to your handcuff key, and find out what was going on. That emergency might be a fight or shooting somewhere—or it might be a killer on the loose. You never knew until you opened the door to the box and picked up the phone receiver. Downtown, the police call boxes were mounted on their own pedestals, neatly painted blue. The department was starting to put radios in the squad cars, the first such system in the state. But the boxes were still essential, especially for beat cops on foot. I patted this shabby one affectionately.

Walking on, I waved away the panhandlers, jive dealers, and

flimflam men who frequented the alley. After dark, things got…
interesting.

On the Third Street side, I ducked into the restaurant supply store. The radio was playing Ethel Waters singing "Stormy Weather."

"Detective Hammons, it's been too long."

He hadn't gotten the memo about me not being a cop, but I let it go and greeted Carl Sims, a young Negro who stood behind the counter. With exotic friendly eyes and a widow's peak where his hair met his forehead, he had arrived from Texas a few years ago. He turned down the radio.

"This is my last day," he offered. "I'm starting my own gardening and painting business."

"That's good, Carl. Tough times, though."

"Don't I know it," he said. "But if I don't start now, I might never have the guts. I've been saving."

"Not in a bank, I hope."

"No, sir."

Theories about the dead blonde were floating around in my head like debris that had yet to form a planet.

"Let's say I had a piece of beef," I said. "How would I take a whack at it to separate it from the…" I hesitated, having never worked in a restaurant or slaughterhouse.

"Like a T-bone? A strip steak and a filet. It's separated by a bone."

"What if I want to cut through the meat and the bone?"

Carl looked at me oddly, but let it pass.

"Well, you could start with this." He pulled down a meat cleaver, a medieval-looking tool with a wooden handle attached to twelve inches of stainless steel formed in a curved rectangle. He slid over a wooden cutting board and handed me the cleaver. I hefted it in my right hand, feeling its weight, then brought it down hard. The cutting board and counter shuddered. The impact left a quarter-inch crater in the wood.

"A skilled butcher can do a lot with that," Carl said. "But he'd still probably use this instead." He moved through the store and came back with something that looked like a hacksaw. "Butcher saw, twenty-inch blade."

I held it closer, lightly running my fingers across the serrated edge. The blade was scary sharp.

"Planning on doing some cooking?" he said. "It's safer to go to a butcher shop and ask for the cuts of beef you want. An amateur could lose a finger or worse."

Or he could cut up a girl and dump her pieces by the railroad tracks.

"Been selling many of these things?" I asked.

Carl shook his head. "We haven't been selling many of nothing. Mr. Johnson is worried about the store. The other restaurant supply, the one on Van Buren, closed last year."

He thought for a moment. "Last week, though, a man came in and bought both a meat cleaver and a saw. Nobody I knew." He shook his head slowly, as if recalling the face or conversation or something more. "He gave me the fantods."

"Fantods?"

"The creeps."

Learn a new word every day, as my pop said. I asked what he looked like.

Carl hesitated. "I don't want trouble, especially not now that I'm about to go out on my own."

"What would get you in trouble?"

He sighed. "I wasn't exactly honest. He was a cop, and I know him. You've always treated me real well, Detective Hammons. But you're the exception. Colored folks don't get an even shake from the police, not even from the colored officers."

"Hell, Carl, I don't even like the cops myself."

He stared past me a long time. Then: "Frenchy."

"Frenchy Navarre?"

He nodded. "Man scares me."

"Frenchy Navarre bought those butcher tools?"

He looked me in the eye. "Yes sir, he did."

Seven

I knew two men in Phoenix nicknamed Frenchy.

One was Frenchy Vieux, real first name Marcellin, who made a fortune as a sidewalk contractor during the 1920s building boom. Walk down nearly any sidewalk in the newer parts of town and you'll find his name stamped in concrete. He lived in a majestic Italian villa–style home with a sweeping veranda on Portland Street, a couple of blocks west of me in the swank Kenilworth district.

The other was Frenchy Navarre, given name Leonce, a Phoenix Police detective. He was a few years older than me. We had never worked closely together, and I didn't know much about him. But his custom-made suits and expensive silk ties from Goldwater's and Hanny's made me suspicious he was at least a little bit dirty. Perhaps had I misappraised the man, and not in a good way.

I walked up to Jefferson Street and slipped into Jones Drugs in the new Fox Theater building, the city's best movie palace—and with cool refrigerated air to boot. They didn't need it today with the temperature hitting a tourist-pleasing 70 degrees. Past the soda fountain, I stepped into a phone booth, closed the door, and called Don at police headquarters.

"Detective Bureau, Detective Navarre speaking," came the unexpected voice.

My paranoia meter shot up several notches, and I hesitated, tempted to hang up.

"Hello?"

I forged ahead. "Hello, Frenchy, it's Gene Hammons."

"Geno!" The voice was friendly. "We miss you down here. I'm stuck on the dragnet for those escapees. It was the county's fuckup. They didn't get out of the city jail."

I contained my boredom and anxiety as he went on. The two jails were on the same floor.

"How's the peeper business?"

"Ups and downs. Is my brother around?"

"No. He's checking a lead on that dead skirt. You hear about it?"

"I read something in the paper."

"Well, she didn't fall from a train. She was sliced up and dumped."

"Nasty business." I fought the temptation to ask him if he'd been using a cleaver and saw lately.

He agreed about the nasty business and was agreeable enough to give me the address where I could find Don.

———

I climbed in my Ford, put the top down, and drove north out of downtown on Central Avenue. The San Carlos and Westward Ho were busy because of players and spectators for the Pro-Am golf tournament at the Phoenix Country Club. What Depression?

North of McDowell Road, the street narrowed and was lined with majestic mature palm trees and handsome homes on inviting shady acreages. Way beyond my budget. Construction of period revival houses that began a few years ago to the west had been stopped as if someone had pulled an emergency brake. No houses were being built anywhere.

A couple of miles farther north, past Central Dairy, I turned right on a two-lane dirt road and was enveloped in citrus groves. It would be a couple of months before their blossoms perfumed the Valley and after that the harvest. It was the next big deal, with the lettuce harvest: 8,700 acres cut, washed, boxed, and loaded in refrigerated railroad cars destined for points back east, already completed. For now, my surroundings were a picture postcard green frame for the bare head of Camelback Mountain, which grew larger as I drove east.

All the time I was in France, with muddy shell holes, shredded trees, and the overwhelming scent of death everywhere, I distracted myself by remembering views like this of our desert oasis so far away across an ocean and a continent, so at peace. Not too much distraction, mind. That could get you killed, especially by infiltrating stormtroopers.

One night a German soldier dropped into my trench, not even seeing me at first. My rifle was stupidly propped too far away, and I ran my trench knife into his gut, twisting it. He wasn't a stormtrooper but a lost boy who looked younger than me, blond and blue-eyed like me, terrified like me. He died hard. Later, when the adrenaline faded, the homesickness kept me sane.

Now it was as lovely and peaceful as I remembered it. "American Eden," the promoters called it, and rightly so, hundreds of thousands of acres reclaimed by the Theodore Roosevelt Dam on the Salt River, followed by four more.

I was born with the century, so I had no memory of the terrible times in the 1890s, when another depression combined with drought and floods almost destroyed Phoenix, with no dam to catch the snowy runoff. But our parents told us. Roosevelt himself visited in 1911 for the dam's dedication. I caught a glimpse of the Rough Rider in an open-top car with Dwight and Maie Heard. He doffed his hat to a cheering crowd. Now he's been in the ground for thirteen years. And after I became a cop, I learned how many snakes populated this Eden.

A little past grandly named but two-lane Chicago Avenue, far out in the county now, I saw Don's car parked beside the road. Down a drive was a two-story hacienda surrounded by dense plantings of orange and grapefruit trees, walled off by tall oleanders. I pulled over and stopped, shut off the engine, stuck a nail in my mouth and lit it, and waited. After fifteen minutes, my brother came stalking out with that long-legged Hammons strut. If you saw us walking at a distance, you couldn't have told us apart. He saw me and shook his head.

"What the hell are you doing here?" He sat in the passenger seat and slammed the door shut.

"Navarre said I could find you here."

"They reported their daughter missing two weeks ago. But they got a letter here a day ago. She's in Hollywood. Wants to break into the pictures. She's the only missing person on file who would fit the description of the girl by the tracks. Pretty blonde. If they want somebody to bring their live daughter back home, I recommended you."

"Thanks, but how old is she?"

"Twenty-one."

"Age of consent."

"Whatever. Like I said, her description matched our body, so I hoped I could clear this case in a hurry."

I didn't like that it was "our body." I said, "What do you know about Navarre?"

He opened a new pack of Luckies—Al Jolson's brand—and lit one, taking a long drag.

"Frenchy's a decent cop," he said, exhaling out the open car. "He can be a hard cop. Tough on the nigg—."

I cut him off. "Why do you use that word, Don? That's not the way we were raised."

"Okay, Mommy."

I shook my head. "Would you trust Frenchy to have your back?"

He gave me a long appraisal, his eyes like a lighthouse fixed on a ship at sea.

"Why wouldn't I?"

"What if I told you he had bought a meat cleaver and a boning saw at the restaurant supply store in the Deuce? Those are exactly the tools that were probably used to cut up that girl. So maybe he's a cook off duty. Or maybe he's a thrill killer who wants to frame me."

"This is my problem, Gene. I pulled your business card from her purse. You're in the clear, unless you really know her and gave her that card and you're lying to me."

I shook my head. "Well, maybe you'll help me with another problem," I said. "Gus Greenbaum."

Don stared hard at me. "And why is he your problem?"

I told him about being hired by Marley. He laid out what I already knew about the gambling wire service.

I said, "Marley wants leverage over Greenbaum."

"There is no leverage," he said. "You need to understand that Gus Greenbaum is a dangerous man. You're an idiot to take that case, I don't care how much money you need. You were an idiot in the first place to get kicked out of the department. You're an idiot to have your business card found in the purse of our body. Goddamn, Gene, am I even related to you?"

I used to idolize my brother. When he joined the Army in spring 1917, I lied about my age so I could go with him. We lived through it and joined the police department together. But I rose faster, made detective first, and was assigned to focus on the toughest murders. I cracked big cases, got plum assignments, and Don didn't try to hide his resentment. He was especially angry that I was named to be Amelia Earhart's "bodyguard" when she visited Phoenix in '30 and gave me a ride in her aeroplane. These things and his drinking and cocaine use strained the relationship, made me see him in a new light. I loved my brother, but much of the time I didn't like him. I did still get postcards from Amelia.

After a long silence, I went back to the original order of business. "First it's 'our body' and then it's 'you're in the clear.' So, which is it?"

He ground out the Lucky in my ashtray.

"When are you going to make an honest woman out of your Dolores del Rio lookalike?"

"Victoria is prettier than Dolores del Río, and she's already an honest woman."

"You know what I mean. All that churchgoing and you're making love to that Mexican girl."

I chuckled. "Don Hammons, the paragon of marital fidelity, giving me advice. Look, I'm not a moralist. Stay out of my private life. Anyway, you're avoiding my question. Here's why I care about 'our body.' If somebody is trying to frame me for murder, then he might kill again once he learns that I'm in the clear. Find a way to point the finger at me more directly. In addition to not wanting another killing, I want to know who the hell is up to this and why. This girl was killed, dismembered, and arranged in new clothes after she bled out. Ever seen a crime like that in Phoenix?" I didn't give him a chance to answer. "Me, neither."

When he next did the classic Don Hammons, withdrawing into silence, I went on. "When you picked me up the other night and took me to the murder scene, you said you wanted my help.

I've tried to give it. She didn't fall from the train. No blood on the tracks or the roadbed, which would have indicated she got chewed up by the wheels of the passenger cars. Too little blood around the body, telling us that she was killed and dismembered elsewhere, then dumped where we found her. No identification. And as I say, in death she was arranged, either to make a statement or because she was so despised by the killer. The wounds were severe but too precise to have been made by swinging a hatchet. They are consistent with a butcher's tools, which were purchased before the murder by one Detective Frenchy Navarre. Who, last I knew, was king of vice cases. So why did he answer your phone just now? I'd say you've gotten pretty good value for your consultation so far."

"Sure." He swiveled and faced me, his back against the door. "Have you been following the Halloran trial? Your girl's testimony sounded crazy as a hoot owl. Judge put a stop to it. Happy Jack got off."

"Big surprise," I said. "Don't change the subject again. Can you get a fingerprint check on the business card without setting off alarms?"

"Maybe." He shrugged. "Give me time."

"What else do you know besides their daughter isn't the dead girl?" I thumbed toward the hacienda.

"Doc Iverson did the postmortem at St. Joseph's. He estimated she had been dead for less than eight hours. The body parts were removed with a sharp instrument, then sawed off at the bones, likely while she was nude. Very little blood was on the clothes, which appeared new, from a Los Angeles department store. No scuff marks on her shoes at all. New polish on her finger and toenails."

"Raped?"

"Unlikely. No bruising or scratches. No skin under her nails.

But she'd had sex within the past week or so. No signs of restraints such as ropes. Doc drew blood, and we'll see if drugs or anything interesting turn up. Stomach contents were a ham sandwich and some chocolates. We fingerprinted her, but so far no hits. She wasn't some roundheels with a prostitution bust in Arizona."

"What about sending them off to the FBI?"

He shook his head. "There's no appetite for going to that much trouble."

"'That much trouble?' This is crazy. Murdered girl, no identification. Doesn't anybody care?"

"Officially, she probably fell from the train," Don said.

I shook my head in frustration. "Distinguishing marks?"

"She had a small cloverleaf birthmark on the inside of her left elbow."

I fired another question: "Cause of death?"

He hesitated, lighting another cigarette.

"Blow to the temple. Makeup concealed it."

I was surprised, but why should I have been?

"Like from a sap," I said. "Like a cop did it. Falling from a train sure as hell didn't cause that."

"You're getting ahead of yourself, getting paranoid."

The image of the woman's mouth, open in a scream, floated across my mind, something I would carry with me to the grave. I asked about it.

"Iverson said the mouth was likely propped open that way," he said. "She wasn't conscious when she was sawed apart."

"Our killer is such a humanitarian. Why hasn't this been publicly disclosed as a homicide? You should go to the press. The public might be able to help. Someone might know her."

"Because the city commissioners don't want another Winnie Ruth Judd scandal making Phoenix look bad." He held up his hand. "Don't start on me, wasn't my decision, wasn't the chief's

decision. The chamber of commerce doesn't want the city's reputation further tarnished when they're rolling out the new 'Valley
of the Sun' marketing campaign."

"Sons of bitches." Or more kindly: "You can always trace all
devilment to a chamber of commerce." Will Rogers wrote it on
the front page of the newspaper, so it had to be true.

I preferred the old motto that had been bestowed on
Phoenix: American Eden. But I supposed that wouldn't attract
tourists.

"There's something else," Don said. He paused. "She was pregnant. Doc estimated it was about six weeks."

Before I could say that this was motive for murder, a man
popped out of the groves thirty feet away. He was as big as a house,
and his face was distinctive, with a long scar and jailhouse eyes
that instantly lit on us. He had a revolver in one hand. With the
other, he waved into the trees, and four other men stepped out
and started our way.

Don swiveled forward and said, "I hope all that choir practice
hasn't made you a pacifist."

"No."

I had just enough time to take off my fedora and use it to conceal me removing the M1911 Colt automatic from its shoulder
holster under my suit coat. One round was already in the chamber.
I thumbed back the hammer. Don's black .38 Detective Special was
out, too, concealed between his leg and the inside of the car door.

By this time, the big man was beside my door, and his friends
were converging.

"Out of the car!" he screamed. "We're taking this!"

He waved his revolver upward.

That was his second mistake. His first was coming here
at all.

I lowered my hat and fired. The heavy .45 caliber slug blew

off his jaw, split open his scar, and kept going as the back of his head exploded in a geyser of blood, skull, and brains. The impact lifted him as if gravity had been temporarily suspended, and he flew up and back before gravity had its way again and he hit the ground with a hard thud.

Out of my peripheral vision, I saw a sawed-off in the hand of a scraggly man coming toward Don. It never made it. Don fired twice into his chest, dropping him. Next, Don opened the door and rolled to the dirt prone, where he put two more shots into the third man, who had the added misfortune of having his gun snag in his waistband.

By this time, I was out and using the door as a shield as a shot went wild. The shooter saw me take aim and panicked, turning to run as I squeezed the trigger three times, spinning him like a top until he landed in a red-stained heap.

The last one looked into the citrus trees, calculating.

"Don't make me kill you." Don said it in a chilly conversational voice. "This is the police."

He raised his hands, eyes torn between terror and defeat.

Less than a minute had transpired.

Twenty minutes later, the road was crawling with deputy sheriffs, then Phoenix cops, then meat wagons. Victoria's Nash came screaming at sixty, a cloud of dust behind it, reaching a hard stop. When our eyes met, she ran without even a camera.

"Gene, my God, are you all right?"

"I am." I gave her the quick story.

She hugged me a long time, and I allowed myself the shakes. My ears were still ringing from the gunshots. Then she went back to her car, fetched a camera, and got to work.

———

The next morning's *Republic* had us in bold capital letters:

COP, P.I. TAKE ESCAPEES IN GUNFIGHT

Then the decks:

**Three Cons Dead
Two Surrender In Bloody Clash**

Hero Hammons Brothers

**Credited With Stopping
Spree After County Jail Break**

Alongside the story was a V. Vasquez photograph. Aside from the cops and meat wagons, I had to say my Ford looked good.

Eight

The most annoying question posed to a Great War veteran was whether you had killed anyone over there. I usually lied and said I was stationed behind the lines in the Quartermaster Corps. Now, however, there was no denying it. Sheriff McFadden assured us the shoot-out was self-defense and that the county attorney wouldn't even present it to a grand jury.

That didn't stop violence from pursuing me into the weekend.

Victoria and I went dancing at the Riverside Ballroom Saturday night. A big band from Oklahoma City was playing swing, and Victoria is a good dancer. We did the foxtrot and the new jitterbug until we were exhausted and sweaty, then a slow number placed us in each other's arms, close. That perspiration only made her more beautiful.

The evening was cold and overcast when we'd arrived at the ballroom. When we came out later it was snowing. Snow in Phoenix! Neither of us had ever seen it, and we goofed around catching flakes on our tongues. That was the best we could do, with most of the snow melting when it hit the ground.

The snow turned to rain as we drove back to town, and when we crossed the railroad tracks on Central, three squad cars went speeding north with red spotlights and sirens. Victoria put down the gas and followed them.

I could only imagine Don's reaction to me allowing myself to be driven by a woman, but she usually drove us in her car, where she kept her cameras. I tuned her car radio to KGZJ, the new police frequency—the first police radio operation in the state. They were responding to a robbery at the Pay'n Takit market on Virginia Street at Central, almost out of the city limits. We were there in less than five minutes. I stayed in the car while she grabbed her Speed Graphic and walked into the scene.

She would probably mostly be taking photos for the department, which irritated her because the city paid less than the AP or UP, and, because of the Depression, the city didn't pay on time. It was strange sitting there, as the uniforms milled around in their peaked caps and Sam Browne belts with shoulder straps, then as the night detectives arrived. That used to be my life not so long ago. I might be the one interviewing witnesses, examining evidence, taking notes, and calming people down. Now I was only a civilian sitting in the passenger seat.

Half an hour later she slid in on the driver's side, handing me her camera to hold, and gave me a quick rundown. It was a stickup gone wrong, with two dead, one of the robbers and a reserve police officer.

For a small city, Phoenix had its share of crime. Earlier that month, Penney's had been robbed right down the street from my office.

I could see my hopes for the rest of the evening evaporate into the night like water on a summer sidewalk. She had to develop film, give most of the prints to the detectives for their case, and one or two for the wire services, and maybe for Monday's *Phoenix Gazette*. She dropped me off at my apartment on Portland and sped toward downtown.

Upstairs, I waited a long time, sitting in the chill air on my sleeping porch, wrapped in a blanket, smoking and replaying the gunfight outside the citrus groves in my head, glad I had retrieved my .45 in time.

Victoria never made it back that night. But I was still sitting there around two when I noticed a match flare up in a dark late-model, four-door Chevy parked against the south side of the parkway. It had been there the entire time I was lounging on the sleeping porch. I stayed another hour, watching. Was it a coincidence, or was I being watched?

On Sunday, I went to early mass with Victoria at Immaculate Heart of Mary church. The Mexican community had built it in the twenties because St. Mary's segregated its masses. As usual, I was the only Anglo there and unable to take communion because I wasn't a Catholic. But my Spanish was good enough to be part of the responses to the priests. My Latin stank.

Then she went with me to the service at Central Methodist, M.E.-South, listening to me sing in the choir. As usual, she was the only Mexican American in the pews, but she was welcome to take communion in our "heathen Protestant" church, as she playfully called it, and did so.

Don could believe what he wanted, but this comforted me beyond the singing: The Apostles' Creed, Doxology, Lord's Prayer, and especially words of forgiveness. I needed the last one. Did I kill anybody over there? You bet—I killed over here, too, and I felt rotten about it, "Hero Hammons Brothers" notwithstanding. Why did the ringleader pick that moment to appear with a gun? And just like during the war, it was kill or be killed. I prayed for the souls of the ones whose lives I had ended, prayed for forgiveness. I prayed for Victoria and for Don. This was not an only-Sunday thing.

After I made it through the war and the Spanish flu, I stopped asking God anything for me. The Lord's Prayer said, "Thy will be done." That was a tough surrender. After the service, we went to brunch.

"You're brooding, Eugene," she said.

"You caught me."

She placed her hand on mine. "It wasn't your fault."

Her family liked me. This was especially true after '31, when Herbert Hoover's Mexican deportation—an effort to lessen the number of job seekers in a free-falling economy—swept up American citizens. Among them was Victoria's brother Feliciano. I went to Nogales and brought him back across the border, pretending he was my prisoner.

The Vasquez family had been in Phoenix for generations, opening a dry goods store in 1884. And they gave me their undying gratitude for saving Feliciano. Whether that would extend to giving me their daughter's hand in marriage was another matter. Her parents were traditional, and I'm sure imagined Victoria married to a handsome Mexican American and having beautiful Mexican American children.

They wouldn't have understood our relationship. I'm not sure I did. She was twenty-eight, well beyond the age of marriage in her community, even in the Anglo world, the postwar revolution in morals notwithstanding. Maybe they would welcome this Anglo preventing their daughter from becoming *una solterona*. She was far from an old maid in my mind, of course. And she had a career as a photographer. When was I going to make Victoria an "honest woman"? I didn't know. It was complicated.

———

On Monday, I enjoyed breakfast as usual at the Saratoga and got into work at nine. Gladys was at her Remington, hammering out the report I had dictated last week—my findings on Gus

Greenbaum for Kemper Marley. It wasn't worth five hundred dollars. Short answer: Chicago organized crime was nesting in Phoenix. Greenbaum had an office in the Luhrs Tower, probably holding his bulky wire service equipment, too. Prohibition had been bad in so many ways, not least because it had provided additional rackets for the mob. Now they were looking for new ways to make money once liquor was legal again.

It was rich that Marley feigned outrage, considering his soon-to-be-legal booze empire was seeded by Al Capone's organization. And his indignation wasn't about lawbreaking—only that he wasn't getting his cut of a lucrative new hustle. He wanted leverage against Greenbaum, and I had found none, unless he could out-bribe the local officials, and that threatened his ambitions with the Outfit. It was a dirty business, and I regretted ever taking the case. Once again for Gladys's amusement, I had to tell the quick version of the gun battle outside the citrus groves. I was sick of it, but Gladys was entranced, for once happy to be working for a private eye as well as a dull accountant. I wished I were a dull accountant.

Inside my private office, the morning mail was waiting for me. Mostly bills, except for one. I used my silver letter opener to slit it open.

The telegram was from Prescott and read:

> GENE HAMMONS=
> MONIHON BLDG PHOENIX AZ.=
> WE WISH TO ENGAGE YOU TO FIND OUR
> DAUGHTER CARRIE A STUDENT AT ARIZONA
> STATE TEACHERS COLLEGE. WE HAVE NOT
> HEARD FROM HER SINCE JAN. 5. PLEASE WIRE
> YOUR ACCEPTANCE=
> EZRA THAYER=
> HOTEL ST. MICHAEL PRESCOTT AZ=

A Western Union money order for a hundred dollars was attached.

Usually, I would celebrate the prospect of new business. But I physically backed away from the paper as if it were a live hand grenade. Ezra Thayer's inquiry might be routine, the kind of thing that was the heart of my PI practice. But I feared the worst: That Carrie was the murdered girl beside the railroad tracks. The homicide that the "Valley of the Sun" bigwigs were trying to conceal.

I put the *Republic* atop it and scanned the news: "Hitlerite Regime in Prospect," read the headline on the top left. Marley would be pleased. Communists and Nazis were battling in Berlin's streets. A prospector had been murdered near Casa Grande and his body thrown down a well. Half a million Chinese troops were trying to eject the Japanese from Manchuria without success.

Only after smoking an entire Chesterfield and slowly walking twice around the office did I sit back down, reread the telegram, compose a response, and call Gladys on the intercom to summon a Western Union boy.

———

The next day, a Railway Express envelope arrived at my office. Prescott was once the territorial capital and the center of a rich mining district. I asked Thayer to send me a photo of Carrie by train—it was the fastest way. In the meantime, I distracted myself by taking the Greenbaum report down to Kemper Marley at his spread on Fourteenth Avenue near Broadway, south of town. His wife, Ethel, was a charming woman who served us tea and made me wonder how she ended up with a thug like Kemper. I guess no man could be a son of a bitch all the time. After she left the room, he read the report like a predator stalking dinner.

"He lives at 321 West Almeria. Nearly new house. But I don't see anything I can use to lean on him."

I handed him an envelope. "That's why I'm returning your five hundred. I'll keep the gold piece for my trouble. Greenbaum seems untouchable, even for you."

"Why can't you do private detective things? Follow the man? Maybe he's a rape-o who likes jailbait. Or a weenie wagger? That would be rich. Or better yet, a homosexual. Why not try?"

"Because I don't want to make enemies of the Chicago Outfit or a guy who came up under Meyer Lansky." I thought about that car parked across from my apartment in the middle of the night. It might have had nothing to do with me. Or everything.

I said, "We're talking about a stone-cold killer here. Look, Kemper, people come to the West to reinvent themselves. Maybe that's partly Greenbaum's story. You're going to be richer and more powerful with your liquor distributorship. If you want a piece of Greenbaum's action, you need to negotiate with Chicago. Offer them a piece of your liquor action."

"What's mine is mine, and I'm keeping it. That's why we have to be vigilant about the communist threat. Do you listen to Father Coughlin on the radio?"

"No."

"I never trusted Catholics, but the man makes good sense about the Reds and the Jews. America needs to wake up. You don't approve of my methods, but what we did to that camp sends a message that Phoenix won't tolerate this. It's bad enough that we're stuck with the lungers in their tents up in Sunnyslope, with that rich do-gooder from Cleveland, John Lincoln, protecting them at the Desert Mission. The more money he gives, the more we'll attract these sick vagrants. It's too damned bad the Klan died out here." When I didn't respond, he gave a reptilian smile. "By the way, what really happened with that young lady who was found dead by the tracks?"

I fought to keep my expression neutral, forced a casual shrug. "I read about it in the newspaper. Sad thing."

"Might be worse than that. I heard she was murdered."

"Where did you get that?"

"I have my sources, Hammons. I own some city detectives; don't think I don't."

I didn't doubt it. I asked why, if this were true, he didn't ask them to help with his Greenbaum problem.

"Because you have brains, Hammons."

Great. Kemper Marley considered me a brain. I tried to steer the conversation gently back, asking which sources had told him about the dead girl. But he leaned in to lecture me on the danger of "bums and communists and shines" on the move across America, that even our womenfolk weren't safe from their depredations.

I silently added Kemper Marley to Frenchy Navarre on my list of suspects. Either one of them could have procured my business card and planted it in the victim's purse. Why either man would want to set me up was a different question.

"I'm not done with you, Hammons," he gave his benediction and tossed the money back. "As I said, it's a retainer."

"For what?"

His eyebrows squirmed. "Something will come up, trust me."

I didn't trust many people, especially after being kicked off the police force. Victoria, I trusted. Don, most of the time. Marley, never. I left the money beside my tea and left, declining his invitation to show me his horses.

Outside with his steeds, he called, "I can take one of these out on the range and survive on jerky and beans for weeks."

I shook my head and walked to the car. He'd be a clown if he weren't so dangerous. But I never much liked or trusted clowns.

Now, after lunch and back at the office, I saw Marley's envelope on my desk again, wrinkled from its repeated journeys like an old man's face. I'd heard of a bad penny. This was a bad five C-notes. Gladys said a delivery boy had dropped it off. I sighed and put it back in the safe.

More important matters required my attention. I tightened my gut and wielded my letter opener like a trench knife, mercilessly slitting open the envelope and letting the photograph and a sheet of paper spill onto my blotter.

It was her.

The black-and-white photograph showed an image of a ravishing blonde in a light-colored dress, sitting on a bench in a garden. She was stunningly alive, with a broad smile. I studied her features, trying to wish this ugly reality away like the morning after a vivid nightmare. But it was no good. The paper answered the basic questions I had asked: nineteen years old, five-feet-four inches tall, one hundred ten pounds, blue eyes, a birthmark on her left arm.

It was her.

The dead girl.

"Our body."

I picked up the phone and dialed. For once, Don answered.

"Come to my office now, please."

"On my way," he said.

———

Don locked on the photograph. His shiny, expensive new shoes were propped up on my desk. He took his time.

Finally: "Ezra Thayer is big in mining. He sold the Monte Christo mines in Yavapai County back in '26 for a million bucks. He might wish he had them back if Roosevelt goes to silver coinage after he's inaugurated in March. The man also lives in Phoenix."

I remembered that now. Thayer was a major player in the

Arizona mining industry. "How could he have a nineteen-year-old daughter? Thayer is older, right?"

"Mid-seventies." He lowered his feet on the floor and reached for the phone.

"Long distance," he said. That would be money I didn't care to spend. "I want to speak to the operator in Prescott, Arizona." He lit a nail while waiting and took a drag. "Hello, this is Detective Hammons of the Phoenix Police Department. Can you tell me if there's a number in the Prescott exchange for an Ezra Thayer?" He spelled both the first and last names. "What about other Thayers?" Then he thanked her and dropped the earpiece into the cradle.

"No Thayer by any first name in Prescott." He dropped his ash into the ashtray on my desk.

"What about at the St. Michael Hotel? That was the telegram address."

He called again. No Thayer at the hotel.

I tried to conceal the squirm of my body in the office chair. "I'm being played."

"Looks that way," Don said. "Out of the blue, you get a telegram asking you to find this girl, Carrie. You ask for a photo and description, and it's our homicide victim. The only person who would do that..."

"Is the murderer," I completed the thought.

"Did you cash the money order for your fee?"

I shook my head.

"Don't," he said.

He was right, of course. I needed to distance myself as far as possible from this case. Still, the metronome of ambition and curiosity that had made me a good detective was swinging, leading me to want to follow this tune where it might go. Maybe the victim really was named Carrie, really was a student at the teachers' college in Tempe. The next step would be to visit the school, talk to faculty and staff, go through yearbooks. Find her real last name—or full name, if not Carrie. Hell, maybe Victoria had photographed her class or some extracurricular club she belonged to. School shots were part of her business.

I laid this out for Don as he kept shaking his head. He said, "This is a homicide. Do you know how close you came to being a suspect if I hadn't snagged your business card?"

"Yes, but now I have a legitimate reason to dig."

"You have a legitimate reason to stay the hell away."

"What are you going to do about it? Your bosses are stonewalling any investigation into this killing, no new Winnie Ruth Judd scandal to taint the tourism business."

He gave me a sour look.

"We've reclassified it as a suspicious death."

After I stopped laughing, I said, "Yes, having your head and arms and legs sawed off is suspicious, even to me. It's too bad no reporter in this town will see it written in the file, and if he did his editors would shut down a story. I know how it works."

Don slammed his fist on the desk. "What is it with you and the Sir Galahad impersonation? Trying to save damsels in distress. Are you trying to atone for Mother's death? She didn't die from anything you did but from the Spanish flu. We were five thousand miles away in the Army and damned lucky it didn't kill us, too. It was especially deadly for young and healthy people our age!"

"I'm doing my job, especially if you won't do yours. And by the way, why would Kemper Marley know that the dead girl wasn't the victim of a fall from the train?"

"What the hell?"

I told him about my conversation. "He says he has his sources in the department. I guess with the money he has to throw around, he can find them. Hope one isn't my brother."

That was a needless dig, but our blood was up.

He stood and stomped for the door. Before opening it, he turned. "Don't do this, Gene. If you do, I might not be able to help you."

"Are you going to do something?"

He stared at me a long moment. "Give me that goddamned business card."

I went to the safe and handed him the envelope.

"I'll get it dusted when I can. That's all I can do for now."

Nine

Choir practice was mostly devoted to preparing our upcoming Easter Sunday performance of the last two choruses of *Messiah*, "Worthy Is the Lamb Who Was Slain" and the "Amen," with its demanding vocal runs. Most people didn't realize that the "Hallelujah" chorus was also in the Easter portion of the masterpiece because it was always sung at Christmas. Anyway, this was hard work, and in the weeks to come we would be recycling anthems from the past two years that we knew well so we could focus on rehearsing Handel. And to think he completed the entire composition in twenty-four days.

I doubted twenty-four days would take me any closer to finding the man who had murdered and cut up Carrie Thayer, or whatever her name was. Still, after rehearsal I drove back to the crime scene. I parked off Sixteenth Street and grabbed a flashlight. It was full dark, a moonless night with overcast and cold. The citrus growers would be worrying about a killing frost if it lingered.

Heading south toward the tracks, a shadow silently emerged to my right. I reached for my .45 and was about to unholster it when I heard my name. It was Jimmy Darrow. He wore a zippered leather jacket, open, with his SP police badge pinned to his shirt and a billy club stuck in his pants.

We made small talk for a few minutes: Jack Halloran's acquittal, a month's reprieve for Winnie Ruth Judd, Governor Moeur asking the congressional delegation to send relief money, women getting the right to sit on juries. Jimmy had a pro and con argument on every subject, or so it seemed. I let him ramble on both sides of these fences.

Then he said, "I didn't give you the whole truth, the other day, about the night that girl was found."

I could tell that at the time but said nothing as he lit nails for both of us, handing me one. After a long drag and painful coughing, he continued. "I was walking east out of the mouth of the yard when I saw a car with its headlights on, facing my direction. It was parked right by where the girl was found." He kicked the dirt. "Don't know if that helps."

"It might. Did you approach the car?"

"No. I was alone, and the car wasn't on railroad property. But after it drove away, I walked over to see why he might have been parked there. That's when I found the remains. The car was there for several minutes while I was watching, but I couldn't say how long it had been sitting there before I came along."

After he had a horrendous coughing fit, I asked if he saw anyone in the car or could identify the make.

"The headlights kept me from seeing anything until he turned north on Sixteenth. Then I'd guess it was a Packard Eight from the silhouette, white walls, the spare tire on the side of the body sitting on the running board."

"Two doors, four?"

"Four. But the window was up, and I couldn't make out the driver or whether he had a passenger. He drove fast."

I stared in that direction, smoking.

"You don't buy that she fell from the *Sunset*." He said it as a statement, not a question.

"No."

I walked him back to my car, where I pulled out a file with the photograph of Carrie. "Ever see her, hanging around the depot, anywhere?" I shone the flashlight on it.

"My God, that's her!" He nervously lit another cigarette.

I pressed, "Ever see her alive?"

"No." He shook his head. "What a shame. Pretty girl. Who would do such a thing?"

After another smoke, he turned back toward the railroad yard while I crossed the two lanes of Sixteenth Street and walked the fifty or so feet to where someone had laid out the body parts so meticulously.

My day had included a visit to Ezra Thayer of Phoenix. I kept it convivial, but he denied sending the telegram from Prescott. He didn't have a daughter or granddaughter named Carrie. He didn't recognize the young woman in the photograph. I had no reason to doubt him.

But someone had sent them. Calls to Prescott were equally fruitless. Given the volume of telegrams and Railway Express, neither Western Union nor the express agent had a memory of who might have sent the wire or parcel to me. It would have been easy for Frenchy Navarre or Kemper Marley or Suspect X to take the train to Prescott and send them back to Phoenix. But it was a lot of time, trouble, and expense.

Now I was in the dark, only the flashlight beam to guide me. Then I saw it.

Someone had been drawing in the dirt exactly where the body parts were found. It was an elaborately designed cross: A skull at the top, with a straight vertical line leading down, a horizontal line that led to a B on one end and a backward S on the other, and finally a long X with curled ends. I placed the flashlight under my arm and sketched it in my notebook. I had never seen anything like it.

The night was very quiet. Not even a sound from the SP yard to the west. I ran the flashlight around for other clues and found only one. Broom strokes on the ground, meant to conceal any footprints.

I couldn't escape the feeling that I was being watched.

Back in the car, I drove up to Washington Street and called Victoria from a telephone booth. She met me half an hour later and took pictures of the drawing in the dirt. And just in time, because a cold, heavy rain started to erase it.

Afterward, we sat in her car with the engine and heater running. Rain sluiced off the windshield like a phantom in the darkness was hosing us down.

She said, "Maybe it was kids."

"Maybe. But how would kids know the exact location of the body? The location was not precisely given in the newspaper. That would be a big coincidence."

"I know." Victoria laced her warm fingers in mine. "I'm afraid, Eugene."

"Of what?"

"For you. This is all so…" She searched for the right word. "Sinister. This girl was murdered and sawed apart. And the evidence in her purse was meant to implicate you. Why?"

I shrugged.

She said, "What if she came by your card herself? What if she were coming to see you for something?"

I'd thought about that. When I set up my PI business, I'd persuaded several businesses to set out my cards on their countertops. I'd handed them out to lawyers, too. But whoever killed her had taken anything that could identify her from the purse.

They either left the card by carelessness or by design. I didn't dare assume it was an oversight. The card was meant to be found.

"I would ask you to let this alone," she said, "but I know you won't."

"I can't." I struggled to articulate a rationale. "The police won't find her killer. Somewhere a mother and father are wondering what's happened to their daughter. And what if he kills again?"

"Then I'm going to help you."

"No!" I reacted too quickly and soon regretted it.

"Don't you dare..." Her dark eyes torched me. "Who did you just call just now? Your brother? No. You called me. As you should have." She pulled a small snub-nosed .38 out of her pocket briefly, slid it back in. "I can take care of myself. You know that, Eugene. And I can help take care of you. So, give me an assignment."

The rain came down harder, settling the matter. Looking back later, I regretted not proposing to her right then.

Ten

The next morning, I put on my best suit and drove east on the Tempe Road. In daylight, it was a different view from the night when I visited the Hooverville: Two lanes of concrete, telephone poles on both sides, farmhouses and outbuildings, and ancient farm equipment. The vast Tovrea Stockyards and slaughterhouse. The strange new birthday-cake castle atop a rocky knoll intended as a hotel by Alessio Carraro. The Depression ended that dream, and "Big Daddy" Tovrea bought the property in '31, just before his death. Now the castle was only occupied by his young widow, Della. Next, off to the left, the Papago Buttes where Victoria and I sometimes hiked.

Across the Salt River, I was in Tempe, then parked and walked across campus to the Old Main building of Arizona State Teachers College. Not so long ago, it had been Tempe Normal, then Tempe State Teachers College, offering a teaching certificate. Since '29, it was also bestowing a four-year bachelor of arts in education. Now it had a new name and would soon have a new president, Grady Gammage, a man said to have ambitions for the school. The sun was out, but the weather remained chilly, in the fifties.

The registrar was a man with a shock of white hair and a lavish mustache that seemed on the verge of cascading down the sides of his mouth. He was suspicious of helping a private investigator until he read my card.

"Gene Hammons," he said. "You were a Phoenix Police detective."

I said that I had been.

He took in a long breath of air. "You solved the University Park Strangler case."

Right again. It was a hell of an icebreaker.

He looked away for a moment and when he faced me again his eyes were wet. "My granddaughter was one he killed. Grace Chambers." He reached out and took my hand in both of his. "She had her whole life ahead of her when this monster took her from us. The not knowing who did it was one of the hardest things. And you got him. It's un-Christian of me, but I was glad when they hanged the bastard." He looked around, but no one was nearby. "Thank you."

I squeezed his hands back with both of mine. "It was my job. I'm so sorry about Grace and the other girls."

Grace Chambers: Sixteen, redhead, pretty, fit his pattern. Disappeared one night and her body was dumped on a lawn at Thirteenth Avenue and Polk Street two days later. Like the others, she had been raped and strangled. In her case, she was also tortured. I was happy to see the SOB swing.

"How can I help you, Detective Hammons?"

I pulled out the photograph and laid it on the counter. "All I have is a name, Carrie Thayer."

He bent down and studied it carefully.

"I've seen this girl." He retreated to a filing cabinet and thumbed through it. Then he pulled out a ledger and went through several pages.

"No Carrie Thayer," he said, which didn't surprise me. I wasn't even sure this was her name. "But she looks familiar. Now we have 875 students. It's harder to keep track."

"Do you mind if I show her picture around campus?"

"No. Not at all. If anyone questions you, tell them I gave you permission."

———

I walked down the steps and into a flock of students changing classes or lounging on the grass by droopy palm trees and sitting on the side of the circular fountain, despite the cool air. "T Mountain"—really more of a rocky butte—sat in the distance. Before the war, I thought about going to college. Teaching held no appeal, so that would have meant attending the University of Arizona in Tucson. And study what? I was a bit aimless, as any good seventeen-year-old should be. Don, four years older, went to Tucson and studied history. He worked his way through the university with a part-time railroad job thanks to our father's pull. He thought about becoming a lawyer but was made an officer when the war came. He was awarded a Bronze Star. Without a degree, I rose to sergeant and got a Purple Heart. Now I surveyed this campus a bit wistfully before getting to work.

It was easiest to approach a group of coeds chatting at the fountain. Easier on the eyes, too. No teacher of mine ever looked like these four.

"You look like a cop," one said, a green-eyed, chestnut-haired wren. The others laughed.

"Am I that obvious?"

"Yes, but you're not bad looking."

"I'm a private detective."

"Oh," a blonde said, "a private dick." More laughter. I joined in.

This was much more satisfying than doing Kemper Marley's dirty work.

"Do you have a roscoe under there?" Wren patted my jacket and felt the .45 in its shoulder holster. Her playful smile froze. I gently set her hand aside, telling her she read too many pulp novels, and showed around the photograph.

"That's Carrie Dell," Wren, who introduced herself as Pamela, said. "I was in several classes with her. But I haven't seen her this semester." The others agreed. The progress was stalled when I asked if they knew anything about where she lived, who were her close friends, or any boyfriends.

But I had a name, at least, to take back up the stairs to get Carrie Dell's information from the registrar.

Halfway up, Pamela called. "Aren't you going to cuff me, private dick?"

"Maybe later," I said over my shoulder.

————

Carrie Dell was nineteen years old, a straight-A student, and came from Prescott. This and other miscellany, plus the names and address of her parents, were in my notebook as I walked back around the pretty shaded campus.

On a lark, I asked directions to the Art Department, where I knocked on a professor's door. A woman in a paint-stained smock answered and introduced herself as Pearl Kloster, instructor of Fine Arts. With twinkling brown eyes and light-brown hair in a chignon, she was somewhere in her thirties.

"Come in, come in. I don't think I've ever met a private investigator."

"We're even, because I've never met a fine arts professor."

She had a spacious office that doubled as a studio. An

unfinished oil painting sat on an easel, a stunning sunset and mountains.

"That's beautiful."

"Thank you," she said. "I'm no prodigy, but I usually drive out and set up outdoors to paint landscapes. Here I teach basics to students who might go on to teach art in high schools. I'm never going to make a living off my paintings. You want to see greatness, go find George Burr. He's a magnificent etcher, lives on Lynwood Street in Phoenix. I'm sure you've heard of him."

"Sorry, no."

I could see her opinion of me drop like the oil gauge of a jalopy.

"He's world famous," she sniffed. "He's been kind enough to lecture at some of my classes."

I showed her the photo.

"Carrie Dell," she said. "She was one of my models. Don't get the wrong idea. She never modeled nude. But I teach a class where students sketch and paint the human form. She's so beautiful. She was a natural. A model has to be patient, hold a pose."

She walked over to a large piece of furniture containing flat file trays, thumbed down to drawer three, and pulled out a canvas.

"Hold it at the edges," she said.

It was a watercolor showing a blonde on a chair draped with a white sheet. Her shoulders were bare and a long nude leg stretched out behind her. Even with her face in profile, it was unmistakably Carrie. This was the first time I had seen her alive in color, the fair skin, golden hair, vivid blue eyes, and magnetic smile. Alive, at least, through the eyes of an artist.

"This is her," she said. "Carrie is a perfect model, because she can sit for an hour at a time while the students work."

I couldn't make out the scrawl at the bottom. "Who painted this?"

"Tom Albert. He's a junior, also plays football. He's got talent. Unfortunately, he also has an attitude."

"Is he in love with Carrie?"

She adjusted her smock and smiled. "Every boy on this campus is in love with Carrie."

I handed it back. "What is she like?"

"Very confident." She gently touched her hair, making sure it was in place. "I only had her for two semesters. I haven't seen her this year."

"What about this?" I showed her Victoria's photograph of the sketch in the dirt of the murder scene, my original motive for coming here.

She ran finger across it.

"Where did you find this?"

"At the scene of a murder."

She drew in a breath. "Oh, my."

"Any help you could give me would be appreciated."

She strode over to a bookshelf and pulled out a folio, carried it to her desk, and paged through it, licking her index finger as she went.

"It looks like this." She swiveled the folio so I could see the image.

I said, "It looks exactly like that."

"It's a 'veve' symbol," she said. "Voodoo. I'm not an expert, but I believe it symbolizes Baron Samedi, ruler of the graveyard and death."

So much for kids playing around.

"I went to college at Tulane, in New Orleans," she said. "One saw a lot of voodoo art in Louisiana. I came here for my asthma. I do hope this isn't connected to Carrie."

"Unfortunately, it is."

And Frenchy Navarre was from Louisiana.

———

Back near the Old Main, four young mugs wearing Bulldog football jackets were admiring my Ford a little too intimately, one sitting in the driver's seat, a cigarette between his teeth.

He eyed me with a smirk. "Hey, Pops, how about you hand over the keys so I can give this baby a spin?"

I reached in and grabbed his earlobe. Hard. He let out a squeal as I dragged him out by his ear, tripped him, and watched as he and the nail tumbled to the concrete.

"How about you get out of my car?"

"Owww, son of a bitch! You can't do that!" He got up but kept his distance. "We're gonna be teachers. We're the future."

"Maybe the future in prison, kid." I slapped Carrie Dell's photo on the hood.

"Do you know her?"

After a few sullen moments, the boys looked.

"Yeah, what about it? You a cop?" This came from a broad-shouldered kid with dark hair. I let his imagination answer the question as much as I wanted to let my blackjack do the talking.

"Her name's Carrie. Carrie Dell. She's T-Bone's girlfriend." He nodded toward the lug I had dragged out of my car.

"Yeah," he said, rubbing his earlobe. "Cute dish."

"Until she broke up with him last semester," said one of his friends.

His features reddened. "She didn't break up with me."

"As much as I'd like to hear about your romantic life, I don't have time." I showed the photo around. "When was the last time you saw this girl?"

"Last semester," one shrugged.

"How about you?" I looked at T-Bone.

He gathered up his wounded manhood and squared his

shoulders. "Before Christmas break. She hasn't been back in school since."

"Why not? Did you call her to check?"

"Nah." He got his smirk back. "Easy come, easy go. Lots of fish in the sea. What's the inside tattle, cop?"

"You tell me? I'm a curious guy. Like what's with the T-Bone bit?"

He grabbed his crotch. "That's what the girls call me."

His friends laughed.

"Such BS," one said. "He works part-time at the stockyards, in the slaughterhouse."

The suspect list grew again. The kid had motive with the breakup, and means with his slaughterhouse skills.

"So, what's your real name?"

He reluctantly gave it—Tom Albert—along with his address in Phoenix.

"You were in art class."

"Yeah, so what?"

"I liked your painting of Carrie," I said. The angry ruddy tone of his face drained away. "Now scram before I get more curious."

They slowly sauntered away, as if the whole encounter had been their idea.

When they had gone, Pamela approached me without her friends.

"Nice touch, handling those pills, Mister Private Dick."

I smiled. "You can call me Gene. What's up, Pamela?"

She smiled. "You like my name. I can tell by the way you say it."

"I do. It's a rare and lovely name." There was plenty more to appreciate as she sat on a concrete bench with "Philomathian" engraved into the back. In addition to her large green eyes and lush auburn-red hair, she was pleasingly small-breasted under a tight wool sweater. Below a plaid wool skirt and above two-tone

high-heeled lace-up oxfords, her ankles and calves were beauti-
fully sculpted. I joined her.

"The name means 'all honey,'" she said, hiking her skirt above
her knees to get sun despite the cold.

"Not just sugar and spice, huh?"

She batted her eyes in a practiced move. "It's a more common
name in England. I'm Pamela Sue, if you must know."

"I like it even more, Pamela Sue. Now, are we here to flirt, or
did you want to tell me something?"

She hesitated, looked around to make sure we were alone.

"Flirting is nice," she said. "But it's about Carrie. Have you
got a cig?"

I pulled out two and lit both, handing her one. She took a long
drag. "God, that's good. The professors don't like to see students
smoking. We're supposed to set an example." She expertly blew
smoke rings.

"Carrie," I prompted.

"Something has happened to her, hasn't it?"

I nodded. I hesitated to give it up but decided to take a chance.

"She was murdered."

"Oh, my God." Pamela put her hand over her mouth. She
shook and looked as if she'd been punched in the gut. You can
tell a lot about someone by the reaction when you first disclose
the homicide of a loved one or friend. I was satisfied that Pamela
was genuinely shocked. I resisted the temptation to give her a
comforting hug.

"She was such a sweet girl, at least at first. From Prescott, you
know. We were good friends her freshman year, but she struck
me as very naive. First time she'd been away from home." More
smoke rings. "Then we drifted apart when she started running
with a fast crowd."

"You seem like a fast crowd all by yourself."

She laughed. "Not like this."

"Tom Albert?"

"Him? He can't decide whether to be a bohemian artist or a hoodlum. He was almost expelled for selling cocaine. I was surprised he wasn't expelled, but I guess they needed him on the football and baseball teams."

"But she broke up with him."

"Word was she was seeing an older man."

I raised an eyebrow.

"Don't ask me his name, because I never knew. Could he have been involved in her death?"

I said I didn't know and asked her to keep the killing quiet.

"Consider it on ice, Gene. You can count on me."

I hoped so.

"Do you have a girlfriend?" She hiked her skirt higher.

"Yes."

"A serious one?"

"A serious one, Pamela. This fast crowd Carrie was running with. Tell me more."

She dropped her skirt and looked out on the lawn.

"Students mixing with older men. Dressed like you. She started going into Phoenix. She had money, where before she was barely getting by like most of us. Sometimes she stayed late and got into trouble with the dorm proctor. I asked her what was going on. Told her to dish. But she wouldn't. She was a very different girl from when she first came here. She didn't want to be a teacher anymore, wanted to go to New York City and be a writer. She was very big on Edna St. Vincent Millay, Pearl Buck, Willa Cather. A pretty eclectic lot."

"Did you read anything of hers?"

"She wouldn't show me. Said she wasn't good enough yet. I think she liked the idea of being a famous writer more than actually doing the work. By this time, last semester, she had assumed this persona. Not at all like the old Carrie, taught to be a good girl. She knew she was beautiful and used it to get what she wanted. She reveled in being the bad girl, cutting classes, smoking openly on campus, breaking hearts, trashing friendships. It was repellant to watch but hypnotic, too, because she was so lovely, you see? Like watching a skyscraper burn down."

"Like Millay's 'First Fig' poem," I said. "'My candle burns at both ends...'"

"A cop knows poetry." She tossed her hair. In the sun it was the color of a new penny. "I'm impressed. Yes, Carrie loved that one. Frankly, I wasn't surprised when she didn't come back this semester. But I had no idea she would end up like this. It's awful. If you're a Sir Galahad, I hope you'll save me and not go for the hopeless bad girls."

I ignored that last line. "Why would Carrie have one of my business cards?"

"God, I have no idea."

I thanked her and stood.

"May I have one of your cards?" she smiled. "Never know when I might need a private dick."

I hesitated, then handed her one.

"If you think of anything else, call me. And be careful."

She smiled. "All honey, honey."

———

I drove back to Phoenix, past the Insane Asylum, with too many clues in my head.

Frenchy Navarre buying butcher tools.

The mysterious telegram and photo of Carrie.

Kemper Marley knowing about a murder that the police department was keeping on the down low.

Jimmy Darrow seeing a Packard parked by where the body was found.

A voodoo marking in the dirt of the crime scene—had the killer returned or was something else going on?

Carrie's boyfriend working at a slaughterhouse.

The fast crowd.

Carrie was pregnant.

A naive girl turned into a fast girl, a hard girl—or a wronged girl?—then into a dead girl.

How much misdirection and coincidence were hiding in all this?

I caught sight of Zoogie Boogie shuffling along by the auto courts and pulled into a driveway in front of him. He tried to turn and make a run for it, but I got out.

"Don't you rabbit on me. Get in the damned car."

His shoulders drooped and he complied.

Zoogie Boogie aka Henry Joshua Porter. He was thirty-five, average height and build with a pinched face. Today he wore a cream sportscoat with dirt on the edges and tan flannel pants well past their prime and way too inadequate for the cool weather. His shoes were blown open at the toes. You could tell the Depression in how many people wore shoddy shoes. He was one of my snitches.

"You get out of Florence, Zoogie?"

He wobbled his head up and down like a child's toy. "I did."

"Only a four-year jolt for knocking over that candy store with a gun. You're a lucky man. Staying clean?"

"Straight and narrow." He held his hands eight inches apart in front of his face and moved them up and down in formation. "Keepin' it straight and narrow. Except, when I went in the joint the economy was roaring along and now…" He dropped his hands in his lap.

"Well, it'd be a shame if I patted you down and found some

reefers. Your probation officer would have you back on the next bus to prison."

"Please, Detective Hammons..."

It was so convenient that few people knew I had been cut loose from the cops. I actually felt sorry for Zoogie Boogie. He was a vet and came back from France with severe shell shock, which probably contributed to his inability to keep a real job.

America was forgetting its Great War soldiers. The grand monument in Kansas City was dedicated in 1926. The British did it better with the inscription on so many of their memorials: "Their names liveth forever more." They lost 744,000 to combat deaths, the French almost 1.2 million, the Germans 1.8 million. In America, where combat deaths totaled 116,500, people were eager to move on.

He continued pleading, "Show a man some compassion..."

"I'm a compassionate guy," I said. "Tell me something I can use."

"Like what? Prohibition's going to end. There go the bootleggers. I wonder if booze will cost more or less?" He was hardly dressed for the chill, but he started sweating.

"That girl who fell off the train..."

He held out a shaking hand. "You got a smoke?"

I handed him a Chesterfield and my lighter.

After he handed back the lighter and took a long drag, I pressed him.

"What about the girl?"

"Word is she was murdered, cut up in pieces. This is your business."

"What word? Where'd you hear that?"

"It's on the street."

"Whose street? Not mine."

"Don't do this."

But I was going to do this. When he started to get out, I pulled him back in, hard, and slammed the door.

"Cop told me. You should know, too."

"What cop, damn it?"

After a very long pause, he barely whispered, "Frenchy Navarre."

"Tell me about Frenchy. What did he say, exactly?"

His eyes widened. "You want me to snitch on another cop?"

"I do."

"You his buddy?"

I shook my head.

"I run errands for him sometimes. He gives me a few dollars. He mentioned the dead girl in passing, that's all. Said I needed to stay away from the railroad yards, a maniac was loose."

I wondered, not for the first time, if Frenchy was the maniac.

"What errands do you run?"

He rolled down the window and blew a plume of smoke outside. "Navarre is a bagman for the city commissioners and the cops. You ought to know that. And nobody messes with him. You ought to know that, too."

So much to learn. I asked where he got the payoffs.

"Gus Greenbaum. He's paying cops and the city commissioners to look the other way from his gambling wire and from bookies. Greenbaum and the Chicago mob have moved in. There's so much money that sometimes Frenchy uses me. Don't ask me where people get money to gamble in the Depression, but there's a lot of it out there. Frenchy told me to stay away from the railroad."

"Have you been breaking into boxcars? The bulls won't like that if they catch you. And they will. They'll remake your face with their billy clubs"

"No, I swear. I collect for Greenbaum south of the tracks, down in darktown."

"How does that sit with Cyrus Cleveland?" He was the most powerful colored gangster in Phoenix.

"Sits fine with Cyrus," Zoogie said. "Greenbaum had a talk with him. Cut him in on the action. Now all his shine bookies are part of Greenbaum's network. Cleveland will do fine. He has other rackets: procuring whores, selling heroin and terp."

I lit my own nail and let that sink in. "Does Navarre know you're my snitch?"

"No." A vigorous shake of the head. "I swear."

"Good. Keep it that way." I let five beats pass. Then, "Is he a killer?"

He stared out the window. "A month ago, I saw Frenchy do a beatdown on a bookie who was holding money back. Used a sap, you know, a blackjack. I heard bones breaking. Teeth flew out of his mouth. When he turned to me I hightailed it, but not before I saw that look in his eyes. Same look I saw on the faces of the murderers in Florence." He flicked an ash out on the sidewalk. "Draw your own conclusions. What are you going to do? Go after a brother officer? That'll be the day. You guys stick together like flies on flypaper. Kill people. Beat confessions. Plant evidence."

"Does he have a girlfriend?"

"He's married."

"So? Young thing. Blonde. Pretty."

"What do you want from me, Hammons? Want me to make things up?"

I shook my head, peeled off twenty dollars, and handed it over. "I want you to nose around about that dead girl. Quietly."

"That's the only safe nosing with Frenchy," he said.

I let Zoogie go, and he wandered west on Van Buren Street, past auto courts that should have been full of tourists this time of year but were barely hanging on. I slipped into a phone booth, closed the door, fed in a nickel, and shared information with

Victoria. She had used her police connection to wander around headquarters and, when the Hat Squad was out, dig through files. Unfortunately, she hadn't found much, not yet at least. No missing person report on Carrie. None on similar young women. The file on Carrie's murder held one sheet of paper.

Next I called my brother. Driving downtown, I took stock.

Frenchy the bagman. Payoffs were a necessary evil in keeping the peace. Cops collected from selective illegal enterprises, and the money went to politicians, the city treasury, and other cops. The bribes were an incentive to look the other way, but also served to contain, monitor, and control illegal activity that was going to happen anyway. This maintained an equilibrium between otherwise law-abiding citizens and their vices. That was the old theory, at least. I tried to stay away from vice cases—other detectives, including my brother, thrived on them. But I had to take my share of the cut. Otherwise, I would have been suspect and might not have gotten backup when I needed it, or worse. Now it was my nest egg.

But Greenbaum was a new element, with plenty of money and juice from Chicago. And Frenchy Navarre was his bagman.

Eleven

I took a table at the Hotel Adams coffee shop to wait for Don and read to distract myself. The paper had a story about the Navy successfully staging a mock surprise attack on Pearl Harbor by planes from the carriers *Saratoga* and *Lexington*. Honolulu residents who witnessed the war game were reportedly "thrilled."

It was more interesting than Phoenix's daily diet of news about debt negotiations with Britain, what President-elect Roosevelt might do come March, and the Japan-China conflict. The local newspaper had barely a peep about the dire economic situation. Will Rogers's two or three paragraphs on the front page mentioned the Depression more than the news columns. The rare "good news" business story received big play. But nothing about people starving, the county relief fund empty, or the businesses closing every month right here. Nothing about the refugees from the Midwest desperately moving through town—if they could avoid Kemper Marley's welcoming committee. And not even the peep of a peep about dead Carrie Dell.

The waitress brought coffee, and I ordered a hamburger. Across the room, a dozen legislators were debating around a large, round table. Voices raised, then whispers, arms gesticulating emphatically. The subject was the governor and the highway commission. Cigar smoke pumped above them like a factory going full out. When I looked back, the man standing before me wasn't my brother but John J. McGrath, the chief of Ds. I reflexively stood and came to attention.

"Sit, Gene." His voice was gentle and his manner professorial. It was a devastatingly effective personality trait in gaining confessions. The only things that made him look different from the faculty at the teachers' college were the shoulder holster and a pair of handcuffs and a nipper in his belt beneath the off-the-rack suit of an honest cop. The nipper was a neat tool, a nonlethal item used to whip around a suspect's wrist and tighten to put pressure on a nerve in the hand and cause compliance. They disappeared as he buttoned his coat and sat, ordering coffee.

I sat. "I was waiting for Don."

"I know," he said. "Your brother asked me to talk some sense into you."

"How thoughtful of him."

McGrath smiled sadly. "Oh, my young friend, I am so sorry about the way things turned out. I had such high hopes for you."

McGrath had been on the force for more than twenty years, possessed a photographic memory, and had introduced modern scientific investigation methods, including a department identification bureau. He had always played straight with me—until the Judd case.

"I'm doing okay," I said.

"That's what I hear. But I want you to know that I really fought for you. I tried. Wanted to make you take two weeks' vacation during the trial. Get you out of the line of fire when the testimony started. But the higher-ups were afraid Ruth's lawyers might call you, or the Hearst press in L.A. might have gotten to you. The layoff was forced on me."

"It's okay, Captain. I'm a happy ending kind of guy. The bigs got their conviction, even though the evidence showed she acted in self-defense, and there was no way she could have cut up those bodies and stuffed them in trunks by herself. I'm not sure Judd's lawyers were even smart enough to call me. And I got to start a new business in the worst economy in American history." I smiled.

"This came for you at headquarters." He passed over an envelope. I could tell from the regimented stationery, if you'd apply such a genteel term as "stationery," that this was from an inmate in the State Penitentiary at Florence. Hoping like hell it wasn't from Ruth Judd, I opened it, relieved to find my jailhouse correspondent was Jack Hunter.

I arrested him for a holdup, and he was doing a fifteen-to-thirty-year bounce for intent to commit murder. Jack had escaped five times. I read:

Detective Gene,

Come see me. We can talk about the train girl, Carrie. It will be worth your time.

I stashed it. "Jack Hunter, can't be important."

"Ah, the escape artist." McGrath smiled, but the expression didn't last. "Don tells me you have a client who wants to find a missing girl, and she might be the one who fell from the *Sunset Limited.*"

"She didn't fall from the *Sunset,*" I interrupted. "She was brutally murdered."

He continued: "I won't ask the client's identity. But what have you found?"

I opened up the file, laid out the photos, and told him. It took fifteen minutes and several bites of my hamburger.

When I was through, he waited a good five minutes. Then he said, "You've been a busy boy. No wonder I gave the toughest homicide cases to you."

"I appreciate that, Boss. But this is where you say 'thanks' and 'we'll take the investigation from here.'"

He shifted uncomfortably. I felt as if a nipper had wrapped around my wrists.

"What?" I said.

"It's not that simple." He pulled out a pipe and meticulously filled the bowl with tobacco, tamped it down with a silver pipe tool, and slowly lit it.

"Don has explained to you how the commissioners and the chamber of commerce don't want Phoenix back in the national spotlight for another lurid murder. I don't agree, but I have to take orders, same as everyone else."

"What does that mean?"

Behind a haze of cherry-flavored tobacco, he said, "It means the case is classified as a suspicious death."

"So that's it?"

After a pause for another puff: "What if I authorized you to go to Prescott and do the death knock? I'll put together a hundred dollars from petty cash. The girl's parents deserve to know what happened."

"I'd want that authorized in writing."

"You don't trust me?"

"I trust you, Boss. But I don't trust the people who sign your paycheck. You have to take orders, same as everybody else, remember?"

"I'll send over a letter this afternoon."

"And what happens then?"

He looked at me like I was the stupid boy in class, repeating that the case was classified as a suspicious death.

I pushed back, trying to keep my voice calm and measured. I felt anything but that inside. "Cap, this girl was sawed apart elsewhere, and her body parts were dressed, dumped, and arranged, moved just inside the city limits. Her purse had money but no identification." I neglected to mention that my business card was also in her purse.

I continued: "She was obviously murdered somewhere else and placed near the tracks. Now, maybe she fell in with the wrong people and this was a one-off. She and her family still deserve justice. You taught me that everybody matters. Or, we have a savage murderer on the loose, and he'll kill again. He won't give a damn what the chamber of commerce thinks."

"It's been more than two weeks since that happened," he said.

"You know that doesn't mean anything. The University Park Strangler only killed when new moons coincided with Catholic martyred saints' dates. Thank God the chamber wasn't so touchy then or we would have ignored that, too."

He winced. "You know, crime has actually fallen during this Depression."

I stayed on the subject. "Who knows what sets this monster off? We do know Carrie was killed by an expert blow to the head. Like from a sap or a blackjack. Like from a rogue cop. Maybe the same cop who got her pregnant."

McGrath sighed. "You've obviously given this a lot of thought. I'm not saying you should investigate this suspicious death…"

"Murder."

"Murder. I'm not saying you should investigate it. You could let it go. That would be the smart thing. But I know you. So, my point is, if you're determined to go off the reservation…"

He reached in his pocket and placed a folded handkerchief on the table. Inside was my old badge.

"Maybe that will open some doors," he said. "But tread lightly, Gene. It doesn't mean you're back on the force."

"I understand." But I didn't.

He reached across and touched my sleeve. "Don't forget Haze Burch."

"I never would."

"This work can bite you when you least expect it."

After he left, the phoenix bird on my gold detective shield stared at me for a long time before I slipped it in my pocket. Over at the round table, the lawmakers were sounding lubricated, laughing and joking.

I thought about the chief of D's last words. Haze Burch was the first Phoenix Police officer killed in the line of duty. On February 5, 1925, he came upon two men siphoning gasoline from a car. They shot him at Eighth Street and Jefferson, then got away. I was on duty and was one of the responding officers. He was dead by the time we arrived. The pair were not petty thieves. They had previously murdered two cops, in Texas and Montana. Haze was killed by what he didn't know.

I pushed away the half-eaten hamburger, feeling very alone.

———

Ten minutes later, I was back at the Monihon Building, where a postcard from Amelia Earhart was awaiting me: She was speaking before a group in Seattle. Signed, "Missing you" and her first name signed like an airplane's loops across the sky. I missed her, too. Gladys also informed me that Harry Rosenzweig called and wanted me to come by.

I walked up First Avenue to the jewelry store and stepped inside. Barry Goldwater waved from the far end of the counter and went back to a hushed conversation with a well-dressed man. Del Webb was visiting with Harry, who waved me in.

"How's the private eye business?" Webb asked. He was dressed in one shade of khaki: slacks, shirt, and zip-up coat. He even had a khaki hat.

"Murder," I said.

"Mine, too," he said. "Only twenty-six building permits issued in all of January. When I finish the mansion that I'm building in the Country Club neighborhood, I'm tapped out. But I have high hopes for FDR. Get federal money flowing into this town for roads, public buildings—I told Carl Hayden we need an underpass for Central at the railroad tracks—and I'm going places." Hayden was one of our U.S. senators. Webb started singing, "Happy days are here again..." off-key.

I clapped him on the shoulder. "From your lips to God's ears."

Harry gestured me to the counter.

"I sent a query to Hamilton for the watch you brought in. With the serial number, they had a record of the original buyer. Don't know if this helps, but..." He handed me a slip of note paper with I. Rosenzweig & Sons letterhead. Written neatly was "Ezra T. Dell" along with a purchase date of 1917 and a jewelry store in Prescott.

"Does it help?" Harry asked.

"I believe it does." I slipped the paper in my pocket. He went to the back room and returned with a Rosenzweig's box. It held the watch I had found in the dirt of the burned Okie camp, now polished and sitting on a bed of felt.

I added it to my pocket. "How much do I owe you, Harry?"

"Don't worry about it."

"Come over here, Gene." Barry beckoned me to the far end of the store. He was clean-shaven now. I thanked Harry, wished Del good fortune, and they went back to gossiping.

Barry said, "Gene Hammons, meet Gus Greenbaum."

I took in a sharp breath but kept my cop face as I shook the hand offered by a man with a tough face, wide-set eyes, big ears, and a flamboyant gold pocket square hanging like a tongue out of his front suit coat pocket. He had an iron grip, and I returned it. This was a long handshake as each of us took the measure of the other. He wore expensive gold cuff links. His nose looked like someone had inserted a lightbulb in the end of it.

"Your legend precedes you, Hammons," he said, an expensive Cuban double corona in his mouth. "The homicide cop who was fired because he knew the truth about Winnie Ruth Judd, the trunk murderess."

We let go at the same time. My hand ached, but I didn't let it show.

"Don't believe everything you hear, Mr. Greenbaum," I said. "What's your line?"

He painted an image in the air with the cigar. "Sporting news. Everybody loves sports."

"He's a real-life gangster," Barry blurted, impressed. Greenbaum smiled wider.

"Don't pay any attention to him." Greenbaum's dark eyes were fixed on mine, trying to assay my reaction. "Goldwater here has a very vivid imagination." He looked me up and down. "You're a private dick now. That's good. I could use a man like you."

"I appreciate that, Mr. Greenbaum..."

"Gus!" He made a punctuation point with the cigar.

"I appreciate that, Gus. But I'm not taking any new clients at the moment."

"Well, if you change your mind..." He reached inside my suit coat and slipped a business card in the pocket. It was close enough for him to feel the M1911 Colt in its shoulder holster. His smile never changed.

Twelve

Two days later, Victoria and I took the Santa Fe Railway to Prescott. The city—pronounced "PRES-cut," although some used "Pres-kit"—was a mile high, and we dressed for the weather. Or so we thought. My father, the loyal "Ess-pee" conductor, would have been horrified by us riding the rival AT&SF, but it was the only way north aside from a rough and, especially in winter, dangerous highway.

This railroad from Phoenix made a long climb all the way to Ash Fork, where it connected to the Santa Fe main line running to Los Angeles and Chicago. We left the oasis and desert as the sun was setting, charging through Wickenburg, which was holding its annual rodeo, climbing into High Country meadows and pine forests that we could barely see in the dark. At Skull Valley, it seemed as if the whole town came out to meet our train. The food in the dining car was excellent, per Santa Fe Fred Harvey standards.

Victoria, her black hair tumbling out from beneath a stylish slouch hat, bought a *Fortune* magazine at Union Station and read it as we rolled along.

"Look at this!" She folded over a page. It held a photograph showing a spectacular view of New York City and a steel eagle perching out, with an opening at the top and a woman halfway out the opening, holding a camera.

"That's the new Chrysler Building," she said. "And the photographer there is Margaret Bourke-White. She's a staff photographer for *Fortune*."

"You could do that."

She smiled and hugged me. "I believe I could."

The locomotives faced an especially hard lift getting to Prescott, which was a major subdivision point on the railroad. Fortunately, our coach windows were closed, so we didn't get showered by soot from the engines. In summer, the Phoenix elite that didn't flee to California came to nearby Iron Springs to flee the heat. The last time I had come here, Prescott's railyard was clogged with locomotives and cars filled with ore. But that was before '29.

Now, as we stepped out before the imposing passenger depot, the yard was nearly empty. A full moon showed Thumb Butte standing to the west covered by stubby piñon trees, but otherwise the rich mining district around Prescott was in as deep trouble as the one in south-central Arizona around Globe and Morenci. The United Verde Mine in Clarkdale had closed in '31, and the others nearby had shed workers as the price of copper collapsed.

The crew pulled off the locomotive to add water and fuel oil while express and mail were unloaded from the baggage car. A slushy, dirty snow was on the ground as we walked to the waiting room, gusts of cold mountain wind hitting our faces. High mounds of snow were piled nearby. Inside, a woman immediately approached us. Older, slender, bent at the back, wearing a furry turban.

"You don't look like you're from here."

I made introductions.

"I'm Miss Sharlot Hall," she said, giving a firm handshake, but not like Greenbaum's viselike grip. "I'm the town historian. You're from Phoenix. You stole our capitol."

"You can have it back," Victoria said.

Miss Sharlot Hall gave a shoulder-bobbing laugh. I asked her how things were in Prescott.

Her face grew serious. "The closing of the copper mines has put thousands of people out of work in the state. It's no different in Yavapai County. Likely worse." She made a sweeping gesture with her right hand. "We have unemployed miners in the hills trying their hands at placer mining. Sometimes they make a few cents, a dollar at the most. Gold played out here long ago. We have gas moochers come through. The city offers to let them work off their expenses by chopping weeds and doing odds and ends. But very few accept the offer. Banks are in trouble."

"It's the same in Phoenix," I said.

"President Hoover sent Prescott fifty thousand dollars in work relief," she said. "Reconstruction Finance Corporation. We used it for local men only. That was important. And it ran out. At least we got the courthouse walls washed."

The RFC funds didn't last long in Phoenix, either. I changed the subject to Carrie Dell.

"Such a sweet girl, smart and beautiful, too," Hall said. "She's at the teachers' college in Tempe."

"When was the last time you saw her?" I said.

"It's been almost a year. She didn't come home last summer. I heard she got a summer job at the Biltmore Hotel outside Phoenix. Just as well."

"And why's that?"

She squared her small shoulders. "I'm the town historian, not the town gossip!"

I flashed my buzzer, and her dudgeon collapsed.

"Oh."

"We're looking for Carrie's father."

She shook her head. "Ezra. It's no wonder Carrie didn't want to come home. That man. Ezra Dell is a drunk." She huffed. "We'll have plenty more when Prohibition is over."

Victoria gently asked where we could find him, and she gave us an address. It was different from the one I'd copied from the college records.

"I tried to get him in the Pioneers' Home. But they wouldn't take him, because he wouldn't stop his drunkenness and cavorting with bootleggers." She looked us over. "I hope you brought warm clothes."

We thanked her and started out.

"I'm so glad Carrie is all right," she said. "It's better that she's away from here."

Town historian or gossip, I saw no need to set her straight. She would find out soon enough.

———

Outside the station, at the foot of Cortez Street, Prescott looked like a prosperous little city, despite the hard times and having one-tenth the population of Phoenix. Paved streets, sidewalks cleared of snow, streetlights, solid multistory buildings leading toward the Yavapai County Courthouse. More people were in Western wear, and not for show. It was how they dressed. A couple of horse-drawn wagons competed with automobiles for space at the curbs. These had mostly disappeared from Phoenix in the '20s. The town was winding down for the night.

We checked in at the Hotel St. Michael at the corner of Gurley and Montezuma streets, using the names Mr. and Mrs. Gene Hammons. We decided to leave questions about the hotel as origin of the telegram about Carrie for later and went upstairs to get warm.

The next morning, a look outside the window showed more than a foot of new snow on the ground. My sweater, leather jacket, and jeans were maybe enough, but not my shoes. Victoria was similarly unprepared, as any Phoenician would be. After breakfast, we went to a store and bought winter boots with zigzag soles to keep our footing in the snow, mufflers, and gloves. The hundred bucks from Captain McGrath was drawing down.

Then we set off in search of Carrie's father. I had done many death knocks. They never got easier, and you never knew how the parents, siblings, or other next of kin would react.

We walked several blocks west, beyond the Pioneers' Home, to find the address on Park Avenue. Amid Prescott's many Victorian and craftsman homes, this property was little more than a shack beneath a tall ponderosa pine. The snow leading to the porch had no footprints. But smoke was coming from the chimney, and one window showed the glow of a light.

We mounted the creaky steps to the porch and prepared to knock. I cocked my head for Victoria to stand away from the door. I did the same on the other side. You never knew when someone might shoot through the door. I knocked, three times, loud.

The door exploded with automatic-weapons fire, the unmistakable sound of a Thompson submachine gun. Victoria crouched, a terrified look in her eyes. I fell to the porch. She did the same. When the firing stopped, the bullet holes in the wood of the door outlined a cockeyed circle, which then fell out. It would have been funny, if the situation were not so deadly.

"Mr. Dell!" I called. "It's Gene Hammons, Phoenix Police. I need to talk to you about your daughter! Put down the Tommy gun and open the door."

I got on my haunches, the .45 in my hand, and waited. In a few minutes, the door squeaked open, and we beheld a gaunt man in overalls with a scraggly white beard that had tobacco stains on it. He was unarmed, so I holstered my weapon.

"C'mon," he said, and turned back inside. We followed him. "Sorry 'bout that. Never know when revenooers will come back here for my still. Had to rebuild it twice already. Want some?"

We took a pass.

The living room, if you wanted to call it that, was crowded with ancient furniture, heavy and dark, and it smelled of gun smoke, alcohol, and piss. A surprisingly well-made fire presided on the hearth. I took the Tommy gun, removing the magazine and the round in the chamber. Then I joined Victoria on a sofa losing its stuffing. He sat across on a tumbledown love seat.

"Hello, pretty lady. Are you police, too?"

"Police photographer," she said. "Victoria Vasquez."

"Ah. Big-city stuff. Now what's this about my Carrie?"

I showed him the photograph of the live girl, the picture that had been sent to me from Prescott. He took it in his left hand and identified it as his daughter. Then I gave him the bad news. As is often the case, he first denied it. Must be a mistake. It was no mistake. After a pause, he sagged and began weeping, his bony shoulders heaving. Victoria sat next to him and put her arm around him.

When he could speak, he asked for the details. I gave him a highly sanitized version, and this brought on more sobbing. He reached for a bottle on the side table and uncorked it, taking a deep pull, stifling a belch. Sharlot Hall was correct: he was a juicer.

He held up the bottle. "Want some?"

We declined again.

"I'm not a good man," he said finally. "I know that. But I tried to do my best for her after her mother died in '23. That was when

I started drinking, though. I thought she'd be better off down in Tempe. She'd be the first in the family with a college degree. Had her whole life ahead of her. Who would want to do this to her?"

"We don't know yet," I said. "Did she have any enemies? Anyone who would wish her harm?"

"No! My God, no. She was the sweetest girl. Everybody loved my Carrie."

"Any boyfriends here?"

"Nothing serious."

I asked if we could see her room, and he led us down a hall, opening a door.

Unlike the rest of the house, Carrie's bedroom had bright wallpaper, a well-made bed covered with stuffed animals, neat student desk and chair, a trophy, phonograph, and records. On the walls were pennants for Prescott High and the Arizona State Teachers College Bulldogs.

I leaned to Victoria and whispered, "Diaries, letters, photos, anything that might be useful. Look under the mattress and beneath drawers."

She nodded, and I steered Ezra Dell back to the mess of a living room.

I told him about the telegram I received from "Ezra Thayer," asking me to find Carrie.

He simply said, "Oh."

"What 'oh'?" I stood close to him, one arm on each side, nowhere for him to go. It was easier for me to breathe through my mouth. I wondered how long since he had a bath.

"I sent it," he said. "Sent down the picture, too. Thought you were a private detective."

"Never mind that. Why did you want me looking for her?"

"I was worried. Hadn't seen her for months, then she stopped writing, stopped wiring Mrs. Carter money to buy me groceries.

I understand why she wanted to keep her distance, my drinking and all, but she still wrote. Until she didn't. That got me scared."

Any parent would be, but something about his manner made me suspicious. I let my arms fall, and he walked back to the living room and took a swig. I followed.

"Why did you use the name Ezra Thayer?"

"I thought it might get your attention. He's a somebody, and I'm a nobody."

He was enough of a somebody to send the hundred-dollar money order.

"That was money Carrie sent me from her summer job. She was worried I'd spend it on booze, but I managed to save it." He belched. "Well, I forgot about it. So, it was there when I needed to hire you."

"Ever have any trouble with the police, besides the Volstead Act?"

"No!"

My tone seemed to sober him up.

"What about you and Carrie? How'd you get along?"

"We got along fine. She disapproved of my binges. Hell, it's not my fault. Life handed me a bum hand. But like I said, I did the best I could for her."

"Never hit her?"

"No! Not once!" He wanted to reach for his jug but stopped himself. "I didn't kill Carrie, if that's where you're going, copper. Why… How…?" Then he was sobbing again, but I didn't offer any comfort.

Then, "Two weeks ago, I got a letter. No return address. It had a lock of her hair and…"

I gently coaxed: "And what?"

"A typed note that said, 'Your daughter is dead and burning in hell.'" He barely got it out before the weeping consumed him.

I walked behind and put a hand on his shoulder. The rest was as I would have expected, if he wanted to make my job as complicated as possible. He burned the letter, kept the lock of hair. Didn't go to the cops because he didn't trust them. Wired the college but never heard anything except she didn't enroll in January. And he looked me up as a shamus to find out if the worst had happened. Parts of his story sounded screwy, but I didn't make him for a killer, certainly not one with the abilities of the man who killed Carrie Dell with a sap and dismembered her. It was all screwy enough to be true.

I remembered the watch, pulled it out, and showed it to him. "This is yours."

He took it in a shaky hand and stared at it like an amulet, bright as new thanks to Harry Rosenzweig.

"This was my railroad watch," he said. "I was a conductor on the Santa Fe, before…"

"My pops was a conductor, too."

He momentarily brightened. "Then you understand. Life-and-death responsibility. I wasn't always this way. I gave the watch to Carrie so I wouldn't hock it. I wanted her to have it. Where did you get it?"

"In a hobo camp outside Phoenix."

"I don't understand."

Neither did I. "We have to keep it for now as evidence."

"It's just as well."

"You'll get it back," I said, "She had a job at the Arizona Biltmore?"

He nodded. "Last summer. I don't know why anybody in his right mind would want to be down there that time of year. But I knew she didn't want to come back here, with me like I was."

I asked him about the end of the fall semester. Did she return to Prescott for Christmas? He shook his head.

"And you said she wrote you…"

"Yes, every week at least. But the letters stopped after around the end of the year. I started to worry, but at first I figured she'd cut me off. It's what I would have done. Then that envelope came."

"Did you save her letters?"

He heaved himself up and toddled to a sideboard, bringing back a stack of mail.

"Mind if I keep these?"

"No. What kind of monster would want to hurt her?" Tears again.

"I don't know. But I promise we'll get him."

It was the same promise I made to the family of every homicide victim. Only this time, I wasn't sure I could deliver.

He stared out a smeared window. "I can't afford to bury her."

"We'll find a way to help." That was another promise I didn't know how to keep.

Was there anyone we could call for him? No, his wife was dead, Carrie was his only child, and his brother in San Francisco had cut off contact.

Afterward, as we walked down the snowy street, Victoria said, "You're praying for him, aren't you?"

"Yes. Of course."

"How do you keep your faith with all the terrible things you see?"

I changed the subject. "You handled yourself well under fire."

"Thanks," she said. "That's never happened to me before. Here's what I don't understand, Eugene…" I slipped on the ice, and she caught me.

"What don't you understand?"

"Sudden sounds make you jump. A car backfire or a slammed door. Thunder. But back there, you were a cool cucumber."

I smiled. "I don't know. When the stakes are high, maybe I fall

back into the training and experience of a combat infantryman."
I had never cared for the nickname doughboy. "The same was
true in the gunfight with the jail escapees."

"Aren't you afraid?"

"Yes. Only a fool isn't afraid."

"Good." She linked her arm through mine as we plowed the
snow with our new boots. "I was terrified."

———

Victoria took some photos of the courthouse and downtown
Prescott. Back at the hotel, the desk clerk handed me a note.
Ordinary paper. The handwriting—I'd seen it before but
couldn't remember where. I scanned it and laid it flat on the
countertop for Victoria as he checked in another guest.

"Don't touch it."

She read in a whisper, "You're in dangerous territory,
Hammons. Stop before it's too late." She leaned closer. "What
does that mean?"

"It means we've been followed."

When the clerk was free again, I asked him who had given him
the note. He didn't remember. He had stepped away and found
it sitting on the counter when he came back.

We went upstairs and read through Carrie's letters and diary.
The diary was faithfully written every day, at least a paragraph, but
only through high school. She made elliptical references to her
father's "illness." Otherwise, the content was what you'd expect
from a girl her age.

The letters to her father were about school, how different
Phoenix was from Prescott, and each one pleaded with him to
take better care of himself. The last one was dated a week before
her murder. The letters from the fall semester were shorter than

she had written the previous year. They were not in keeping with Pamela's description of an aspiring author or artiste. I'd have expected pages of reflections, observations, and stories. Instead, they contained little more than what a postcard would hold.

That night, although mindful that someone might be watching us, we enjoyed a fine dinner at a nearby Mexican restaurant. We sat at the back, both of us in a booth facing the door. Just in case.

"It doesn't smell right," Victoria said over cheese-and-onion enchiladas, refried beans, and Mexican rice. "Everybody up here says Carrie is such a sweet girl. But how does that jibe with the house we saw, with the alcoholic father?"

"Or with the transformation that was described by her friends at the teachers' college," I said.

We tried to piece together a timeline of Carrie's last months but it was full of holes. Then we went back to our room, warmed up, and tried not to break the old bed.

Thirteen

The next morning, I wanted to take another run at Ezra Dell. Maybe the shock of his daughter's death had worn off enough to jog his memory, or a long, cold night alone had made him willing to tell us something he had withheld the previous day.

But when we hiked up to Park Avenue, two cars were sitting in front of Dell's house, the door was open, and a policeman stood on the porch. I was cold already but now a chill ran up the back of my neck.

"You'll need to stay back," the cop said. "What's your business here?"

I held up my badge. "Phoenix Police."

He looked barely out of high school and worked to conceal being impressed, curious, or plain disgusted with the interruption. "Stay." He said it as if we were two pooches and disappeared inside. No smoke was coming out of the chimney.

In a couple of minutes an older man in plain clothes came out and waved us forward. Introductions were made. He was the Prescott Police chief. I abbreviated myself to Detective Hammons and again recklessly flashed my buzzer. But it would get me further than showing up as a private eye.

"Dell is dead," he said. But I suspected that already. "Suicide." That, I seriously doubted, but I had to handle this gently. No "big-city know-it-all detective" from me.

"Would you mind if I looked, Chief?"

He didn't welcome me inside without an explanation of what brought us there the day before. I gave him the short version of Carrie's murder, without all the details.

"Well." he stamped his feet. "Would've been nice professional courtesy for you to check in with the local police."

"I'm sorry about that, sir," I said. I could be deferential, but I couldn't change the fact that I was a head taller than him. "It was a routine death notification…"

"Nothing routine about a murder," he snapped.

"No, sir. We should have contacted you when we got to town."

That seemed to mollify him somewhat, but he looked Victoria over.

"Miss Vasquez is a police photographer who's been involved in this case," I said.

"I'd be happy to retrieve my camera and take photos here if you'd like," she said. "For your departmental records."

"Looks cut and dried to me, forgive my pun." Was he flirting? But then he seemed to change his mind, deciding it was proper to add to his departmental records, such as they were. "That'd be real nice, Miss."

Victoria gave me a sardonic look and started off.

"Wait, Miss," the chief said. "I'll have Officer Gibbons give you a ride downtown and bring you back."

After they slid off down the snowy street, he turned and let me follow him inside.

As I suspected, the fire was dead and the stove cold. It felt chillier inside than outside, but maybe that was imagination. My bleak anticipation for what I would find.

Ezra Dell was seated in the same stuffed chair as the day before, but far beyond the comfort of his liquor. His throat was slit, a seeming bucketful of blood down the front of his shirt and pants, and into the upholstery. His head was lolled back, eyes glassy. In his right hand was a straight razor.

"See," the Chief said. "Suicide, like I said. Looks very straightforward."

It looked all wrong to me.

"How did you find him, if you don't mind me asking?"

"Got a call, check on him. Assumed it was a neighbor who didn't want to deal directly with Ezra, who could be nasty. When Gibbons got here, the door was unlocked and he walked in and found him just like this."

He pulled out a cigar, bit off the tip, and lit it. "Not the first suicide here since the hard times set in. I'm not at all surprised with Ezra, poor bastard. He was a conductor on the Santa Fe, you know. But the drink cost him his job. He really went downhill after his wife passed away. I knew him well in those days, a decent man. I'm surprised he didn't kill himself earlier with the booze he made in his home still. Then, the news about his daughter, well, that obviously pushed him over the edge."

I studied the wound, ear to ear. "That's a very precise cut for somebody with as shaky hands as Ezra had."

"Maybe. Hadn't really thought about it."

Having investigated many suicides, I knew that slitting one's throat was exceedingly rare, much less being done with such exactness and going all the way across. One suicide I remembered was characterized by a cut that barely made it halfway. Once the man hit his carotid artery and it started gushing blood, he dropped the razor and, in a moment of regret, tried to stanch the bleeding. Too late, of course, but that was a normal involuntary reflex. Only someone with the greatest discipline and steely determination could replicate the scene before me on his own, and I'd never seen it. A straight razor was a poor weapon with the danger it would fold back on the user's hand. That didn't keep it from being used in many a fight in Paris Alley and Darktown. I kept these observations to myself for the moment.

I thought about Ezra's actions the day before. "Wasn't he left-handed, Chief?"

The chief looked at the straight razor in the man's right hand and bit into his cigar. His his face turned red. After a long pause: "Yes, yes, he was. Goddamn."

I pointed to the wound. "Look at the steady cut all the way across, including to the end on the right side of his neck. I've never seen anyone cut his throat and be able to complete it that way." Going to the back side of the chair, I pantomimed how a killer would hold Ezra's head up and neatly slice his throat open, hitting the carotids on both sides. "This is what happened."

"Well, shit. It's a homicide."

"Yes, sir." I asked him about Carrie. Once again, I heard how wonderful she was. "Prettiest girl in Prescott. You knew she was going places. What a terrible thing. Only child. Now the entire family snuffed out."

I asked if his people had checked the rest of the house.

He shook his head, and I immediately went to Carrie's bedroom. Someone had obviously tossed it. Drawers were open, the mattress was disturbed as if the intruder had been looking underneath it, pillows askew, the trophy on its side. Beyond the door, I heard Victoria return and start to take photos.

I'd brought more than bad news. I'd brought a killer, who followed us. Sometime after we left Ezra alive, he knocked on the door. Thinking it was us returning, Ezra opened it without his previous...caution. Then the killer had tried to pry information about Carrie, about what we had told him. He was gathering intelligence, tying up loose ends.

Maybe he pretended to be a cop or was one. However it went down, Ezra appeared seated trustingly as the man kept talking, walked behind him, produced the razor. Or maybe Ezra had drunk himself asleep when the killer arrived. Either way, it was over quickly. And it was a damned good bet this was the same man who left the threatening note for me at the hotel.

To satisfy myself, I went into the bathroom. Sure enough, Ezra—who hadn't seemed to have shaved in months—had his own straight razor, sitting peacefully inside the medicine cabinet. I pointed all this out to the chief, who ordered his minion to take notes.

"What now?" he asked.

I was on my haunches, looking around the living-room furniture, under tables and beside chairs.

"Yesterday, Ezra greeted us with a Tommy gun," I said. "It's gone."

The young cop stared at his boss, whose cigar had long gone cold.

Fourteen

We returned to Phoenix overdressed and overheated in time for me to read that Jack Hunter had been stabbed to death at Florence Prison. A fight with another inmate. A baseball bat was involved, too. Otherwise, nobody saw anything or knew the origin of their quarrel. The shiv that killed him hadn't been found.

This would be routine as prison violence goes if not for the note Hunter had sent me at Police Headquarters, promising information about "the train girl, Carrie." He wanted me to visit, writing that it would be worth my time.

Now there would be no visit, unless I wanted to commune with a corpse. I was left to speculate. He knew her name and, apparently, something about her murder. Prisons were rich in gossip and intelligence. Did Jack know her killer's identity? Had another prisoner spilled to him, leading him to write the detective who helped put him away? Would he want a deal—privileges, reduced sentence—if he informed?

I would never know.

Somebody was tying up loose ends. Three murders, and the case was still classified as a suspicious death. I was plenty suspicious all right.

Jack Hunter. Twenty-six and he'd never reach twenty-seven. What a waste.

The newspaper also reported that eleven men were jailed for violating narcotics laws. Somebody hadn't been paid off. But, as McGrath assured me, crime was down during the Depression. Another article celebrated that thirty-five hundred men were employed in state mines as of this past December. Nowhere in the story did it tell how many thousands of miners were unemployed. I put Ezra Dell's watch in my safe and dictated to Gladys a report for Captain McGrath on my Prescott assignment.

Not for the last time, I wondered if it was time to stop. I had performed the death knock. My work should have been done. Could have been. But, no. I was a stubborn SOB.

Victoria and I divvied up next steps. I would go to the Arizona Biltmore and ask about Carrie's summer work there. Victoria would return to Tempe and try to find Carrie's possessions, left behind at the end of the previous semester. First, she needed to complete a commercial job for the McCulloch Brothers. Commercial photography paid the best, and the McCullochs had the business cornered, so when they tossed her an assignment, she always took it. This one was for photographing a car dealership.

I put on my best suit, a fedora, and a topcoat. We brought the cold with us from Prescott. Certainly not as cold as up there, but cold for Phoenix. High of forty-eight and low of twenty-five, the kind of chill that only happened a few times a year here. The heater in the Ford made short work of the outside weather as I drove north. Crossing the Arizona Canal, I left the oasis behind and was in the desert. Nothing out here but the tuberculosis camps at Sunnyslope, a few played-out mines, and this new hotel amid the saguaros and beneath Squaw Peak.

The Biltmore was impressive, four stories tall with stylized geometric bricks, the work of architect Albert Chase McArthur and influenced by Frank Lloyd Wright. It opened at the height of optimism, a few months before the stock market crashed. Now, I came up the curving concrete driveway flanked by plantings and surrounded by winter grass, then slipped the valet a quarter and let him take the car.

Inside, I went to the front desk and discreetly showed my badge to the clerk, asking for the manager. I wondered how many times I could flash that button before it backfired. McGrath had authorized me to poke into this case. But he had deniability. Nobody had my back.

Half a dozen guests were gathered in the swank lobby wearing expensive new Stetsons. They were grousing about the weather. Soon an officious little man in a gray double-breasted suit appeared and led me to his office. He was using a pearl cigarette holder. I took off my fedora and followed him.

"I hope there's no trouble, Detective…"

"Hammons."

"We scrupulously follow the liquor laws, Detective Hammond, even though Prohibition is on the way out."

I thought about correcting him. Hammons was an unusual name. But I let it be. I said, "Scrupulously, except for the Men's Smoking Room on the second floor."

He smiled. "Oh, you know about that."

"And I know about the red beacon on the roof you turn on when there's a raid, and the secret passages that let speakeasy guests exit to their rooms. As I recall, a nearby suite was favored by Clark Gable and Carole Lombard." Some of the best booze I kept at home was appropriated from periodic raids at the Biltmore.

"Look, Detective Hammond, we don't want any trouble. The Depression is trouble enough…"

I cut him off. "I'm not here about hooch. It's about her."

I slid across a photo of Carrie. It was a straight-on shot taken from Ezra's house in Prescott and showed her to best advantage, straight blond hair with bangs, expressive eyes, a white button-down blouse, and knees showing below a tan skirt.

"That's Cynthia," he said. "Lovely girl. She worked here last summer as a waitress. The slow season but we have air-conditioning. She was a good employee. Never missed a day. She's in college in Tempe."

Cynthia.

I slid the photo closer. "This girl was Cynthia? You're sure?"

He flicked ash off his cigarette. "Yes, of course."

Not only was she staying in Phoenix instead of going home, she was using a false name.

I asked him for her address, but he told me she was allowed to use a room at the hotel itself, deducting the rent from her earnings. It was off-season, so the Biltmore had extra space.

"Did she have gentlemen callers?"

"Absolutely not." He drew himself up to his full height, which was a good head shorter than me. "We have rules, and she always abided by them."

"Like the rules about liquor." I smiled. "Did she serve in the speakeasy?"

He nodded.

Then I asked to speak with anyone who worked with her and might have been a friend.

"I hope Cynthia is okay..."

"I'm afraid not. This is a homicide investigation."

He went pale. "Oh, my."

In a few minutes, he produced a willowy brunette named Margaret. She sat in the chair beside me.

"This is Detective Hammond," he said. "Of the Phoenix Police. I'm afraid something has happened to Cynthia."

"Oh, dear," she whispered, her plain face contorted in a frown.

I nodded at the manager. "Would you mind giving us a few minutes?" He hesitated. I added, "Alone." He reluctantly shuffled out, closing the door.

"Margaret, I want you to be straight with me." I leaned in. "Nobody needs to know anything you tell me."

She nodded.

"Tell me about Cynthia."

"Well, she was good at her job. She very nice to me. I wasn't used to such a pretty girl treating me well. She gave me money when I was broke. She always seemed to have cash."

"Where did she get this money?"

"Her father was in mining. I don't know why she had to work. But she was a hard worker, never made out like she was a rich girl."

I took a chance. "Her last name was…?"

"Thayer."

Like father, like daughter? Had Ezra Dell come up with this scheme, or had Carrie taught him to use it?

Margaret caught my mind wandering. "What's going on, Detective?"

"As I said, this is a homicide investigation. Someone attacked… Cynthia…last month and then dismembered her body. She was also pregnant at the time."

The shock radiated down Margaret's body. I asked her if Cynthia had any enemies, anyone who might wish her harm, any grudges. No, no, and no. Perfectly loved Carrie/Cynthia.

"I don't buy it."

She looked away, but I cupped her chin with my hand and made her look at me.

"Come on, Maggie."

"That's what my friends call me."

"Then think of me as a friend."

Tears began. "Men like her," she said. "Liked her, I mean.

Cynthia went out a lot at night, when the manager had gone home."

"Where did she go?"

"She wouldn't tell me. But a man always came to get her. He'd bring her back late."

"What man?"

Now she was crying full out. "I don't want to get in trouble."

"You're not going to get in trouble. What man? What did he look like? Did you know his name?"

After a long silence, she gave a massive shrug. "All I knew was what she told me. He was a policeman. He wore a hat like yours."

———

I was almost back to town on Seventh Street when a police car came behind me, turned on his siren, and pulled me over. My first thought was that I had used the damned buzzer once too often, and I would be carted off to jail in handcuffs.

"Detective Hammons," the uniform said, bending into my rolled-down window. We shook hands.

"Hey, Watkins. What's up?"

"Detective Muldoon has us looking for you. The squeal just came over the radio. You know where the Triple-A junkyard is?"

"Yep. Seventh Avenue and the tracks, right?"

"That's the place."

I gunned it south before Watkins even got back to his car. I stayed on Seventh Street past Van Buren, where the Phoenix Union High School students were lined up at the Nifty Nook burger joint. "Twenty-Four-Hour Service," a 7-Up sign proclaimed. A crossing guard held us up as a covey of coeds crossed, laughing and talking, making me think of Carrie aka Cynthia and her cop friend. Then I went south to Washington Street and turned west, brooding over what Muldoon wanted of me.

At Seventh Avenue, I waited for a long freight train then crossed the seventeen railroad tracks and pulled into the junkyard. I saw Turk's broad back and Frenchy Navarre, along with some uniforms. I took a deep breath, set the brake, and stepped out onto the hard soil. The uniformed officers nodded and let me pass.

"Geno!" Frenchy clapped me on the arm. He was wiry and intense, with a precise manner. He could be fussy and autocratic on the job, but if he liked you, he was pleasant. "I'm glad they found you. We put out a dragnet. A friendly one!" He laughed, high-pitched and sinister, but maybe I was imagining the last part.

Turk Muldoon came over. He was angular and lanky at six-foot-three, possessing hooded icy-blue eyes. His gaunt face was grim.

"Take a look at this."

He led me to the wreck of a Model A and pointed to a body resting against the old car's rust-caked door. The man's throat had been neatly slashed and his head pushed to the left, with blood on his cream sport coat and flannel slacks.

Zoogie Boogie.

His legs and arms were in the perfect posture of rigor mortis.

"I thought you'd want to know," Muldoon said. "Him being your snitch and all. When was the last time you saw him?"

"His trial," I lied, not knowing quite why. "I didn't realize he'd gotten out."

Muldoon sighed. "He might have been safer in Florence, lad, even with what happened to Jack Hunter. We hear Zoogie was collecting gambling money in jigtown."

"Coon probably robbed and killed him," Frenchy said. "They all use razors. If it was nigger killing nigger, it'd be misdemeanor murder." He roared with laughter.

Muldoon rolled his eyes and winked at me. I was two places at once: Here, and back in Prescott, where Ezra Dell had been murdered. The colored population there was negligible.

I reached under Zoogie's shirt and found a money belt. Inside was a wad of bills. I counted ninety bucks.

I held it out. "And your colored killer left this?"

Nobody spoke as I handed the money to Turk. I walked around the car, following furrows in the dirt, and a few feet away behind another junk car was a lake of blood with several spurts from where the blade first hit the artery.

"He was killed over here, see?" I said. "Then the killer dragged him to the car and leaned him against the door. Make it easier to find him." I walked back to the body and examined his hands and arms. "No defensive wounds. Whoever killed him took him from behind. Either he was surprised or he knew the killer and felt safe turning his back. It was at least four hours ago, see the rigor setting in?"

"This is another reason we needed the best homicide detective on the force," Turk said. "Or used to be on the force. Dumb move by the bosses, letting you go."

I shrugged. "Lot of detectives here for a colored slitting the throat of an ex-con."

"It's the first homicide in the city this year," Frenchy said, propping up his fedora and pulling his pocket watch from a chain that went to his vest, checking the time.

"Second," I corrected. "The girl who was dismembered by the railroad tracks."

"I heard she fell from the train," Turk said. I let it be. He said, "You hear that Jimmy Allen died?" He was the night captain. "Dropped dead in his chair, talking to Joe Youngblood one minute and the next he's gone. Bad heart, but only fifty-five. Maybe that leaves an opening for you to come back."

"I doubt that."

"Never know," Turk continued. "The Chief likes you. Everybody does."

I was skeptical about that, too.

Leaning back down, I closed the lids over Zoogie's dead eyes. First Ezra Dell, then Jack Hunter, now this. Tying up loose ends. Preventing men from giving me information. This was why detectives didn't believe in coincidences.

As Frenchy and Turk examined the blood spatter, I reached in Zoogie's other pocket and found a slip of paper and a key. I thought for a second, then clandestinely pocketed them.

"He was your friend?" This came from an unfamiliar voice. I turned to see a young priest.

"I guess I was as close to a friend as he had. His name was Henry Porter, Father…"

"McLoughlin," he said. "Call me Emmett. Do you know if he was Catholic?"

"I don't know."

"No matter." He knelt beside the blood sinking into the hard soil and began administering last rites in a quiet voice. "Through this holy anointing, may the Lord in his love and mercy…"

"Two cops, a private eye, and a priest," Frenchy said. "Sounds like the beginning of a joke. All we need is a rabbi." He chuckled in a low voice. "I say we go brace the first suspicious jig we see, beat a confession out of him, or get him to roll on somebody. Case closed. Can't be letting white men be knifed in Phoenix, even no-account shitbirds like Zoogie Boogie. Sends a bad message."

I put my hand on his shoulder and walked him a few feet away. "What do you know about voodoo, Frenchy?"

This time he bent over laughing, holding his ribs.

"Geno, you got me in stitches." He switched to a bayou accent. "You thing yo' Cajun friend from N'Awlens know about de Ouanga an' de spells, de dragon sticks an' de gris-gris?" He pronounced it *GREE-gree*. And laughed hard. Then he pulled the watch from his vest pocket again, checking the time once more.

I was quite the comedian, but looking back at the dead body propped against the junk car, I was filled with a mixture of sadness and anger. I knelt down and from memory drew a crude representation of the distorted cross I had found at the crime scene where Carrie was laid out.

"What about this?"

Frenchy studied it, and I studied Frenchy.

He shook his head. "I don't know, *cher*. But it looks scary as hell."

Fifteen

After a few minutes, I pulled out and started back toward downtown. This time the road was blocked by a passenger train slowly entering the tracks into Union Station. Del Webb was right—we did need an underpass at Central. In my rearview mirror, I saw Frenchy's dark Chevy come out of the junkyard and turn south. I decided to follow him and pulled a U-turn.

This would be tricky on a two-lane road, so I gave him plenty of distance. A hay truck helpfully pulled in front of me, offering concealment. The South Mountains loomed blue-brown ahead of us as we left the city, passing farmhouses and pastures, then dipped down into the dry Salt River, a quarry to the left with water in an excavated portion. I wondered how deep that hole went and what might be in it: bodies, cars. Frenchy wasn't searching for an innocent Negro to frame, at least not now.

At Broadway, Frenchy turned right. So did the hay truck. My luck held as I spun the steering wheel and followed on the dirt road. I had a gut feeling where he was going.

Sure enough, Frenchy pulled into Kemper Marley's property. The hay truck continued on, and I made a snap decision to pull into a stand of cottonwoods about thirty feet away. I got out, quietly closed the door, and went into a grove of grapefruit trees on the west side of the Marley house. It was just in time to hear Kemper yelling.

"What kind of fool are you, Navarre? You stupid son of a bitch!"

Frenchy said something I couldn't make out. Then his blood was up and his voice louder. "I don't let any man talk to me that way!"

I moved closer in a crouch and watched. The two were standing beside Navarre's car. Marley had confronted him before he even got up the path to the house.

"I'll talk to you however I want, Frenchy. I own your sorry ass."

Frenchy was insistent. "You said you wanted to send a message to that kike! What better message than taking out one of his bagmen?"

"I didn't tell you to kill anybody," Marley said. "This only brings more trouble. I have to work with Chicago, not fight them. I need leverage against them, not a war, you damned idiot."

I crouched a little lower. There it was: Frenchy had cut Zoogie Boogie's throat. My snitch would have been compliant around a member of the Hat Squad. Not only that, but trusting a man he was collecting money for, not knowing what was coming. And, with a razor, Navarre would make it appear as if the killer was colored.

"Gene Hammons was there," Frenchy said.

"What the hell? Why?"

"Zoogie Boogie was Hammons's stool pigeon back in the day, before he went to prison. Muldoon called him down. There was nothing I could do to stop it without it looking suspicious."

"What did Hammons say?"

"He's a smart cop. Dangerous smart. Found the place I slit Zoogie's throat and the drag marks where I brought the body.

And he found a money belt with cash in it. Gave it to Muldoon as evidence."

Marley cursed.

"Hell, I didn't know he had that on him," Navarre protested.

If only Marley knew that Frenchy was playing both sides. Zoogie Boogie told me Navarre was Gus Greenbaum's bagman. Now here he was, acting as Marley's lieutenant.

Marley said, "What about his brother? Was he there, too?"

"No, Don's probably hitting the gonger in Chinatown. You don't have to worry about him. This case was just me and Turk Muldoon and some uniforms. Captain wanted two detectives on the call. It's the first homicide of the year."

"Except for that girl, Carrie."

My hands clenched into fists.

"What's going on with that?"

Frenchy said, "Deep six. The department won't even acknowledge it."

"I want to know if that changes, got it? Last thing I need is for Gene Hammons to start nosing around in her killing. And meanwhile, Muldoon has that money you missed on the ex-con. He'll be suspicious."

"I know," Navarre said. "I went through Zoogie's pockets. I wanted to make it look like a robbery. But the junkyard owner came around, don't ask me why at that hour. This was when I was still talking to Zoogie. We hid and kept quiet. Finally, the owner split and I turned Zoogie around and used the razor. How could I know he was wearing a damned money belt?"

"What the hell were you thinking?"

"Easy. Say it was a robbery. Muldoon won't talk to him, tell him about the cash. So it looks like a robbery. Then you could tell Greenbaum his men might not be safe in Niggertown without your protection, see? It would send a strong message. But you'd be the man on top, willing to help. Chicago would notice, too. I thought it through. This will still work for you."

"Are you insane, Navarre, or only a jughead? You 'thought it through' about as much as a gelding 'thinks through' his nuts before they're cut off. Gus Greenbaum would kill your ass without a second thought, cop or not. Same with me. His people carry Tommy guns, not razors. He'd see through any explanation and retaliate if I even mentioned this to him. You'd better pray you can find a jigaboo you can blame it on and make it real public."

"All right, all right. I'll give one a tumble. It won't be hard."

"And never say a word about the truth of this—ever! Got it?"

"Yeah."

"Do you?" This was a roar.

"Yes, Kemper. I've got it."

"You're no good to me doing foolish things. I have other flat-foots I can use. You're not my enforcer. I have muscle when and where I need it." I heard him spit. "You're nothing special, Navarre. You'll forfeit a month's pay from me because of this stunt."

"Damn, I need that money," Frenchy pleaded. "I've got gambling debts."

"Then you should have thought before you killed Greenbaum's man. And if your gambling debts are to some bookie in town, you're lining Greenbaum's pockets. You're stupider than I thought."

Marley stalked toward his house, and I rose up a few inches for a better look. Frenchy's face was bright red and scrunched in anger, resembling an overripe tomato. He plainly wanted to say more but kept silent. Then he climbed in his car and drove off trailing dust, fortunately for me, going west away from where I was parked.

I gave it a good ten minutes, then returned to my car and drove downtown.

———

I went back trying to figure out Navarre's scheme. Zoogie Boogie told me he worked for Frenchy, collecting in the colored part of town. Frenchy was Gus Greenbaum's badged bagman. He was also in Kemper Marley's pay. To hear Navarre tell it, his thinking, if you wanted to dignify it with that word, was what he said. Kill Zoogie and give Marley a chance to offer protection against shakedowns in Darktown. As if Greenbaum needed protection. Frenchy was a fool, as Kemper had said. Or something else was going on.

For one thing, I couldn't get past the money left on Zoogie's person. Beyond slitting the man's throat, stealing his cabbage would be the priority of making it appear as a robbery, making it look like Greenbaum's men were unsafe south of the tracks. But the bills and money belt were left behind.

Also, when I braced Zoogie a few days ago on Van Buren, I asked him to find out the lowdown on the street about Carrie Dell's murder. He was a good snitch, diligent, before he went away for the robbery. Now, on probation, he would have every incentive to stay on my good side and dig. Maybe too deep. Maybe Zoogie was sitting on important information for me while I was in Prescott—and Frenchy found out about it, needed to silence him.

If so, why the trip to Marley and brag about killing Zoogie? My best theory was that Kemper was nagging him for results, same as me, and Frenchy decided to improvise his murder of Zoogie as something done to help Marley get leverage over Greenbaum. Otherwise, why kill one of his own collectors in Darktown?

And I was being watched. That much was clear from the events in Prescott, as well as the car I saw parked in front of my apartment, the occupant helpfully lighting a cigarette to reveal himself. Maybe that man was Frenchy and he leaned on Zoogie to learn what he knew about Carrie, then slit his throat. If all this was so, Navarre was a great actor, playing my friend with the whole "Geno" routine. I knew it sounded like a reach.

Once again, I tried to figure out Marley. He was a major landowner and kept buying more as people were forced by the Depression to sell. With his legal liquor distributorship, he would add exponentially to the wealth he had acquired as a bootlegger. A young man, he was probably one of the richest people in the state. How was that not enough? Yet he wanted the Chicago Outfit to cut him in on the betting wire service. I didn't get it. With a fraction of his holdings, I'd be happy to retire and marry Victoria. Maybe it wasn't merely money. It was power he was after. He was no Dwight Heard, who used his fortune to help build a city. But Heard was in the ground, and now we were all supposed to bow to Kemper. Even Barry Goldwater and Harry Rosenzweig seemed intimidated by him. I had his money burning a hole in my safe and wondered what he'd want for it.

The key from Zoogie's pocket was attached to a worn fob for the Golden West Hotel. It was a two-story building that dated back to territorial days on East Monroe Street downtown, a sleeping porch built over the sidewalk. Now it was dwarfed by the new Professional Building, an art deco tower that housed the still-solvent Valley Bank.

Inside, the desk clerk was on the phone. I held up my key and mouthed, "Any mail?"

He reached behind him into the cubbyhole and handed me an envelope. I took it and quickly headed upstairs before he got off his call and had time to realize I was too well dressed to be the typical guest of the Golden West.

The hallway smelled of desperate men.

I started to slip the key in but pulled out my pistol just in case.

Then I opened the door, surveyed an empty room, quietly shut it, and turned the lock.

The space was tiny, barely enough for the single bed, small chest of drawers, and a chair. Through the thin walls, I heard snoring. The guests must have shared a bathroom down the hall. I went through his minimal wardrobe hung in an open closet. Two pairs of pants, four shirts, no shoes. His pants pockets were empty. Next I tossed the place more methodically, looking under the mattress, pulling out drawers, and checking beneath and behind them. Nothing.

Suddenly I heard voices coming up the stairs.

"I was on the phone, but I'm pretty sure he came up a few minutes ago…"

No place to hide.

I went to the window, opened it, and stepped out on the fire escape. It swayed under my weight. I closed the dusty curtains and then gently pulled down the window—but not far enough, for the door opened. I thought about going down, but no. I gingerly took the rusty stairs to the top landing. The roof offered escape, but I bent down and listened.

"I don't get it." This was the voice of the clerk. "I could have sworn he came in, Detective."

Detective.

He might be doing a routine follow-up to the murder. But considering I took the key, how the hell did he know where Zoogie was staying? Unless it wasn't part of the investigation and it was Navarre, who either already knew where Zoogie roomed or had pried it out of him before running the razor across his carotid.

Sounds came out the partly closed window as the room was ransacked. What would I do next? I leaned against the old masonry, trying to make myself invisible as the window below came up and a fedora popped out. Frenchy? Muldoon? Don? I couldn't tell. Damn, I couldn't remember the hats worn at the junkyard. Its owner looked below, but not above. Somehow the decades-old ironwork of the fire escape didn't creak or groan with me imposing on it. The window slammed shut.

I gave it a good fifteen minutes, then took the fire escape all the way down to the alley.

Out on the street, I leaned against the Professional Building and lit a nail to calm my nerves. I pulled out the envelope, and it had my name on it. Opening it, I found a single business card. Decorated with a saguaro cactus, it read:

Summer Tours

Cynthia

3–7222.

A big clue from a dead man. Maybe Zoogie had the presence of mind to know his room might be tossed if something went wrong, that he might be searched if he kept it on his person. So he gave it to the night clerk to place in his cubbyhole at the front desk.

Then I remembered the slip of paper from Zoogie's pants pocket. I unfolded it and read a typed message:

Meet me at the Triple-A, midnight.

Walking across to the Hotel San Carlos, I found a phone booth and shut myself behind the folding door. Then I dialed the number on the card.

"Answering service." A woman's voice.

"Is this Summer Tours?"

"We're their answering service."

I leaned in. "This is Detective Hammons of the Phoenix Police Department." Just to be safe, I gave Don's badge number.

"Are you Summer Tours or are you a commercial answering service?"

This got the woman's attention. She said they answered for sixty clients, ranging from doctors to locksmiths. I asked about Summer Tours. I listened as she opened a drawer and thumbed through it.

Coming back in five minutes, she said Summer Tours had engaged them this past May, paying five dollars a month. But they had stopped paying in January and were in arrears.

"That happens often these days," she said.

"Do you know what Summer Tours was?"

"Something to do with tourism, the girl who opened the account told me."

I asked for a description: Young, blond hair, blue eyes, pretty. Cynthia Thayer. She paid three months ahead in cash. Customers would leave their names and phone numbers, and she would call daily to retrieve them.

"Would you happen to have a log of those calls and the numbers?"

"Oh, yes. We keep records for all our customers."

I asked if I could take a look, expecting her to demand a warrant.

"Of course," she said and gave me her address.

Sixteen

Victoria came over that night. She brought news from her visit to Tempe, too, carrying a box. She placed it beside the sofa and I poured us Scotch. Thanks to my name as an introduction, the registrar gave her this container that held Carrie's belongings, left behind in her dorm last semester. Besides some clothes and shoes, it held a notebook of her writing, a diary, and letters.

"Jackpot," I said.

She clinked my glass and sipped. "I hope so. I have another box of very expensive clothes still in the car. As for this, it will take some time to go through it. You have quite an admirer in that coed named Pamela."

"She's a kid."

"I'm not jealous. Much." She punched my shoulder. "I did some sorting this afternoon. A few letters from her father. Some from a neighbor in Prescott. She sent money to the woman to buy groceries for her dad. I guess it was a way to keep him from using the cash to buy booze or build another still. Then things got interesting. She had a number of love letters."

"From her boyfriend, the one who works at the slaughter-house?"

"They don't read that way. Young men are needy. These are written with more assurance. I guess an older man or men."

"Who?"

"That's the problem. They're only signed, 'Your Admirer.' And the envelopes they came in were discarded, so no return address or even a postmark. But do you have that note from Prescott, saying you were in dangerous territory?"

I went to the desk and retrieved it. Victoria pulled out one of the notes from Carrie's things and leaned against me, holding them side by side.

"Different handwriting," she said.

I read the note:

Dearest C.

I know you'll be pleased with your cut this month, which I enclose. You can share it with your friends as they deserve. This will not go on forever. I promise. Keep trusting me. In the beginning, I remember that you were eager to try. But I sense you are having second thoughts. Hang in their, dearest. It won't be much longer, and we'll be set with a nice nest egg and we can run away and start a new life.

Your Admirer

I read it again. "What the hell does this mean?" I told her about what I had learned at the Biltmore, including her friend Margaret saying an older man would fetch her at night and that he was a cop. And our Carrie was going by Cynthia. Both starting with the letter C.

"Could she have been embezzling from the hotel?" I said.

"Maybe," Victoria said. "Makes sense. Even in the hot months,

I bet the Biltmore makes plenty. It might be involved with the speakeasy out there. But what about 'share it with your friends'?"

I shook my head. "Maybe she needed help for the inside job. It still doesn't explain her nightly jaunts. Unless the man was her lover and somehow involved in skimming the money. Maybe he put her up to it. Married man, promising to leave his wife if they got enough."

Victoria shrugged. "Maybe. Still, it doesn't seem right."

"How so?"

"I can't put my finger on it, Eugene. Woman's intuition. We need to read more. I'll leave these with you." She set the letters and diary on the coffee table.

I gave more of a rundown about my day, showing her the numbers and names I had copied from the answering service for Carrie's mysterious business.

Finally, I had to tell her about Jack Hunter, Zoogie Boogie, Frenchy Navarre, and Marley. She closed her eyes and gripped my hand. Each piece of information felt as if I was delivering a kidney punch.

Finishing her drink, she stood. "I've got another McCulloch Brothers job early tomorrow. It's not hanging out from the top of the Chrysler Building, but it pays the bills."

"I'm needy," I said, touching her skirt.

"You'll have to wait, young man." She paused. "I can't get that Margaret Bourke-White photo out of my head. There's got to be more to life than photographing crime scenes and quinceañeras. If she can get on the staff of a major magazine...wow."

"I said you could do it. Maybe you'd let me tag along. I'm sure New York needs another shamus."

"I need to build a better portfolio than I have, or nobody will take me seriously. In the meantime, please be careful, Eugene."

I walked her to her car, where we enjoyed a long kiss. Then she drove around the parkway and headed east toward Central Avenue.

I stepped into the shadows of the porch to watch her go. That was when I saw a dark car sitting across the slim linear park come to life, headlights on, pulling out and driving in the same direction.

I ran to my Ford and swung around, headlights off, and followed him. It might be a coincidence, but I wasn't taking chances.

Out on Central, I marked his taillights going south, the same direction as Victoria. He caught the green light at Roosevelt Street, then it turned amber and red. I ran it and kept my headlights off until there was enough traffic that I could turn them on and blend in. A quarter mile farther south, with neon decorating the business district ahead, he turned right on Van Buren Street. This was the same route Victoria would take to reach her bungalow, which doubled as her photo studio.

I hung back, watching his taillights as we crossed Seventh Avenue. When he turned left on Tenth Avenue by Woodland Park, my gut tightened. Victoria's house was close. I turned off my lights again and cruised slowly down the darkened residential street.

In quick succession, I saw Victoria park, unload her equipment, and walk past the trunks of palm trees to her bungalow. The dark car waited for her to go in, shut off his lights, then crept past. I parked at the curb fifty feet behind them.

Then he pulled a U-turn at Adams Street and came back. He pulled into a spot south of Victoria's house far from a streetlight. And sat there.

I gave it fifteen minutes, then climbed out on the passenger side of my Ford, gently closing the door and walking south, mostly concealed by palm, olive, and pepper trees on the narrow parking lawn between the sidewalk and the curb. I left my apartment without my regular pistol, as well as a coat, and the cold penetrated uncomfortably. But I had the .38 Detective Special from the glove box. Now I held it in my right hand, keeping it down against my leg.

The street was quiet except for train noises from the tracks a few blocks south, locomotive whistles and cars coupling, then silence. He stayed in the car, a dark four-door Chevy, so I took my time. With the temperature around freezing, fog wafted from his tailpipe. His engine was on.

Then I was parallel to him, concealed by the lazy fronds of a lush, low Canary Island date palm. Ideally, I would have liked to keep walking, then approach him from a blind spot to his rear. But the tree cover didn't extend down the street. A nail glowed through the driver's window but not enough to show a face. The four-door Chevy looked similar to Frenchy's, to Don's, to a thousand cars in Phoenix.

I walked fast, stepping off the curb, coming straight at him. But it wasn't fast enough. He saw me and pulled out. I grabbed the driver's door handle with my left hand, but he gunned it. The door was locked. For a second, I thought about hanging on and trying to make it up to the running board. But I couldn't get my foot up in time, had only the barest grip on the door handle, and would have been dragged down the street. The next thing I knew, I was spun around and deposited on the cold pavement. When I looked up, he was a block away and moving fast, lights off, no chance to catch a license plate.

Then he was gone. Who knew the trick of camouflage by driving with your lights off? Cops and criminals. In my mind, the two were rapidly blending together.

Another thing about that Chevy sedan: It had the spare tire outside on the running board. Jimmy Darrow, the railroad bull, said the car he saw pulling away from where Carrie's body parts were dumped had the same feature. He said it might be a Packard. But what if he were wrong? Hell, even my two-door ragtop had the spare placed that way.

I walked to Victoria's house to tell her what happened. She tended to the bloody scrape on my left hand.

After I left, I stayed in my car for an hour, watching. Her light went out. I walked through her alley. Sat in the car again. Nothing stirred.

This was familiar terrain beyond the fact that Victoria lived here. North of Van Buren was the University Park neighborhood. At one time, the Methodist Church planned to build a university there. It never happened, but the name stuck as it became a residential subdivision. It had been the center of the murders that became my most famous case. They happened on quiet nights.

Now, no one else came down her street. I finally gave up my watch and drove the empty drags of Phoenix, half aimlessly, half chasing four-door Chevys. Finally, I went home, put on a Duke Ellington record, and started to read some of the material Victoria had retrieved from the college.

As a homicide detective, I often imagined the victims speaking to me. I would talk to them in my head, sometimes out loud: "Tell me how you died. Tell me what happened. Who did this?" It was a useful mental exercise in the investigation.

This time, Carrie was speaking to me through entries in the two-inch-thick diary, written in blue ink, feminine cursive. I would soon realize that some of the contents were more personal than I expected. I picked some random diary pages to get a flavor.

———

CARRIE DELL'S DIARY 5/15/32

Tonight K was giving her dewy smile as "Edward" laughed, his cigarette holder at a jaunty angle. P was blowing smoke rings, projecting disinterested bravado. She is all sardonic irony. I caught two lovebirds in the hallway outside the kitchen. The party was only getting started.

This is so easy it's scary! We're up and running like

my wild palomino when we raced through the woods in autumn. Dad always said I should run my own business, work for myself. But I bet he never had this in mind. With the right connections, Prohibition makes everything possible. People are such hypocrites. The biggest moralists are the biggest libertines. Scratch that prissy, churchgoing surface and there they are. Revealed! Naked as can be. Someday I'll make them characters in a novel. Times are hard, but big money is to be made from this crowd, with the right partners. I think I've got them. Now if I can keep trusting them. My bet is that money will ensure that.

So far, the business is operating as I intended. We've started with a core of a dozen regular clients. I checked out each one myself, made sure the connection was right and tight. You wouldn't believe who some of them are, and Cynthia's not telling. Confidentiality is what we're selling. Am I a poet and don't know it? The Biltmore job is the perfect cover. Better than that, really. My business actually complements theirs.

Carrie Dell is a long way from Prescott and not going to end up as a teacher. I can feel the sidewalks of Greenwich Village under my feet, being on the arms of handsome beaux in the jazz clubs of Harlem. But…must not get uppity, girl. Always watchful. Always on guard.

CARRIE DELL'S DIARY 9/20/32

He tells me to call him Frenchy. But I love his real first name. Leonce. It has music to it. My Frenchman. My Cajun lover. The appeal of an older man, and, no, I'm not looking for a daddy. His forty years vs. my nineteen. So I call him Leonce and he always laughs.

He's so much more interesting than the college boys who want me. He's worldly, dangerous. I always went for the bad boys. But his bad side is real, *earned*. He's a real detective, too.

He tells me about the police, and it's exciting. His fellows on the "Hat Squad," he calls it. I sit in the car and watch them. The ones he talks about the most are Turk Muldoon, Don Hammons, and his brother Gene. That's the detective who caught the University Park Strangler. Leonce is envious. Gene is also tall and handsome, and Leonce is envious of that, too. It's an itch my Frenchman can't scratch. I know the advantage that good looks convey. I wonder how Gene uses his?

We go to fancy dinners and speakeasies, and he introduces me as Cynthia. It's a name I found in the newspaper women's page. I like it. I can tell he's worried, though, that people might see us together and tell his wife. He hates her. She hates him, at least to hear him tell it.

My group is envious. They want to know who this man is. And he's interested in them. It makes me proud and territorial, a little jealous.

Tonight we got a hotel room and he finally took me. I didn't resist. He likes his love rough. I acted as if it was my first time. He wondered about that because it didn't hurt, no bleeding. Maybe all that horseback riding already "broke me in." Ha! I was barely drunk and remembered every second. How his muscles flexed and tensed. He told me he loved me. How the tables turned as we went on. He doesn't know that he isn't my first *affaire*!

The taker became the taken.

Afterward, when I told him I was a virgin, he didn't believe it. He was wondering what lovers—mythical

Adonises in his head—had me before him, were handsomer and more skilled than him. I could tell. And I ain't telling. It showed me I could make him jealous, too. Oh, if he only knew the truth.

I'll wrap him around my thumb.

CARRIE DELL'S DIARY 11/1/32

Big Cat is my best lover and my biggest risk. Tonight he exploded on me, slapped me. I punched him in the nose and I thought he was going to kill me. I'm not making it up. I could see the murder in his eyes, and I know he's capable of it. He could do it and nobody would ever know, he'd get away with it. But I was able to play sorry girl and cry and pretty soon we were in bed. "I'll make you laugh instead of cry, baby girl," he said. I'm nobody's baby girl.

Big Cat has muscled in to take a bigger share of profits. I don't like it. This isn't the agreement. But, as he said, "What are you going to do about it, baby girl?" For the first time, I feel over my head. How will he react if I tell him that I've missed my period?

Seventeen

The next morning, I woke up with Carrie's diary on my lap and the phonograph needle scratching. As I bathed, shaved, and dressed, I thought about the diary. Navarre was mentioned by name. But who was Big Cat, a man Carrie was afraid of?

Carrie-Cynthia wrote with a tone far beyond what I expected from a nineteen-year-old girl. But Pamela said she had literary aspirations. Maybe I'd known the wrong nineteen-year-old girls.

I stuffed the letters, journal of writing, and diary in my briefcase and headed to work.

Downtown, people were talking about it on the street before I got to the newsstand outside the Monihon Building. Two black decks in capital letters on the front page of the *Arizona Republic*:

ROOSEVELT ESCAPES DEATH
AS ASSASSIN SHOOTS FIVE

The president-elect was visiting Miami when an Italian bricklayer opened fire at the Bay Front Park. Chicago Mayor Anton Cermak was expected to die. Four others were wounded, including a detective shot in the head.

I had never been to Florida. The attempted murder of Roosevelt, and a sidebar about the Secret Service detail at the White House being doubled, added to the sense of dread as the Depression worsened. Even Will Rogers's pithy two paragraphs didn't ease the feeling.

This wasn't the only news. Outside Los Angeles, a bandit boarded the eastbound *Sunset Limited* and robbed passengers until he faced an armed conductor. Both men exchanged fire, with the robber killed and the conductor badly wounded. The story said the Southern Pacific would combine the *Sunset* with the *Golden State* and the train would arrive in Phoenix at 7:15 a.m. today— old news, because it was already past nine. Crime was down in the Great Depression.

It was a good thing the national morticians' group was going to hold its convention at the Hotel Westward Ho. At least the cold wave was easing, with Phoenix forecast to hit 72 degrees today.

Upstairs, Gladys nodded toward my office.

"Your friend is back."

I doubted it was a friend, and sure enough Kemper Marley was pacing around the room, fussing with the safe combination. He showed no contrition when I caught him.

"Going into the safecracking business, Kemper?" I put my hat on the coatrack and sat at my desk. "Phoenix is notorious among safecrackers. The detectives interrogate them with blows from phone books. Hurts like hell. If you do it the right way, it never shows a bruise. Safecrackers avoid Phoenix."

He barely heard me before launching into a lather. "You hear about that damned Frank Roosevelt? Almost got himself killed. Then where would we be? I'm telling you this country is on the verge. Immigrants like the assassin in Miami. Communists everywhere. Fascists. At least fascists believe in free enterprise. You watch how Herr Hitler turns Germany around, cleans up those

Reds and Jews. It might come to that here, you know. Blood in the streets. We're closer to it than most people realize."

The ball-peen hammer sat in the client chair. He was in his come-to-town outfit of a black suit, vest, and tie.

"I want to get some private investigating from my retainer, Hammons."

"How's that?"

"Frenchy Navarre. What do you know about him? Is he trustworthy?"

I leaned back and considered my approach. How about straight on?

"Frenchy, huh? I hear he's Greenbaum's man, collecting from the bookies in Darktown. One of his runners got his throat slit yesterday, body dumped in a junkyard by the tracks. Was that your work, Kemper? Send Gus a message?"

Navarre had killed Zoogie Boogie. I wasn't feeling charitable. And I was armed with the information I picked up while listening to Kemper lay into Frenchy yesterday.

Marley was momentarily thrown off-balance. That gave me time to light a coffin nail, as much to irritate him as for my pleasure.

He finally said, "What if I wanted to hire him?"

"To do what?"

He waved the smoke away with his hand. "Errands."

Errands, my ass. "I'd say you'd be playing a dangerous game by hiring an untrustworthy, dirty cop."

His lips curled up. "I like dirty cops." The smile didn't last. "But I don't want somebody who would play a double game, give Gus Greenbaum intelligence about me. Or do something stupid like killing Greenbaum's line rider and making it seem like I ordered it."

"Well, there you have your answer."

"Tell me about the dead girl. Carrie's her name?"

I leaned forward. "What makes you think that's her name?"

"I've already told you I have my sources."

"Then what do they tell you?"

"They say she was meticulously cut up, head, arms, legs, and laid out by the railroad tracks at Sixteenth Street, south of Eastlake Park. There wasn't enough blood there, so she was killed and sawed up somewhere else, then taken to be dumped. Nineteen years old. Pretty. A student at the teachers' college. And she was pregnant."

I exhaled a plume of smoke, considering the depth of his information, who might have told him these things, most of which I had discovered. The only things he didn't mention were her being from Prescott with a drunken father, working last summer at the Arizona Biltmore, and setting up a tourist business. Those were details in my report to Captain McGrath.

He also didn't know about my business card being in Carrie's otherwise nearly-empty purse. And he didn't mention the Hamilton railroad watch I found in the Hooverville that his gang laid waste. Was he capable of ordering a prison hit on Jack Hunter, who had information for me? You bet.

"You know, Kemper, if I was still a police detective and heard all that, you'd be my prime suspect. First, I'd put you in the interrogation room for a tumble. And I'd have a search warrant by this afternoon and we'd go over every inch of your property looking for evidence. Who knows what we might find out there? We'd search your whorehouse, too. You couldn't buy your way out of it, either. Not murder of a pretty white coed."

I'd started this to feel him out, but the more I talked the more plausible he actually became as a suspect. Sure, Carrie mentions Navarre in her diary. But who the hell knew where her adventure was going, the men she was attracting? Was Marley the man named Big Cat?

Marley's eyes started blinking quickly. But he managed that reptilian smile.

He said, "Then I guess it's a good thing you're no longer a cop, Hammons."

I slapped my badge down on the desk. "Guess what, kiddo. You were misinformed. And I have one assignment. Find the monster who killed this girl."

The face froze.

"You know things that only the murderer would know."

"But my sources…"

"Save it," I interrupted, standing and walking to the safe. I spun the dial and opened it. Then I came behind him and roughly slid the envelope containing his money into his coat pocket.

"Now get the hell out of my office. The next time we meet things might not be so friendly."

———

Marley bumped into Don while exiting the office. Don watched him go, then closed the door.

"What's with Kemper Marley?"

"A little attitude adjustment."

My brother chuckled, sat down, and used the tallboy lighter on my desk to get his Lucky Strike going.

"Roosevelt was one lucky son of a bitch."

"Let's hope that luck lasts," I said.

He tossed an envelope on my blotter. Looking inside, I saw my business card with powder revealing prints. The card he had removed from Carrie's purse, which was part of the stage dressing at her death scene.

"As you can see, I got it dusted," he said, stretching out his long legs.

"And?"

"The good news is your fingerprints aren't on it. You had the good sense to only hold it at the edges. Otherwise, nothing. No matches on file."

"With criminals in our files."

"That's the point," he said. "The individual who put that card in the girl's purse hasn't been arrested here."

"And you won't send it to the FBI?"

He shook his head.

"Ask McGrath!" I rubbed my stiff neck. "You could at least pretend to give a damn. What about fingerprints of cops?"

He took a long, thoughtful drag. "What are you getting at, Gene?"

"You know damned well. I think the killer might have been a police officer, with that expert blow to her temple. Kemper Marley and a college student also in the running. Neither of those two have been printed."

He started to speak, then saw the badge on my desk.

"What the hell is this? Where did you get this?"

"The chief of Ds."

"Jesus Christ, Gene. Are you back on the Hat Squad?"

"Not officially."

He smashed out his smoke and immediately lit another.

"You're investigating the girl's death."

"Murder," I said. "And yes, it's the only thing I'm investigating."

"Oh, my fucking God." His shoulders relaxed. "Well, walk me through it."

I did.

After I was done, he lowered his head and looked me in the eye. "Your spy trick out at Marley's place has Frenchy confess to killing Zoogie Boogie. Do you want to try getting the county attorney to prosecute a decorated police officer over a stool pigeon? The stupidest lawyer in Maricopa County could raise a mountain of reasonable doubt."

I said, "Too bad Frenchy's not Ruth Judd."

He smiled and continued, "Greenbaum sounds like an interesting cat. This girl is full of secrets and trouble. Otherwise, everything you have is speculation and circumstantial. Jack Hunter's an interesting lead, him knowing about the girl and ending up on the wrong end of a shiv. I like your sniffing out potential suspects by the butcher tools, but you'd need to find and match the actual ones. Ideally, you'd locate the place where the girl was dismembered, too. Then the man following you, or men, all the way to Prescott and outside your apartment. They might be related to the murder. Or they might be about the Marley-Greenbaum contest to throw weight. Or something else."

This was my brother: He might be on the pipe, a cocaine snowbird, a drunk—but he never lost his penetrating intellect, never got lost in the woods, was a detective's detective.

I remembered the time soon after I joined the Hat Squad, when Don and I were hanging out at Union Station one afternoon. Two men came in on the Santa Fe, unremarkable to me but not to my brother. He stopped them after they picked up a trunk at baggage claim. When they were confronted, they started stammering and sweating. They voluntarily opened the trunk, revealing gold ore. Don nodded at me to put them in handcuffs, and we took them to the shabby headquarters at old City Hall.

There he sweated them for six hours in the clubhouse, finally getting their confession to stealing the gold from a prospector near Bouse, a tiny railroad stop a few miles from the Colorado River on the Santa Fe line that branched off northwest from Wickenburg. He wired the sheriff in Yuma County, and learned the prospector wasn't merely the victim of a robbery but dead, killed with pickaxes. Another six hours, and they crumbled under

Don's calm, focused questioning. They admitted to the murder, but claimed the mastermind was a third man. Don wired the police in Los Angeles, who picked him up. He took the bounce at Florence, and the two we arrested got off with life.

He stubbed out the third Lucky. "How can I help, Gene?"

"You could check these prints against cops."

He sighed. "When a man joins the department, he gets finger-printed partly so we can rule him out if he touches something on a crime scene. They go into his personnel jacket, and it's locked up. Unless McGrath gives me permission, this will take a lot of time, and a lot of discretion."

"That's how you can help."

———

After Don left, I arranged Carrie's collection of love letters by date. The last one was dated two weeks before her death. It was typed.

C,

I've never begrudged you your freedom, your indiscretions. Our enterprise has made us all plenty of money. Me, your little friends, you most of all. All this has come thanks to my protection, don't forget that.

But now your silence is killing me. I know I haven't yet left my wife. It will happen I promise but I also have to think about our children. Your too young to understand how complicated these things are. They take time. I thought we had discussed this and you agreed to wait.

And have you been faithful to me, hardly. Yet I've stood by, knowing how you are. You and your older men. Trying to

*find father figures to make up for the drunk whose your real
father. I get you baby girl. You tell me that your pregnant.
How do I even know that the child is mine?*

*Now I hear nothing from you. Not one letter or call. Do
you take me for a fool? I know your a little schemer, C. Don't
think I don't. Don't think you can cut me off and cut me
out. Don't say you weren't warned. I'm watching you when
you don't know it. Write me. Call me at work tomorrow.*

And this one had no signature. I couldn't match the handwriting. It did contain misspellings like the "Admirer's" note.
But plenty of people spelled badly. One thing was sure: He was
no longer her admirer. Something had radically changed in their
relationship. What was the enterprise and who were the "little
friends" involved? The note was a clear threat, even to murder. I
carefully refolded it. My mind went to Navarre, of course. He was
married. As a cop, he could offer protection. Now I needed to
find a sample of his handwriting to compare with the love letters.
If his fingerprints were on these notes, it would be compelling
evidence that he was the killer.

But I would have to read more. I didn't want my growing
hatred of Frenchy to blind me to the possibility of other suspects.
And the typed note used the term "baby girl," which appeared in
Carrie's description of Big Cat, not Navarre.

If this was the trail that led to her murder, horrible as it was, it
meant we weren't dealing with a monster who would strike again.
The man who had killed Carrie was monster enough.

Eighteen

I started to compare that final, nasty billet-doux with the last pages of Carrie's diary. Skipping to the end of a book wasn't usually my style, but I'd make an exception here. I could always go back through more methodically.

The intercom buzzed.

"A man is on the phone," Gladys said. "He won't give his name but said he needs to speak to you immediately."

I told her to put it through and picked up.

"I've got your girl." A gravelly tone. Someone disguising his voice. "If you want to see her again, go to the phone booth inside the Gold Spot Rexall at Third Avenue and Roosevelt. I'll call you in ten minutes. Then I'm going to run you around, and I'll tell you what I need for you to do to get the pretty photographer back. If I see any cops, she'll be on the wrong end of my saw, just like Carrie. I'll be watching you. Not all the time, but you won't know when. Get moving."

Then the line went dead. A cold spike of dread went into my gut as I checked my wristwatch. I fumbled Victoria's number. It rang and rang. Fifteen times. No answer.

I grabbed my suit coat and fedora, checked the magazine in

my pistol, and ran out of the office. Down on Washington Street, I turned north and sprinted. No car today. No time to wait for the Kenilworth streetcar. Dodging honking cars at Adams, Monroe, and Van Buren streets, then I was out of downtown pounding the sidewalk as hard as I could. Seven blocks and a half mile to go. My watch told me I had five minutes. I was sweating by the time I threw open the door to the drugstore. The pay phone in back was ringing.

"Don't touch that," I commanded the old lady about to answer. She backed away and huffed off.

The same voice: "You got a workout, Hammons."

"What do you want?" I said.

"So impatient," he said. "Good things come to those who wait. Get over to the phone booth outside the Bayless market at Central and Moreland. I'll give you five minutes."

I said, "If you hurt her, I'll kill you."

"You wasted thirty seconds." Then the line went dead.

This was an easier run, a long block along the narrow Portland Parkway, past my apartment. Then I crossed Central, again holding out my arm and causing angry motorists to stop. I worried that one might not see me—or wouldn't care—and send me to the hospital or the morgue.

Bayless was busy. The phone booth was empty. I stepped inside, closed the door, and checked my watch. A minute to go. I pulled off my suit coat. Between the run and the sunny day, I was plenty warm. I checked my surroundings. Only shoppers, all women, coming and going with their groceries. They paid me no mind. No parked cars I could see through the windows, much less four-door Chevys.

Five minutes went by, and the phone was silent.

I lit a nail and leaned against the wall of the booth. Anybody who wanted to use a phone here was out of luck. I should have stayed with Victoria last night, should have accompanied her on the commercial shoot. Should have. Should have.

"The wrong end of my saw, just like Carrie." It had to be the killer.

Ten minutes more passed and still silence. I looked at the pay phone, willing it to ring.

At fifteen minutes, I fed a coin in the phone, heard it fall into the machine, and called Victoria again, getting no answer. It kept my nickel. Damned Ma Bell. I flipped through the phone book. Banged the phone, inserted another coin, and I called the McCulloch Brothers studio.

"I'm looking for Victoria Vasquez," I said.

In a moment the most beautiful sound in my life came across the wire: her voice.

"Victoria? Are you all right?"

"I'm fine, Eugene. What's wrong?"

In the distance, I heard sirens.

"I think I've been duped. Do you still have that .38?"

"Right with me."

"Good. Please be careful. I love you."

I hung up before she could respond. I was afraid to know what she might say. Then I ran to my apartment, got in the Ford, and drove toward the Monihon Building.

Three blocks away I could see the fire engines and smoke.

By the time I got there and parked, firemen were setting up fans at the door of Boehmer's drugs on the first floor. A plume of smoke was wafting as far as Kress. I found Gladys amid the crowd that had gathered on the sidewalk. She was wearing her cloche.

"They say someone set off a smoke bomb in the drugstore. We thought it was a fire."

I cursed and ran for the stairs.

"I locked up!" she called.

But that wasn't enough. By the time I reached our landing, I was coughing and out of breath, my eyes burning from the smoke. But I could see someone had used a pry bar to wrench open the old wooden door to the outer office. I pulled my M1911 and thumbed back the hammer. Then I slowly pushed the door open.

The outer office was undisturbed, and no bad guy awaited me. The accountant's door was fine. The same could not be said for mine. The door to my inner office had received the same pry-bar treatment, with the knob and lock sitting on the wooden floor. Again, I carefully pushed the door fully open and traversed the room with the barrel of my gun. Whoever had been here was gone. The safe was undisturbed, while all the drawers of my desk were thrown onto the floor and given a quick shake. He didn't have enough time to get in my filing cabinet, which was locked anyway.

But Carrie's letters and diary were gone.

He was a cool operator, knowing I had taken the streetcar to work and was without a car, so he could run me around on foot, get me out of the building so he could set off the smoke bomb in the pharmacy, watch people evacuate the upper floors, then make his move. Crack open the doors, make a quick ransack of my office with the biggest prize sitting right on top of the desk. He might have made the call to me at the Rexall from right here, with firemen and bystanders down below. Very slick. Very nervy.

I holstered my gun and stared at the disaster that was my empty blotter. How could I have been so careless? If I had ten minutes to get to the Rexall, what difference would it have made to pause a few seconds and lock up this critical evidence in the safe? But at the time I was only thinking of Victoria, fearful she would end up dead and dismembered.

Now I was left with a good memory of the snippets I had read of Carrie's last months. It was so little to go on, leaving far more questions. As I opened windows in the office to let the smoke vent, I imagined the burglar tossing Carrie's love letters and diary into an incinerator. I tasted the ashes and cursed under my breath.

———

Angry and anxious to retake the offensive, I drove south across the tracks to where the Mexican part of Grant Park turned Negro. The individual houses were small and old, many going back to the 1890s or earlier, some on meticulously cared-for lots, others on weedy dirt. I knew some of their floors were dirt and outhouses were common. But given the age of the area, for most of the year it benefited from an abundant shade canopy.

At Hadley Street, I spun into a dusty lot before a tar-paper building with double screen doors. Don't be fooled by the Barq's root beer strips on the door handles—"Drink Barq's, It's Good"— this was a colored speakeasy and juke joint.

I could hear jazz coming from a jukebox and laughter, but when I stepped inside, all went quiet. Three pool tables, a jukebox, tables and chairs, a bar. Six young colored men stared at me. One started a military-like drill with his pool stick, while his friend tossed a cue ball in his hand. It was as white as he was black and would find an easy mark on my forehead, if the cat with the pool stick didn't get to me first.

He said, "Lost your way, Officer?"

Suddenly the entire door behind me was filled with a giant. Cyrus Cleveland doffed his hat and stepped in the room.

"You boys stand down." They sullenly went back to playing pool. He motioned for me to follow him. We went into his office in the rear, and he shut the door. With an expert spinning toss, he landed his homburg on the coatrack.

"They don't mean any harm," he said. "You smell like smoke."

"You have amazing powers of observation, Cyrus."

He smiled the finest dental work in the state. "The great Gene Hammons reduced to working as a private shamus. All because he would have told the truth about Ruth Judd."

"Yeah, well, Ruth is going to hang, and I hung out my shingle." I sat and he eased his bulk into a fancy leather executive chair behind an expensively appointed desk.

"I was actually coming to see you." He slapped down a C-note on the leather-edged blotter. "I need to hire a detective. Somebody killed my boy Zoogie Boogie, slit his throat, let him bleed out like a pig. Can't let that go unpunished." He stretched out his arms. "As you know, I'm a preacher, among other things. And I believe in forgiveness and reconciliation, communion with the Lord, the New Testament. You still singing in the choir at Central Methodist?"

I said that I was.

"You sing well for a white boy. But, as I was saying, there are times, and this is one of them, when I go Old Testament."

"An eye for an eye…"

"Exactly."

Cleveland might or might not have been ordained, but from this tar-paper palace he had presided over the colored rackets in Phoenix for the past ten years. He hovered at the border between crime and the city's small Negro business and professional class, which included college-educated doctors, teachers, and ministers.

On the legit side, he owned a funeral home, was a member of the NAACP and Colored Masonic Lodge, and mediated disputes south of the tracks. He was an investor in the *Phoenix Tribune*, the Negro newspaper, until the Depression killed it. He was also a silent partner in the Rice Hotel and Swindall Tourist Home, which catered to Negro travelers who weren't allowed to stay at white hotels.

His reputation for violence was enough that he rarely had to use it. The story where he staked a rival out in the desert atop a red-ant mound and covered him with molasses—it might have been true or not, but people believed it either way. And he was the richest colored man in town. I had a grudging respect for him because he was a veteran, too.

This was going to be the easiest hundred dollars I ever made, but I circled around.

"What was Zoogie to you?"

"He collected from my bookies."

"Why use a white man for that?"

"Because the white man's ice is always colder, Hammons. Zoogie was a mess, but when he got out of stir he came to me and I put him to work. I'm an equal opportunity employer. I figured my boys would show him more respect when he came calling, and they did. Send a Negro for that, and they'd know him, he might be hesitant. But send a white boy, and they'd cough it up."

"Maybe one of them didn't respect him."

"No way. It'd never happen. Disrespecting him would mean disrespecting me."

We fell silent. Somebody sure as hell had disrespected Zoogie.

Finally, I said, "I hear you're Greenbaum's man now."

He tilted his head, amused.

"I'm nobody's man but my own. I do have a partnership with Gus on gambling. It's a new world, Hammons. The Chicago Outfit is losing out with Prohibition going away and Capone in the pen in Atlanta. He has the clap, you know. Anyway, the profits are going to be in consolidating gambling nationwide through the wire service. They gave me a nice cut."

"I'm sure," I said. "But why does Greenbaum give a damn about penny-ante bookies in Phoenix if he's responsible for the whole Southwest?"

"He likes to keep a tight grip. Wouldn't look good to the Outfit if his backyard was messy."

Tight grip Gus.

"Well, I can solve your case easily. Zoogie's throat was cut by Frenchy Navarre."

Cleveland's body tensed. "How do you know this?"

"I heard Frenchy bragging about it to Kemper Marley. Kemper blew a gasket. He's afraid of Greenbaum but wants part of his action."

Cleveland's eyes narrowed. "'Hell is empty and all the devils are here.' Goddamn Frenchy. That shit Marley. He pays me to procure colored girls for that whorehouse he runs. You know, he's got a wall peek there so he can take photos of what's going on in each room and who's doing it, from businessmen to politicians."

"I guess that helped ensure he'd get the first liquor distributorship in the state."

"Indeed." His big head nodded. "What I don't get is that Frenchy is Greenbaum's bagman. Why would he kill Zoogie, who collects for me as part of my partnership with Gus?"

"To hear him explain it, he wanted to pin the murder on a colored man, make it seem like Greenbaum needed protection south of the tracks and Kemper could provide it, as long as he got a cut from the wire service."

His bass voice went down an octave. "That's crazy."

"Nobody ever accused Navarre of being a genius."

"I tell Gus this and Frenchy's gonna end up in the riverbed with a dime dropped on him."

"A police officer?" I said. "Killing a cop is dangerous business, breaks the code, brings down heat, and takes away a valuable asset. Even a stupid, double-dealing police detective is worth more alive than dead."

Cleveland thought it over. "You're probably right. But that

doesn't preclude a well-administered beating. And Frenchy's promise that this murder goes unsolved, not pinned on an innocent Negro. That's my code."

I'd love to watch that. Cleveland reached across for the C-note but I pulled it away.

"You got your money's worth." I wrote out a receipt and handed it across.

"Heh." He stood, the signal we were through.

I stayed seated. "What do you know about the girl who got killed and had her body dumped by the railroad tracks a month ago?"

He pulled a cigar from a humidor on his desk, cut it, and slowly lit it with a match. It was Cuban—quality will tell.

"I know that a Negro doesn't want anything to do with a pretty, white, blond dead girl. We've never had that kind of lynching in Phoenix, and I don't want to be the first one. Race relations are pretty good here, considering. But these are crazy times. Communists. People who think Mussolini is the way to go. Okies and hoboes coming through, gas moochers..."

I let him go on. He sounded like Marley. But he knew Carrie was pretty and blond with no prompting from me.

When he wound down, I said, "What about the white man having something to do with the pretty, white, blond dead girl? You hear things."

The perfect smile reappeared. "It's like back in the trenches, Hammons. A man hears lots of things. Funny, though, is he never hears the artillery shell that kills him. But I'm not worried. You're the man who caught the University Park Strangler."

Nineteen

At eleven thirty p.m. on Thursday, January 10, 1929, the west-side patrol car driving on Van Buren was flagged down by a frantic man, who led the officers to his house at 324 N. Twelfth Avenue. His daughter was dead, murdered. The blue light and horn sounded at headquarters, and more officers headed that way. I was the sole night detective and arrived a little before midnight. It was cold out, and even most speakeasies were closed.

Edna Sawyer was seventeen years old, pretty with flame-red hair. She had been raped and strangled in her bed. Her periwinkle-blue flannel nightgown was pulled all the way up, exposing pert breasts, parted fair legs, a ginger bush, and a pool of semen on the white sheet. I ran the gawking uniforms out of the bedroom, instructing one to sit with her parents—her mother had found her and her father had called headquarters and then ran a block to busier Van Buren, where he was fortunate enough to find the police car cruising.

Captain McGrath arrived with a beautiful, raven-haired female photographer. She had no hesitation in bossing me around as she took shots of the crime scene. It was the first time I met Victoria. Don and Turk Muldoon came soon after. I briefed them and, as the youngest member of the Hat Squad, prepared to step aside when Turk put a hand on my shoulder.

"You were here first, lad," he said in his rich brogue. "You're the primary."

At the exact same moment, I felt a thrill—and a terrible responsibility fall upon me.

After they left, I shut the door and surveyed the scene, making detailed notes and sketches.

Entry was obvious. The killer came in through an unlocked window facing the backyard and caught the girl sleeping. Her brothers and parents were also asleep but separated from Edna's room by the bathroom. A sock stuffed in the girl's mouth took care of any screaming as he prepared to go about his work. But she must have fought. Her nails were bloody and flakes of the attacker's skin were underneath them. In return, he punched her in the left eye. He must have been straddling her. Afterward, he exited the same window, leaving it fully open.

Through the door, the mother was wailing, and the father was angrily demanding a doctor. But Edna's body was cold.

We didn't realize it at the time, but this was the first victim of the killer who the press would call the University Park Strangler.

The postmortem confirmed the obvious: Death by strangulation, genital bruising, penetration. She fought hard enough to break one fingernail. The killer would have received a nasty gash on his face. But he was very strong. Edna's windpipe was collapsed, as was the cricoid cartilage surrounding it. The pathologist said it took forty-five pounds of pressure to produce such damage. He also speculated that the killer had been in no hurry, slowly strangling her.

With the sock stuffed in the girl's mouth, I assumed the rape preceded the strangulation. But the doc, who had worked at the coroner's office in Los Angeles and seen such cases before, said it was possible that the murderer was raping Edna while he was slowly crushing her windpipe. "It's part of the excitement for him."

He turned her to show me a small cross carved into the exact middle of the small of her back. It looked as if it was done with a penknife rather than resulting from some accident, and it was fresh.

"He marked her," the doc said. "Mutilation is part of the M.O. of a lust murder."

I had never heard the term before, I told him.

"It was first used by the Austrian psychiatrist Richard von Krafft-Ebing in the 1880s," he said. "The killer receives intense sexual gratification from killing someone."

"A nice pair of nylons always does the trick for me."

"You cops and your black humor. Lust murderers can be much worse that this. Genital mutilation. Cannibalism. Inserting objects into the victim's orifices. Necrophilia. This killer is only strangling with great force and cutting the victim, but you should be prepared for worse."

I left him with the body, but the cross stuck with me. It wasn't like a typical one found in Christian churches. With the two arms meeting in the middle, it reminded me of the simplified iron cross the Germans were using by 1918. The *balkenkreuz*, or beam cross. Were we looking for a war vet or a German immigrant?

Edna was a straight-A student at Phoenix Union High School, popular, a cheerleader. She was the oldest of three children. Captain McGrath assigned three of my Hat Squad colleagues to interview her friends, teachers, and steady boyfriend. He was the son of Chauncey McKellips, president of the First National Bank of Arizona and had an alibi for Thursday night. The detectives also started rounding up suspects with morals offenses and transients. Migrant farmworkers were mostly gone for now, the lettuce harvest complete and more than four thousand carloads shipped by rail.

A crime such as this had never happened before in Phoenix, much less in a pleasant Anglo middle-class neighborhood only a few blocks from the state capitol.

On Monday afternoon, with two hours of sleep and fueled by the sludge that passed for coffee at headquarters, I went back to the house on Twelfth Avenue and interviewed her parents in more detail. They were shattered, sleep-deprived, but cooperative. Edna's father worked in insurance and her mother was a housewife. Neither had sensed anything unusual about their daughter, no indication she was afraid, no enemies, no strange men following her. They always closed the blinds and curtains at night. But on cool nights, Edna liked to open her bedroom window slightly and sleep under a thick comforter.

I took a careful inventory of her bedroom. It was untouched since the attack, her parents complying with my request to leave it alone. With the sun streaming in, the room became clearer. The bedclothes had been thrown off Edna and folded on the floor. With the body removed, I noted the bloodstain dried on the middle of the sheet; this was a hellish way to lose her virginity. I went through her closet and drawers, her mother trailing me. "Tell me if you see anything out of place or missing," I said.

"I don't see her knickers," she said. "Edna always slept in them. She was a modest girl." Then the tears came. "Who could do this to her?"

It took time for her to focus again. "Wait, where is Theodore?"

"Theodore?" I was thinking of a cat or a dog.

"It's a Teddy bear she's had since she was a little girl. He was always in the bed next to her pillow." She fussed around the room. "He's gone!"

The killer took trophies.

———

Almost a month later, on Saturday, February 9th, he killed again. Dorothy Jameson was raped and strangled in a Spanish-colonial revival house on Taylor Street, a quarter mile from the first killing. She was an only child who lived with her grandmother, who was hard of hearing. The woman didn't discover her body until the morning when Dorothy, usually an early riser, wasn't already up.

Some elements of the crime were identical: The sock in her mouth, nightgown pulled up, and bedding folded. He came in by an unlocked bedroom window. The second victim was a redhead, although not a natural one. Dorothy had small firm breasts and delicate, "cute girl" features like Edna Sawyer. She had the same cross carved into the small of her back.

But the evidence revealed some differences, too.

He took more care and time with the assault. The girl's wrists were tied with rope to the headboard. The rope strands were cut to exact lengths and brought by the killer, as was the sock. Perhaps the gash he received in the first attack made him want to restrain the victim. Had he spied on the house to know the grandmother was nearly deaf, thus giving him more time for the attack? Her legs were raised and knees bent with her feet on the mattress, as if he arranged her that way after the rape. This time he didn't have to worry about being overheard by parents and siblings.

Dorothy had a cat that slept with her. Her grandmother said she always kept her door partly open so the animal could come and go. But Dorothy's door was closed and the cat was hiding under a chair in the living room. The killer somehow immobilized the girl, or she was a hard sleeper, then shooed away the cat and shut the door. This was the second victim whose family didn't own a dog. Did the killer know this in advance? Of course he did. He reconnoitered his targets.

Unlike the first scene, where the ground below the window was covered with grass, the Jamieson home had a flower bed.

We were able to get a clean cast of a footprint, a tennis shoe or sneaker, size eleven. Don guesstimated that the wearer was a well-built man, at least a hundred-eighty pounds.

When I went through the bedroom with Dorothy's grand-mother, a pair of the girl's knickers was missing. So was a stuffed animal, a puppy with a red ribbon around his neck. I also went carefully through the girl's diary, but it gave no clue that she was afraid, being stalked, or had enemies.

The postmortem was similar to the first victim. Genital bruis-ing and bleeding, slow strangulation by a man with strong hands. It was possible she was raped and then killed. But the doc's com-ment, once again, about the penetration occurring along with choking her to death stayed with me. "Maybe it's the only way he can maintain arousal and orgasm," he said. "Characteristic of a lust murder."

Dorothy was another straight-A student at Phoenix Union High, a clarinet player in the band, member of the pep club, popular. She was sixteen, a year behind Edna Sawyer. Interviews with her friends indicated that she didn't know Edna, didn't have a boyfriend. She was hoping to attend the University of Arizona.

Once again, detectives talked to neighbors, who saw and heard nothing. They hadn't seen any peeping Toms, and the police call logs backed that up. Another roundup of potential suspects went nowhere, either because of alibis or the most promising ones failing to break under heavy interrogation. One whacky who was familiar to us came in to confess. But he didn't know even the basics of the crime, especially the parts we held back from the press: taking trophies, the penknife cross, and tying her hands with ropes. I sent telegrams to Tucson, Los Angeles, San Diego, and El Paso, asking if they had anything similar. Nothing close came back.

As for the rope lengths and sock, they could have been

purchased anywhere. The shoeprint matched a Converse, but that was available in at least a dozen or more stores. Fingerprints from the second house produced no suspects, although they did match the ones from the windowsill of the first murder. It was the same killer, not a copycat.

As with Edna, though, it was as if she had been murdered by a ghost.

Now the city fell into a panic. People started locking their doors and windows, calling us to report "suspicious" people walking down the streets—even though none of them turned out to be potential suspects. Neighborhoods demanded more streetlights. We put more officers in University Park, especially at night, both uniformed and plainclothes. Overtime wasn't an issue. I was going on three or four hours of sleep a day.

Arizona was only a generation removed from the frontier, less than twenty years from statehood, so many people owned guns. More folks purchased them from gun shops and pawn-brokers, whether they knew how to use them or not. One woman in University Park fired her shotgun at a neighbor taking out the trash one night, sending him to the hospital with a few pellets of buckshot in his backside. The newspapers and radio played it up, while the city commissioners demanded an arrest.

But we had nothing but clues that led to dead ends.

———

Don was focused on pervs and peeping Toms, but I wasn't sure. Muldoon interviewed all the teachers the two girls had, turning up nothing but squarejohns and proper matrons. Navarre, not surprisingly, rousted Negroes in Darktown. We spoke with every relative and friend of the two girls, then went back and did it again.

I started compiling lists of janitors and maintenance men at the high school; short-order cooks at nearby restaurants, especially the Nifty Nook right across the street; and workers at other nearby businesses. People who would see the coeds. Everyone willingly gave his name. Everyone wanted to help. Only two on my list had records, one for burglary and another for bootlegging. But the burglar angle interested me. Although this individual committed his crime twenty years ago and had an alibi for the nights of both murders, what about someone else? What if burglary was the gateway impulse that led to murder?

Then we faced the killer choosing University Park as his target. What was this geography to him? Maybe he lived there, or once did. I started compiling burglary reports in the neighborhood. The few arrests led to individuals who were still in prison. One incident stuck out: Back in November, a woman claimed that someone had been in her house while she slept. Nothing was taken but items were rearranged, and an unlocked window was left open, all of which she noticed in the morning. The officer who took the report at the time noted skeptically, "Hysterical female, no evidence of forced entry." The house was two blocks from Edna Sawyer's.

I started wandering University Park at the hours when the girls would have been coming or going to school. I added interviews and names from postmen and dairymen, delivery drivers, plumbers, city garbagemen, Western Union messenger boys, and Central Arizona Light and Power crews.

Finally, I noticed that both crimes happened on nights with new moons. Maybe it mattered, maybe not, but Captain McGrath agreed we should go full-out on the next one, March 11th.

But the University Park Strangler had other plans.

Twenty

"I had never heard those details about the early murders in University Park," Victoria said. "So, you thought I bossed you around, huh?"

"In the nicest possible way."

We were lying in my bed, our legs entwined, listening to jazz on the radio. The room was dark.

"You can't kick yourself for losing the diary and love notes," she said. "You were thinking of me. That's sweet."

"Sweet won't catch this killer," I said. "What kills me…"

"Pun intended?"

"What slays me? Anyway, what frustrates me is that Carrie specifically mentioned Navarre in her diary. There's a good chance the love letters were from him. But a second man is involved, too. Big Cat. She was afraid of him, and he probably wrote her the threatening letter. But I can't go to McGrath now because I don't know enough."

"I know," she said. "But there's also a good chance the love letters weren't from Frenchy."

I raised an eyebrow. She slipped out of bed and walked to the window. The ambient light gave her body an enchanting glow.

"Is our friend in the Chevy out there?"

"No," she said, slipping back in bed.

He hadn't returned since I nearly caught him outside Victoria's house.

She said, "I took the note we received in Prescott, which matched the love letters, and went to headquarters while the detective pool was empty. I pulled one of the case files Frenchy worked on. The writing doesn't match."

"Damn."

"Another man is involved," she said. "Carrie got around. She was living a double life. And she was making a hell of a lot more money than I did when I was her age. Maybe more than now."

———

The next morning, I was still itching to get off first base. Evidence was gone. I felt no nearer to closing the case than a month ago. My other private eye business was dead. It was time to start eliminating suspects. I started at the beginning with Tom Albert, Carrie's former boyfriend.

I caught him coming out of classes, flashed my badge, and walked him toward my car.

He protested. "What's this about? I've got practice in half an hour."

When we reached the Ford, I braced him against the fender and put his arms behind him. Then I slapped on the cuffs tight.

He let out a yelp. "You can't do that! I'm a student."

"Shut up." I shoved him into the passenger seat and slammed the door.

Overlooking the shady campus to the north was Tempe Butte. Whitewashed rocks formed the letter *T* for the Tempe State Teachers College. Until 1925, it had been an *N* for the Normal

School. Maybe soon they'd get around to an *A* for the latest name change.

I drove in that direction up Mill Avenue, then pulled off a little south of the flour mill and railroad spur. Tom was so nervous that even my setting the brake made him jump. That was what I was after. His apprehension grew when I shed my suit coat, revealing my shoulder holster.

"Let's go." I dragged him out and stood him up, then led him by the cuffs from behind toward the bare rocky prominence. His complaints were drowned out by the mill sounds until we were a hundred yards away and climbing.

"What do you want, Pops?"

I said nothing, pushing him on and up.

We reached a primitive trail that led to the top of the butte. My hope was that no students were up here smoking and drinking, requiring an explanation that I didn't want to give. A lie that could come back and bite me. So far, we were alone.

"Carrie," I said. "I want to know everything."

He briefly turned his head toward me and stumbled. He wouldn't make that mistake again.

His voice was choking back panic. "I don't understand, Pops." I repeated my demand and told him if he called me "Pops" one more time, I was going to kick him to death.

That got his attention. "We dated for a few months, okay?" he said. "I met her when she modeled in art class. We went out, became steadies, then she broke up with me. That's all, I swear."

"Why did she break up with you?"

"I dunno. Who knows why girls do anything?"

"Did it have anything to do with you selling cocaine?"

"What? No! That was all a mistake."

I shoved him hard. "You're no student, Tom. You're a criminal. Where did you get the cocaine, and who did you sell it to?"

He struggled to keep his footing.

"Chinatown," he said. "I bought it there and sold it to a few students. I needed the money. It didn't hurt anybody. I don't know why that's a big deal. But after they suspended me, I stopped, and that's the truth. Carrie never knew. She barely drank."

We were high enough up to see over the rooftops of the town center and soon the college campus. The smoke of a steam locomotive trailed south, hauling a freight train through Tempe and toward Tucson.

I didn't say anything more until we reached the summit. The view would have been great in normal circumstances. But the butte fell away from us, an unsettling drop. The whitewashed *T* was below us on the slope.

"It's a long way down, kid." I turned him to see. "I can take off these bracelets and give you a good shove. Maybe you'll break your leg. Maybe you'll break your neck. 'Climbing accident,' they'll say. Nobody will ever know. You snap some bones, still alive for now, but you won't be found for days. With no water, you'll be as good as dead. So close to civilization you can see the lights of town and so damned far. Nobody can hear your cries for help. And with this warmer weather, maybe some rattlesnakes will think it's time to wake up. And there you are."

"Look, Mister, I never even made whoopee with her." He was sweating. "She was straitlaced. At least I thought so. Way smarter than anybody else I knew. Beautiful. And she sure as hell wasn't going to become a teacher somewhere. She had the train schedules out of town memorized."

"But she broke up with you, why?"

"She didn't say."

"I heard she'd met an older man."

"That's what I heard, too."

"Who was he?"

"I dunno!"

"Oh, bullshit. You had to have spied on her. It's what I would have done."

He was turning green and starting to hyperventilate, so I pulled him back and spun him to face me.

"If you get sick on my nice shoes, I'm going to toss you down the butte."

After a few minutes, his color improved and he was breathing normally.

"I saw her with an older guy once. He picked her up. He was shorter than you, dark hair, wearing a suit. That's all, I swear."

"So she left you for him. Big man on campus made small by an adult taking your pretty girl. You saw her draped to be painted in art class, imagined what it would be like to get her totally naked, but somebody else did that. Must have made you angry."

He looked toward the ground. "Sure, it did."

"Angry enough to kill her?"

"What? Gosh, no! What happened to Carrie?"

"She's dead."

He looked sincerely gut-punched. I took off the handcuffs. Next I produced my sap.

"You know what this is?"

He shook his head.

"It's a sap or a blackjack. Police carry them, but anybody can buy one."

He stared at it, stared at me. "I don't..."

"Take it."

He hesitantly wrapped his hand around the heavy end. That's not the way someone conversant in a sap would take it. He'd take the small end and whack me upside the head and I'd be the one rolled down the mountainside. It could be an act. I took it back and slipped it inside my waistband.

"Level with me, Tom. You got mad. You confronted her, things went bad, you hit her in the head with one of these. Teach the little bitch a lesson. You didn't mean to kill her. But that's how it went, right? What happened next?"

He rubbed his wrists. "You're all wrong." Seeing his hands were free, he realized that might not have been a compassionate gesture, and I might be ready to give the big shove. He knelt down on the dirt. "I'm afraid of heights! You gotta believe me, Mister. If Carrie's dead, I didn't have anything to do with it."

"Not a thing? I don't believe you. Maybe you had a buddy help..."

"No!" He looked pleadingly at me.

"You work at the slaughterhouse, right?"

"Sure, so?"

"So why do you have a job when so many adult men can't find work to provide for their families?"

"My uncle works at Tovrea." That was the big feedlot and slaughterhouse operation. "He got me part-time work. Between that and my football scholarship, it's the only way I can stay in school. My dad lost nearly everything in '29. Stocks, you know. Then the building and loan where he was an officer closed. He hasn't been able to find a steady job since then."

It was a good story, if true. I continued: "You know how to cut meat. That would come in handy if you hit Carrie in the head, accidentally killed her, and wanted to make it look like her body fell from a train..."

"What? I don't know what you're saying. I never fought with her, never hit her. My mom taught me to never hit a girl."

I forced him all the way down on his butt. His eyes darted around, looking for snakes while I took in the view. From up here, even a slight breeze made a noise. So did Tom, continuing his denials.

I demanded: "What kind of car do you own?"

"I don't," he said. "Who has the money? I have to hitchhike to work."

If I were still a real cop, I could take my time with him in the interrogation room. But I didn't have that luxury. I was hoping the stress of suddenly being kidnapped and frog-marched up Tempe Butte might have the same effect in less time.

"I've got your parents' address in Phoenix," I said. "Are you telling me that if I get a search warrant and go there, I'm not going to find the place you cut her up? I'll find the bloodstains. That's evidence. I'll find the butcher tools you used to hack her apart, and where you got the clothes to dress her again. That's premeditation. Her breaking up with you is motive. Quick conviction, and you'll hang, Tom. It's not looking good. But if you level with me, maybe the jury will go easier. Crime of passion."

Now the husky football player was red-faced and bawling. "Is that what happened to her? Oh, my God. It wasn't me. I haven't seen her in months. You've gotta believe me, sir. I'm innocent."

Unfortunately for my investigation, I did. He didn't seem to have the ability, cool-headedness, and cruel imagination to plan and carry out something like Carrie's murder. He also didn't fit the profile of someone who had been following me, leaving threatening notes, and setting off the smoke bomb that allowed pilfering of Carrie's love notes and diary.

Still, I asked him where he was the day and night before her body was discovered. He claimed he was in classes during the day and working at the stockyards that night. If it checked out, he could be removed from the list of potential suspects.

I drove him back to campus and let him out. He looked back at me several times as he walked away, no confidence in his movements, wishing I were a bad dream.

———

Tom was the easy mark. Things became more difficult with the others. Kemper Marley knew about Carrie—too damned much. And he was curious about the case, asking Navarre what was going on. He was worried that I might investigate it. Frenchy bought butcher tools, and he was certainly capable of the worst violence. Her diary mentioned him as her lover. If either he or Kemper or Big Cat got her pregnant and she demanded he leave his wife or else—things might have escalated from there. Means, opportunity, and motive.

Unfortunately, bracing them like I had Tom Albert wouldn't work. Both were too cool and connected. Nosing around their properties carried unacceptable risks. I didn't even know who Big Cat was. Making progress would require other means. And every time I seemed close to catching a break, something kicked the solution further away, whether it was the office break-in that got Carrie's writings or the murders of three men.

This last pushed me into a fight with Victoria that night. I told her she needed to get out of town. However much she wanted to help me, however much she was confident with her .38 Special, she was a target. I didn't want her to be the next Ezra Dell, Jack Hunter, or Zoogie Boogie. She knew everything I did, and this would make her especially vulnerable.

Her response was clear and fierce. "There's no way I'm leaving you alone to face this, Eugene! You wouldn't leave it alone and now it's too late, for both of us. We either catch this bastard or he kills us."

No games or manipulative tears from my lover. It was one of the many things that drew me to her. But I also knew I'd never forgive myself if she was hurt or killed. So I manipulated her and didn't feel guilty about it.

She said she needed to work on her portfolio, but only so many photographic opportunities could be had in little Phoenix, a burg people in New York would look down on. What if she took a month's vacation to Los Angeles, a real city that was so much more photogenic? She could stay with her brother there. I would keep her up to speed on my investigation. Then she could come back.

She steamed. "Maybe you want to make love to Pamela while I'm gone."

"You know that's not true."

"What is true with you, Eugene? When Don pulled your business card out of Carrie's purse, all you had to do was walk away."

"And let her murderer get away with it? Find a new way to frame me? Or kill somebody else?"

"Well, too late for that, isn't it?"

I tried to touch her but she pulled away.

Two nights later, I walked her to a dark green Pullman car on the westbound *Sunset Limited*. She tipped the redcap extra for lugging her equipment. I received a chilly kiss, the briefest embrace. Then the conductor called all aboard, the locomotive unleashed its bell and gave two long toots of the whistle, and the long train started rolling. Big wheels with body-cutting flanges rolling against steel rails. The last car, its *Sunset* drumhead lighted, disappeared into the darkness. And I was alone.

Twenty-One

As I walked back to my car on Fourth Avenue, I heard a ruckus on Madison Street. It was the unmistakable sound of a man on the losing end of a fight.

At first they were shadows, four figures in the darkness kicking a man who lay in a fetal position against a boxcar beside a warehouse. As I got closer, I heard his moans as he received each kick. Then bones breaking.

Drawing my .45, I walked closer, fired the pistol in the air, and shouted, "Police!"

The beating stopped, and I was close enough to see four muscled-up white men assessing their fight-or-flight options. I wasn't willing to offer that.

"Don't make me kill you," I said. "Hands in the air, now. Face the boxcar and put your palms on it, keep 'em up. I won't hesitate to shoot."

They shuffled to the AT&SF freight car, which proclaimed "The Scout: For Economy Travel *West*" on the side, and put their hands against it. Their knuckles were raw and bloody.

The victim was on his knees, spitting up blood and picking a tooth from the street. His suit was a mess from where they had pulled the coat down halfway to immobilize his arms as they assaulted him. Keeping the .45 on the thugs, I reached out my other hand and hefted him up. A grateful, if bruised and bloody, face caught the light.

"Thanks, Geno, you saved my life."

Frenchy Navarre.

I left him to put himself together as best he could and searched the crew. Thug One carried a .25 caliber Baby Browning and a switchblade. Thug Two was armed with a "broomhandle" Mauser—I hadn't seen one of these since the war. The third goon was underdressed—only a pair of brass knuckles. Thug Four had a snubnosed Colt Detective .38 in a shoulder rig. It was amazing they hadn't decided to turn all this firepower on me. I might have been able to put them all down, but who knows? I slid the guns into my waistband and the knife and knucks in my pocket.

"Keep your damned hands up and faces forward," I commanded. "At this range, I'll blow your guts all over the pavement." That was true, but I took two steps back. I didn't want one of these toughs to get the idea he could make a clever move behind him and disarm me.

I said, "Guess what, smart guys. You assaulted a police officer. You're going to Florence for a nice, long bit."

Frenchy touched my elbow. "Let 'em go, Geno. It's a long story, but I don't want 'em arrested."

I whispered out of the side of my mouth, "Frenchy, these guys almost killed you."

"I know," he wheezed. "But let 'em go. I'll explain later."

That would be interesting to hear, but I already knew the truth. This was payback from Greenbaum for Zoogie Boogie, or maybe from Cyrus Cleveland, and I couldn't say I was sorry he was getting it.

I holstered my pistol and ordered them to turn around. "Get lost."

"What about my gun?" This came from the first one, who was about my height, swarthy complexion, eyes that showed an intellect somewhere around that of a mule.

I patted his cheek. "You're lucky to not be going to jail, sweetheart. Don't push it."

They walked east on Madison, looking back. I expected the worst, that they would make a run at me, but soon all four were gone. Frenchy was bent over, spitting up more blood.

"I need a drink," he said. "I need to get my car..." He collapsed again, and I lifted him upright, grabbing his mangled fedora.

"First you're going to the hospital. No argument."

I folded him into the Ford and drove to St. Joseph's at Fourth and Polk streets, the closest hospital. Before they ushered me into the waiting area, I assessed his injuries: One eye already turning purple, scrapes on his face, nasty hit to the jaw, bruised ribs. He gave me his badge, gun, sap, handcuffs, and wallet. I explained that he was a police officer.

"Geno." He grabbed my sleeve. "Please keep this between us. If McGrath finds out, I'll be writing parking tickets and directing traffic in uniform for the rest of my career."

Considering this was the man who slit Zoogie Boogie's throat, I felt surprisingly compassionate. "It stays between us," I said. "But who were those goons?"

"Gambling debt..."

And a nun pushed me out of the room.

While the doctors were working on Frenchy, I went outside for a cigarette and unburdened my confiscated weapons into the car. Bing Crosby was singing "Shadow Waltz" from a phonograph playing in a house across the street. Victoria would be well on her way to Yuma by now, with a morning arrival in Los Angeles. I wish I'd offered to go with her.

Hefting Frenchy's blackjack, I wondered if it was what killed Carrie. I dug through his wallet. He was carrying two C-notes in addition to ones and fives. Not bad for an honest public servant—or somebody who got busted up over unpaid gambling debts. Among notes and cards, I found one from Summer Tours. On the back side, Carrie's handwriting said, "Leonce, Big Cat scares me. C."

I slid it back into place. Frenchy was definitely not Big Cat. I wondered again who was.

Two hours later, Frenchy was as patched up as possible. They wanted to admit him for fear of internal bleeding, but he was having none of that. He had three broken ribs, had lost two teeth, and came close to having a fractured cheek and ruptured spleen. He was staggering from a dose of morphine but still winced in pain as I slid his holster and other cop gear back on and put him in the passenger seat for the ride home.

"What the hell am I going to tell my wife?" he slurred as we arrived.

"Lie well. You're a cop and got in a fight. Say you look a lot better than the toughs you took down tonight and threw in jail."

He started to laugh but this turned into a moan from his broken ribs as he wrapped his arms around his battered middle.

"You ever been in love, Geno?"

I nodded.

"I mean really in love," he said. "I had what I thought was a tumble with this young girl. But she caught me like a fish on a hook. 'Course my wife didn't know. Anyway, she made me feel like I was seventeen again, made me forget all the dirty stuff that comes with the job. God, I miss her."

I waited and calculated, then decided to risk it. "What was her name?"

"Carrie." Tears started down his bruised cheeks. Electricity ran up my spine.

"What happened to her?"

"She died. A tragedy."

"What happened?"

Now he was visibly sobbing. "I don't know. I don't know. Wish I did. Feel like it's left me at the end of a long, dark cave with no way out..."

I waited for more, but he stopped himself. I couldn't tell if he wanted to confess to killing Carrie or if he was genuinely innocent.

"What do you do for fun, Frenchy? To relax? You need to take a few days off after what happened. Get your story straight for McGrath and stick to it. Hoodlum ambushed you, you fought, he ran, and you lost him. He'll give you a few days."

"What if he kicks me off the Hat Squad, Geno? We're supposed to be tough."

"Nobody doubts your courage, Frenchy. You're safe."

He furrowed his brow, thinking it through. "I guess I could take time off and cook. Family likes my steaks, my gumbo."

Maybe the steaks explained his purchases at the restaurant supply store. Nothing could explain him slitting the throat of an innocent man. Despite this, I made myself get out and help him from the car to the driveway.

"You gotta get my car..."

"It can wait. You're in no condition to drive. You can barely walk."

"No! Please. Please get it, Geno. It's a '32 Chevy, black four-door, parked near the train station."

He handed me the keys.

"What were you doing down there?"

"Got a tip from a snitch," he said. "But it turned into an ambush."

That might have been true. Or he had followed me and run into unexpected trouble.

———

At the foot of a darkened Fourth Avenue, the lights still glowed from the Union Station waiting room. One or two no-name passenger trains and the westbound *Fast Mail* would still be arriving tonight.

I had dropped off my car at the apartment, fetched a flashlight, and hopped the Kenilworth line streetcar down to Washington Street, walking the rest of the way.

Now, Frenchy's four-door Chevy sat unmolested a block north of the depot. It was the same car I had followed from the junkyard to Marley's house. If I were still a real police officer, I would be burdened by the need of such pesky things as search warrants. Instead, I was your friendly local private eye, with the keys to my "friend's" car. It could easily have been the one watching my place or the one that followed Victoria home. Spare tire on the outside.

I slipped on my leather gloves. Without the attached trunk to search, I opened up the driver's door, flipped on the flashlight, and had a look inside. The glove box was disappointingly neat, with an extra set of handcuffs and road maps. I felt under the seats—nothing. The floor and upholstery looked new, with no bloodstains. I pulled up the back seat and, aside from dust, it was lacking anything, much less evidence that he had used this vehicle to kidnap Carrie and murder her.

Nothing was left for me but to drive the car back to Frenchy's house and leave the keys under the visor for him to find in the morning. That was when a key on his ring attracted my attention. The car key and house key were obvious. But a third one was different: thin, sturdy, brass. It opened a safe-deposit box.

I drove up to the Monihon Building and let myself in. I locked the door behind me and took the darkened stairs up to my office. There I pulled out my cigar box of lock-picking gear and made a clay mold of the safe-deposit key. When I was satisfied it was exact, I slipped the key back on Frenchy's ring. Fifteen minutes later, I dropped off the car in his driveway and walked home through the silent streets, missing Victoria terribly.

Twenty-Two

The next day I rolled into the office early. A wire was waiting from Victoria: She had arrived safely at Los Angeles Central Station. I scribbled a response and left it for Gladys to summon a Western Union boy. I retrieved the clay mold and walked down Washington Street to my favorite locksmith. Favorite because he still thought I was a cop and because he could work magic in duplicating any key. Thirty minutes later, I had the key to Frenchy's safe-deposit box.

But which bank?

Start at the best. I walked up Central to Monroe Street, where the imposing new Professional Building hulked over the southeast corner. On the bottom floor was the lobby to the Valley Bank & Trust, the strongest such institution left in Phoenix.

The lobby looked like a high temple of money, with soaring ceilings, art deco carvings, sleek hanging chandeliers, and walnut teller counters and benches so beautiful they made me feel every inch the imposter. It was almost enough to make you trust banks again. The armed guard was a retired patrol sergeant, so that greased my skids to the vault manager after a few minutes of small talk.

The manager wore a conservative suit and toupee that wasn't fooling anyone. I could use my badge but that might raise issues of warrants, so I decided to brazen it out.

"Leonce Navarre." I shook his hand. "I'd like to get my safe-deposit box."

I held up the key.

"Of course, Mr. Navarre," he said. "Come this way."

Barely believing my luck, I followed him as he waddled to a gate, unlocked it, and did the same with a sturdy polished steel door. Then we passed an immense open vault door and soon were inside a long room filled floor-to-ceiling with boxes. Each had two keyholes.

"I believe you're 1207," he said.

"Sounds about right." I was about to say something about not having been here for a while but who knew? Maybe Frenchy had been here last week and dealt with someone else. I held my breath. The man produced a key and inserted it in the correct box. I did the same with mine. And it turned. The little steel door opened, and he pulled out a long rectangular box. Carrying it to a table in the middle of the room, he said, "I'll leave you to it. Let me know when you're done."

Then he was gone.

For a moment, I stared at the walls containing money, gold, jewelry, important documents—and secrets. Tamping down my curiosity, I focused on the little fortress in front of me and opened the hinged top.

Inside was money: Seven neatly bound packs of hundred-dollar bills. A quick flip through the C-notes in one pack made me sure Frenchy had at least ten thousand dollars hidden away here. I set them on the table. And saw the brown manila envelope.

I carefully undid the string and let a heavy handkerchief fall to the tabletop. Unwrapping it slowly, I saw a blood-caked straight razor. It had been dusted for fingerprints and inside the envelope were four neat latents on an official police form. They were clear partial prints. But no name was listed on the paper. No suspect, no investigating officer.

The packs of money went back in the safe-deposit box. I wrapped the blade in the handkerchief, careful not to leave my own prints, and put it and the paper with partial fingerprints back in the envelope. That went in my suit coat pocket.

As I walked back to the office, it was time to reorder my thinking.

If Frenchy really murdered Zoogie Boogie, why keep the straight razor? The immediate answer was so that he could plant it on the Negro suspect of his choice. But if that were the case, why dust it for prints, lift latents, and put both in a safe-deposit box? That made no sense.

No, Frenchy found Zoogie dead—arriving at the junkyard ahead of Muldoon—and took the razor. Then he claimed the killing to get Kemper Marley off his back. This went a long way to untangling his convoluted explanation about the murder of a man who was secretly collecting for him in Darktown. Someone else did the killing and Frenchy either knew who he was or he was protecting the evidence until he could match the prints.

Back at the office, I locked the envelope containing the razor and prints in my safe. No more carelessness like the kind that had cost me Carrie's diary and letters.

McGrath hadn't responded to my report. On the plus side, he hadn't demanded my badge back.

Some unrelated business came in. A few weeks ago, I would have welcomed it. Now it was an unwelcome distraction.

Barry Goldwater put me on retainer for the Williams Investment Company, which was formed by his family with two hundred thousand dollars of capital stock. What they intended to do—maybe purchase land—and why they might need a private eye were mysteries to me. I felt as if he was taking pity on me. But the four-hundred-dollar retainer fee he offered helped my dwindling treasury. A few weeks ago, I would have stuck the money in the safe and celebrated with a shave and haircut from Otis Kenilworth, a shoeshine, and a movie and prizefight with Victoria. The shave and haircut would have to do.

A man named Street hired me to help him in a dispute with the city. He didn't want to pay an assessment on his property at Twelfth and Van Buren streets, claiming the contract was awarded illegally. It was boring by my standards but it was fifty bucks and easy money. The job entailed working up background on the contractor, the Phoenix-Tempe Stone Company.

As part of the Street case, I attended a city commission meeting in the sparkling new commission chambers at City Hall. I sat in the back and took notes as the city attorney discussed Street's case.

The four commissioners were R. E. Patton, J. B. Guess, David Kimball, and O. B. Marston. These worthies were behind my layoff from the force. I wondered how many saw me sitting there. I wondered how many were in compromising photos taken from the wall peek in Kemper Marley's whorehouse. A case like this gave my mind plenty of time to wander.

Once the meeting ended, I grabbed a late lunch at the Busy Bee Café and got back to the office. Removing the Carrie Dell file from the locked filing cabinet, I turned to the call log for Summer Tours and started dialing.

As a police detective, I quickly learned that there were basically two kinds of cases. One set were obvious, with the suspect already apprehended or easily identified. Most murder victims knew their killers. The second kind were rarer but more interesting. They were cases that appeared random and evidence was scattered, requiring many hours, days, even months of work plus creativity. That was certainly true back in 1929.

Twenty-Three

On Monday, March 11, 1929, the next new moon, the entire force was mobilized to apprehend the University Park Strangler before he killed again. All vacations and leaves were canceled. Twelve-hour shifts with overtime were authorized.

The national press had caught the story, labeling the perpetrator as the "Fiend of Phoenix" but "University Park Strangler" stuck locally. Part of me wondered if it was because people in other parts of the city used the moniker as an incantation to keep the killer there and safely out of their neighborhoods.

Captain McGrath worked out a plan to focus marked police cars on the fringes of University Park, to "give him a sense of safety" inside the neighborhood itself. At the same time, members of the Hat Squad and patrolmen in plain clothes stationed themselves around University Park in parked cars, commandeered delivery trucks, and one empty rental house with good views of the street.

Everybody worked in pairs. Pump-action shotguns and Thompson submachine guns were issued. McGrath kept me with him at our new headquarters, which probably made sense because officers could use call boxes to notify us of the situation.

But I wanted to be on the street. We were all in position as the sun went down.

Yet nothing happened that night.

Just after sunrise two days later, Wednesday, a homeowner at Thirteenth Avenue and Polk Street called. A girl was on his front yard, half dressed, not moving. By the time I got there, the street was crowded with people, police cars, and an ambulance. But she was long dead. Her head was turned at an angle, cherry-red hair swept back, eyes staring at us reproachfully. On her stomach with her blouse off, I made an immediate check: The cross was carved in the small of her back.

"Goddamn it!"

Muldoon knelt down and put his big arm around me. "Easy, lad. We all feel that way, too. But civilians are around."

It was the only time I ever lost my composure on the job.

As the girl was sent off for the postmortem, we fanned out to interview everyone within two blocks of the body dump. Nobody saw anything. Not even the milkmen who were out that early.

More information allowed us to sort out the basics. She was likely Grace Chambers, sixteen, who never came home from the movies the night before. Her parents felt it was safe for her to see the pictures at the Rialto with her steady boyfriend, Ben Chapman. It was her birthday, and they also wanted to reward her for perfect grades this year. They felt safe because they lived in the Las Palmas neighborhood, north of McDowell Road, miles from University Park.

When neither Grace nor Ben came home by nine on Tuesday night, as agreed, her parents notified the police. Because of the letdown the night before, headquarters was short-staffed, the desk sergeant made a report and said he would send a car to interview the parents—but somehow it never happened. A fight in the Deuce distracted the patrolmen on duty. As McGrath said sourly, "The right hand didn't know what the left hand was doing."

Ben Chapman, seventeen, varsity athlete, choir member, was the prime suspect. That certainty, borne of desperate policemen, wasn't dimmed when Ben's '28 Buick was found parked outside the Arizona Citrus Growers warehouse on Jackson Street an hour later. But it was not to be. Two hours after Grace's body was identified by her parents, Ben Chapman was found bludgeoned to death out in the county, inside an orange grove. Mexican farmworkers discovered him. He was beaten badly. Don guessed a baseball bat. His hands were tied behind his back with rope.

As in the prior cases, Grace had been viciously raped and strangled, her underwear taken. But the killer had more time with her: She was not only tied up with a rope, but also with barbed wire. Her body had multiple cigarette burns. Her bottom had been whipped with a belt or whip, hard enough to leave bruises and bloody welts.

The pathologist guessed she was first bound with rope, perhaps at the same time as her boyfriend. He was a well-built young man, so it raised the possibility the two had been forced to give in at gunpoint. Then the killer made Grace tie up Ben, and she was restrained by the killer. As always with victims, they held out hope: *"This is only a robbery. He'll let us go if we do what he asks."*

The fingerprint tech went over Ben's car, and the latents were sent off to the FBI. Victoria took photos of both scenes.

Here the evidence petered out into our speculation. Did the killer take them both somewhere and force the boyfriend to watch as he tortured and raped Grace? Then what? Beat Ben to death before her eyes, finish her off, and leave her in University Park? Then dump his body outside the city limits? Quite a night's work and plenty of risks of being discovered, but possible. Frenchy raised the possibility of two killers, one following the other, who drove Ben's car. Then both could make a quick escape.

The heat came quickly, from the city commission, the chamber of commerce, the newspapers, and two sets of well-connected parents. It came from inside headquarters, too. Three members of the fifteen-man Hat Squad had daughters around the age of the strangler's victims. Senior patrolmen and sergeants, too. And those weren't shy about voicing frustration and recriminations.

On Thursday, a typed letter came, addressed to the Chief of Police Matlock:

> *The Phoenix Police can't solve the greatest crime ever to hit our city. Doesn't speak well for your new city hall and police headquarters building.*
>
> *It's me, you clowns. I'll get your tiresome little hidden tricks out of the way: I take their knickers and stuffed toys. I use a sock to keep them quiet. I carve my brand in their backs. I used barbed wire on the latest girl.*
>
> *Believe me now? I am HIM.*
>
> *You thought you had me all figured out. So predictable, you flatfoots. But I nabbed two lovers this time and had my way with both of them. Took them to my lair, isn't that what the reporters will call it?*
>
> *Made him watch while I did things to her. Nice and slow. Made her watch while I did things to him while he cried and pleaded, then killed him. Then it was only us. I was naked and bloody. She was screaming and begging right to the end. Nobody could hear her. I delivered her body to the neighborhood like the morning newspaper.*
>
> *Speaking of THAT... I'm sending a copy of this letter to the papers and radio stations.*

*I'll kill again and you can't stop me. It will be worse
every time.*

Given the specifics, this letter was definitely from the killer.
The paper contained no fingerprints. Chief of Police Matlock
succeeded in getting every news outlet to spike the letter. The
one exception was the *Los Angeles Examiner*, owned by William
Randolph Hearst. It printed the letter in full, headlined: FIEND
OF PHOENIX SPEAKS!

We didn't have time to deal with the reporters. This was the
donkey work of being a detective. In addition to making another
run at the neighbors around where Grace's body was dumped, the
farmworkers who found Ben, and family members, we spoke to
everyone conceivably involved. Ticket girls, ushers, concession-
stand workers, and the manager at the movie theater. Identified
the last ones to see them alive and correlated these witnesses
against the same for the previous victims.

Yet it produced no suspicious matches. People at the movies
that night came forward, but they didn't notice anything or anyone unusual. Again: Teachers and friends at Phoenix Union High
were interviewed. We tried, unsuccessfully, to match the barbed
wire that had been used to wrap around Grace Chambers's wrists.

Tips came in by the scores, and we had to run each one down to
its inevitable dead end. Then turn it over to another detective for
another try. Four goofies and hopheads came forward to confess.
None possessed the information we held back from the newspaper reports, but that still meant hours in the new interview room,
plus printing them to compare against the existing evidence.

I took the letter to the chief apart sentence by sentence, word
by word. "Talk to me, you bastard," I said under my breath. The
person who wrote this was either the killer or intimately knew
him, was an accomplice. Very confident. "She was screaming and

begging right to the end. Nobody could hear her." That indicated an isolated location or a soundproofed room.

I made notes. What *did* we know? All the victims went to Phoenix Union, none to St. Mary's or the colored high school, much less the schools in outlying towns. The killer was strong. He prepared his attacks in advance. For example, he never chose a house with a dog but did pick one with a deaf grandmother. He had a connection to University Park.

"He's neat, almost fussy," said Victoria, who by this time had become my friend and confidant. "The comforter or blanket and sheet wasn't thrown off in a heap. It was neatly folded. He took trophies from the first two, but otherwise their rooms were undisturbed. Barbed wire will hurt, but it won't cause extensive bleeding."

I made neat reports and forwarded them to Captain McGrath, as if my every addition to his "in" tray was a fresh nail pounded in the strangler's coffin. Hell, the coffin was empty.

After a week, the case went cold again.

McGrath assigned me, Don, and Muldoon to continue working on it full-time, while other detectives went back to cases that had been holding. We had four dead students, no viable suspect. The city commissioners fired Chief Matlock in May and replaced him with David Montgomery, captain over the traffic division, who made it clear that nobody on the Hat Squad was safe from meeting the same fate. He stared at me, the youngest detective, as he made this announcement.

Dead ends multiplied: A second check found no previous arrests of the high-school teachers, not even of the many deliverymen and tradesmen who spent time in University Park. The same was true of Phoenix Union High janitors and maintenance staff.

Prowler calls increased, but arrests were few. In many cases, someone called after seeing a neighbor take out his trash or work in his backyard after sundown. One suspect had a burglary conviction in Texas, but he had the best alibi in town for the time when Grace Chambers and Ben Chapman went missing: He was in jail for drunkenness and vagrancy. Finally, the FBI report came back: The prints on the Buick were not in their extensive files.

Yet somewhere in all this noise was the fact that would break the case.

I knew I wasn't alone among the detectives in feeling guilty for partly wishing the Fiend of Phoenix would strike again, but this time we'd get him before he killed the victim.

City leaders considered canceling the Masque of the Yellow Moon, scheduled to begin April 25th. But their consideration lasted about as long as a drunk thinking about quitting the bottle. The Masque might have started as a high-school event, but the Junior Chamber of Commerce had turned it into a parade and festival aspiring to nip at the heels of Pasadena's Tournament of Roses. People came from all over the state. The final night of this harvest celebration—a vast pageant going all the way back to the Aztecs—filled the Phoenix Union High's 10,500-person-capacity Montgomery Stadium.

So much money was flowing into Phoenix, to build the new office towers and hotels, start new businesses, and increase land under irrigation and the yields of the farms and groves. Never mind that Mexico was in turmoil, with rebels seizing Nogales, Sonora, and *federales* bombing them. That seemed far away from the Roaring Twenties in the states, and especially in this state.

The last thing Phoenix political and business leaders wanted was to dampen the good times by canceling the biggest event in the annual life of the young city. The mayor demanded the chief promise him Phoenix would be safe from this "maniac nonsense," and he did. Once again, the entire force was mobilized. Fortunately, a full moon began on April 23rd. The Masque came off safely, and May was strangely quiet except for the real harvest rituals. In a single day, the Salt River Valley sent one hundred seventy-five refrigerated railroad cars off to help feed the nation. And that was just lettuce—we also picked, packed, and shipped oranges, cantaloupes, watermelons, onions, dates, grapes, strawberries, and beets.

I had to make a break instead of waiting for one.

McGrath blew up when I first took the idea to him. Only Muldoon agreed. Turk pulled me aside and said, "Always trust your gut, lad, and sometimes fight for what it's telling you. It's the best weapon a good detective has."

Finally, McGrath agreed.

Juliet Dehler worked in the records department. She was twenty-one but looked much younger. She was petite, pretty, red-haired. In my work with Juliet, I'd been impressed by her intelligence, maturity, and most important, moxie. Over lunch at the Saratoga, she readily agreed to help me in my plan. I issued her a .38 snub-nosed for her purse and took her into the desert to teach her how to use it. She also got a police whistle to hang around her neck, hidden below her blouse.

June arrived. Phoenix Union High School graduated 407 students, the Valley shipped its first-ever carloads of apricots on the Santa Fe Railway to New York City, people had to shake out their shoes for scorpions, and wealthy men sent their wives and children to California or Iron Springs. Juliet took to the streets of downtown and University Park two or three times a week. Although the summer heat was oppressive, the city cooled down at night.

She dressed like the victims the strangler favored, feminine and middle-class stylish but never like looking like a roundheels. She went to movies in air-conditioned theaters; shopped on Thursday nights, when the stores stayed opened late; took the streetcar to the Carnegie Library; walked "alone" to a rental house in University Park we'd commandeered as her "home." She made herself visible.

I was watching, of course, tailing at a safe distance. Sometimes Don or Muldoon joined the tail. Juliet attracted plenty of attention, whether from young whistling wolves or the summer bachelors freed for the hot months of their families.

Nothing dangerous happened, however. Not a sign of a perv or rapist, much less the strangler. That changed on the night of Friday, June 28th.

Twenty-Four

Back in '29, Turk Muldoon told me to always trust my gut. My much more experienced gut was now telling me that Carrie Dell was running a call-girl service out of the Arizona Biltmore. She was doing it under the protection of a vice detective who loved her, Frenchy Navarre. Pamela said Carrie was running with a fast crowd. Indeed, she was.

The gut was informed by more than a good breakfast at the Saratoga as I wrote a letter to Victoria. Over the past two days I ran down the list of incoming calls to Summer Tours. I dialed each, innocently saying I had reached a wrong number once they answered.

The numbers took me to switchboard operators at the state capitol, city hall, a bank, two respectable law offices, the Grunow Clinic—where Winnie Ruth Judd had worked as a medical secretary—and Central Arizona Light and Power Co.

I wondered how many legislators, doctors, lawyers, and executives were clients of Summer Tours. The only thing missing from the lineup was an Indian chief. In one case, the number was answered by a woman who said, "*Racing News.*" Greenbaum? *Fast crowd.*

Several calls were made from rooms at the Westward Ho, San Carlos, and other hotels. Every few days a call came from the Arizona Biltmore, but I suspected that was from Carrie. Several had repeatedly called Summer Tours, a few only once. The total individual numbers calling totaled thirty-five between May and September last year.

Two numbers didn't require a call because I already knew them. One was the number to the detective bureau at police headquarters. The other was Kemper Marley's line.

Only one number gave me pause: It rang directly to Barry Goldwater's home on Garfield Street.

Barry was one of the handsomest men in Phoenix. He could have any woman in town that he wanted, and if the stories were true, he'd already had quite a number of them. Why would he want a prostitute? I'd never been with one, not even when I was a soldier. I was afraid of getting the clap. The mystery continued when I worked vice cases, although I suppose the appeal of no-strings-attached sex was strong for some and the only option for a married man. Still…Barry?

Maybe my gut was wrong. Carrie's business might have been involved in liquor or gambling. Maybe Summer Tours was simply that—pretty girls chastely on the arms of lonely older men at restaurants. I was too cynical to buy that.

That afternoon I walked over to Goldwater's, which occupied a four-story building with Dorris-Heyman Furniture Company at First Street and Adams in the heart of the retail district. I purchased a silk tie with an abstract design to protect myself from Barry's scolding once I found him.

He was alone in his office, feet up on his desk, working a crossword puzzle.

"The pressure-filled life of a department store executive," I said.

Barry's face lit up, and he set the puzzle aside.

"Gene! Come on in. I hope you came to shop…"

I held up the necktie.

"Ah, very good. What's up?"

"Tell me about a young woman named Cynthia."

"Cynthia?" He wasn't a good liar, and I told him so.

He lowered his legs to the floor, sighed, and said I'd better shut the door.

He ran his hands through his wavy dark hair. "How do you know about Cynthia?"

"That's not her name, for starters."

He opened his mouth to speak but closed it.

"Her name was Carrie Dell. Blonde, blue eyes, about five-five, beautiful, from Prescott, and a student at the teachers' college."

"Goddamn it all to hell, Gene. What are you trying to tell me? The description sounds familiar. Unforgettable, really. But what's this about being a student and from Prescott? Cynthia was a writer, visiting last year from Cleveland. She's the granddaughter of John Lincoln. You know, the Lincoln Electric millionaire? His wife has tuberculosis, and he brought her to the Desert Mission in Sunnyslope to recuperate. She got much better. Now he's giving big bucks to the mission, promoting Phoenix for health-seekers. Anyway, I got to know Cynthia last summer."

Oh, Carrie was an even better liar than I gave her credit for.

I pulled out a Chesterfield and asked if I could smoke. He asked for one, too, and I lit us both.

"Barry, what do you mean you knew the girl?"

"What do you mean?" His voice was angry.

I didn't back down. "You damned well know what I mean."

He quickly cooled. "Did I sleep with her? Sure."

"Did you pay for it?"

His face reddened. "That's not the kind of thing I usually do, but…"

I asked how much.

"Three hundred. It was worth every penny. Even though she made me use a condom."

Now it was my turn to fight for words. That was an astounding sum. The highest-priced call girls who worked the hotels in Phoenix during the height of the tourist season charged fifty bucks. The girls at Marley's disreputable house charged far less and netted even lower sums because of Kemper's overhead charge.

"Don't get the wrong idea, Gene. I really like this girl. I've never met anyone quite like her. She's smart as hell. Creative. Are you sure she lied about her name and all?"

I nodded and asked how he met her, expecting him to mention Summer Tours.

He said, "She's a friend of Gus Greenbaum."

Big Cat?

I waited until he was willing to meet my eyes.

"Well, she's dead, Barry. Murdered."

His hand shook and ash fell on his tailored vest. He didn't even notice.

I sat in one of the chairs facing his desk. "I hate to have to tell you, my friend, but you were taken in." I gave it to him straight, and although it was inconceivable that Goldwater killed her, I asked him where he was on the day she was murdered. He had an alibi, working at the store all day, then a party at the Arizona Club on the ninth floor of the Luhrs Building. He grew angry at having to answer until I spoke next.

"She was pregnant, Barry."

When I finally stood and exited the office, I'm not even sure Barry was aware that I had left.

Twenty-Five

I am in Belleau Wood again. Unlike so much of the tree-denuded front, this forest is almost untouched in 1918. Until now. The poilus are urging us to retreat back to the trenches, but we move ahead, fixing bayonets. Our job is to protect the Marines' flank.

The darkness is giving way to daylight, but you'd never know it from the trees and low fog. The scent of decomposing bodies is everywhere. You never get used to it. Our skirmish line moves two hundred yards when we run head-on into the Huns.

I fire my rifle, but the bullet slithers out slowly from the barrel and falls to the ground. Then the German is upon me, and I am unable to get my bayonet in a position to repel him. He's fast, but I'm impossibly slow. My buddy brings him down with a bayonet but then his face disappears into a mist of blood and I am alone. Artillery starts falling while I tremble uncontrollably.

Next we're in dugout fighting positions, night has returned. I'm lying amid skulls and goo with rats running across me. The rats and lice bite. Our company dog goes on point; he's been trained not to bark or even growl. When he goes on point, an attack is coming. Victoria is here, kitted out like any infantryman. She's maybe ten yards away in a shell hole. I call to her, move toward her on my belly, working my elbows and legs to stay low, but when I get there she's gone.

Back in the line, we wait. The dog growls now, but the field is strangely quiet. No artillery barrage. What if mustard gas is coming? I can't find my gas mask. I grip my rifle. The word is quietly passed: Fix bayonets! But stormtroopers are already inside our perimeter, black eyes beneath coal-scuttle helmets. Two of them are upon me, and my bayonet has disappeared. He had a German war dog with him ready to pounce. I know I'm going to die…

———

When I woke up, sweat covered my body. As I got my bearings, I thanked God I was in my apartment. When I had these night-mares and Victoria was with me, she said I started making an eerie sound. It was my screaming and shouting in the dream, barely making it into the real world. She woke me with diffi-culty. Shaking and calling my name was no good. She finally realized the way to bring me around was to push hard against my body, rocking me awake. She was afraid I might come out fighting, but I never did. She was my saving angel.

But she wasn't in the bed tonight. The moon streamed in through the window, and I pulled up the covers as the sweat quickly evaporated in the low humidity of the Phoenix night. That was when I heard a sound that might be mistaken for rodents in the walls. But this was a nearly new building. Someone was picking the lock to my front door.

Wearing only pajama bottoms, I put my feet on the cold floor and slipped the heavy M1911 Colt semiautomatic from its holster and thumbed back the hammer. The sound of the lockpick tools became more distinct, and I heard the front-door lock's tumblers begin to turn.

Deciding to stay in the bedroom, I made myself one with the wall beside the open door, holding the cold steel of the pistol against my face, arm crooked. The front door quietly opened, then shut. A heavy tread came inside and moved toward me. Then a silhouette was inside the bedroom, and I brought the M1911's barrel down to the silhouette's temple.

"Move and I'll blow your brains all over the room."

I stepped back and pivoted to face him, keeping the pistol aimed. He was tall, broad-shouldered, and smelled of expensive cigars.

"Back out into the living room, very slowly. Keep facing me."

He did as told. Now the ambient light was enough to reveal my visitor.

Gus Greenbaum smirked at me.

"I must be losing my touch."

"Sit down, gangster."

"You need to show some respect, Detective Hammons. What if I have some well-armed associates waiting right outside the door?"

"Then they're going to find their boss on the floor without a head, and I'm going to kill them, too. Respect is earned, and maybe I'm the only guy in Phoenix who doesn't get excited by your presence, but you'll have to live with it. Or not."

Greenbaum muttered something and sat on the sofa. He started to turn on the floor lamp, but I stopped him. I had night vision and had recently been in hand-to-hand combat with German stormtroopers.

We sat in silence until he started to reach inside his coat.

"Ah, ah, ah." My finger was on the trigger.

He froze. "May I smoke?"

"Why not? But reach very slowly."

He carefully removed a cigar from his coat pocket and bit off the end.

"If you spit that on my carpet, I'll shoot you."

He let it fall in his palm, dropped it in the ashtray, then lit the cigar with a match, a long circular motion until the tip was red as a smelter. As if my dream had foreshadowed this moment, Greenbaum looked at me like a rottweiler assessing how easily he could rip out my throat.

"What brings you to my humble lodgings, Mr. Greenbaum?"

"Gus," he instructed. "May I call you Gene?"

I didn't see why not.

"You have me all wrong, Gene. Your pal Barry Goldwater has a very active imagination. In reality, I'm a businessman, serving a need with the latest technology. You and Barry may imagine that I'm taking over this town with a Chicago typewriter, but that's silly. Phoenix has welcomed me with open arms. Goldwater and Rosenzweig have opened doors. I'm welcome at the chamber of commerce. This is a great place for my new service's Southwest operations." He tapped his finger and an inch of spent cigar embers dropped into the ashtray. "All my relationships are transactional, see? The power of money will outdo the power of a Tommy gun any day."

"You're a pretty good lock picker."

He smiled. "An old trade I learned many years ago. I'm sure you can do it, too."

That much was true, even though we were on different sides of the law.

"So why pick my lock?"

After savoring his Cuban, he spoke. "I didn't expect to find you at home. I supposed you were off with your girlfriend. See, I have a problem. I foolishly got involved with a girl who got herself killed. She went by Cynthia, but I learned her name was really Carrie Dell. I gave her a loan to help get her business started, and she paid me back in more ways than one. But something went wrong and she was murdered. A little birdie at police headquarters told me you were investigating that killing, even though you're officially off the force. I assumed you might have some of her records that might be embarrassing to me."

I set the .45 beside me and lit a nail. "That might implicate you as her killer?"

"Not at all. Killing is bad for business, especially the way the poor girl was sawed apart."

I had to admit the Dell homicide was more like a lust murder, like the University Park Strangler, than an organized crime hit.

I said, "Maybe I can help if I know what you're looking for?"

He chuckled. "You'd like to help put me in the gallows for killing her. Nevertheless, Carrie might have written down my name and phone number. I'd prefer that not become public record."

"Why do you care?"

"Because I'm enjoying becoming part of respectable Phoenix. I like this little city. It's going places. The truth is I was going to find this information and pilfer it."

"Is that so, Big Cat?"

He looked confused enough that I knew he was not Big Cat.

I said, "My problem, Gus, is that somebody set off a smoke bomb below my office and used that distraction to steal the records I found from Carrie." I lied about his phone number in the list from the answering service. "So whatever worries you was taken. My expectation is that whoever took it has already stuck it in an incinerator. I don't think they're going to give it to the newspapers, and what if they did? Carrie is still classified as a suspicious death, not a homicide."

"Or they're going to try to blackmail me. Look, Gene, I'm a married man. A divorce lawyer could make sure my wife could take half of what I own. I don't need that distraction. And I answer to people in Chicago who wouldn't like it at all."

It was such a prosaic answer that I almost believed it. "A guy like you could arrange an 'accident' to eliminate your wife. Otherwise, I expect you know how to handle blackmail, Gus. But if you hear from someone in that racket trying to lean on you, let me know. I can help."

He set the cigar in the ashtray.

"I expect you could." He leaned forward. "Now, if you won't plug me, I'd like to stand and leave and thank you for the conversation."

"Not quite yet," I said. "You know how Carrie was murdered. Please don't tell me about your buddies on the force feeding you information. I know all about Frenchy as your bagman. He went off the reservation and got quite a hammering for it."

"That was Cyrus Cleveland, my man on the South Side. I agreed something had to be done. But Frenchy pinning a murder on a Negro didn't sit well with Cyrus, so I let him set Navarre straight. What's your point?"

I said, "Who murdered Carrie Dell?"

He shrugged. "A psycho. This was deeply personal. The year I was born, 1893, Chicago held a world's fair to celebrate Columbus reaching the New World. A very big deal, the White City. Only trouble was a guy named Dr. Holmes who built a hotel catering to single women. And he murdered them there. I'm told it had soundproof rooms and mazes. He confessed to murdering twenty-seven, but it might have been two hundred. He dissected some. Maybe Carrie ran into a Dr. Holmes, and if that's true you have more victims. Or…"

I studied his face but it was grim, unreadable.

"Or?" I prompted.

"There is no 'or,' Hammons. Just a figure of speech. Carrie ran into a maniac. Phoenix is turning into a real city."

After he was gone, I locked the door and propped a chair against it. A long hour passed before I fell asleep, the pistol under my pillow. I dreamed of taxicabs.

Twenty-Six

Friday, June 28th, 1929. Juliet took in a double-feature at the Fox and walked west on Washington in a crowd as the other theaters let out. I followed half a block behind. It looked to be another fruitless night, and McGrath would shut down my attempt at baiting the killer.

Then a taxi pulled up and paced her.

I heard the driver lean out and call. "May I take you somewhere, pretty lady?"

She came two steps closer to the curb. I thought: *Do not get in that cab!*

It might have been innocent, but I realized here was one thing that had evaded our attention: a driver and vehicle that could go anywhere without raising suspicion.

Suddenly, he opened the door and started to wrestle her inside. She yelled and kicked him.

Then I was there with my Detective Special out. Don was soon at my side and we braced him against the taxi with difficulty. Although he had a meek face and average build, he was strong as hell. It took both of us to get him in cuffs, with a nipper for good measure. He argued, then begged to be let go. But the game was up.

In the back seat were ropes, barbed wire, a sock, and a rag soaked in chloroform. A penknife was in his front pocket.

We sweated him for twelve hours until finally, under my continued questioning, catching him stumble through lie after lie, as he told and retold his activities on the dates of the murders, he broke. It happened when I lied to him and said his wife refused to support his alibi that he was home the nights of the murders. And when I told the truth: We found a soundproof room added to his garage. Then he spilled.

By that time, other detectives had executed a search warrant at his home, finding the knickers and stuffed animals taken from the first two victims, as well as a bloody baseball bat. His typewriter matched the taunting note sent to the police chief. His wife expressed surprise, then outrage that we suspected her husband of such heinous crimes. But I suspected she knew all along.

He wasn't a taxi driver—that cab had been stolen specifically to snatch Juliet, who he had been watching. He was a clerk at a building and loan. Each of the female victims had opened passbook savings accounts with him. This was the link we didn't find.

Emil Gorman, forty-five, was a model employee at the building and loan, shy, kept to himself. He didn't have so much as a parking ticket. His neighbors on East Pierce Street were similarly surprised that Gorman was suspected of being the strangler.

With one exception: an elderly woman with a habit of watching the street saw him leave late at night on the date of Grace Chambers's disappearance. She remembered because it was also her daughter's birthday. He didn't return until early the next day.

His arrest and confession were national news. The Hearst *Examiner's* headline: FIEND OF PHOENIX CAUGHT!

Although Gorman confessed to all the murders, I always wondered if there were more. Maybe he got his taste for it on prostitutes nobody would miss. University Park seemed only sinister coincidence. The first girl lived there, and it was fertile hunting ground. Then he liked the name bestowed on him by the press.

It was the case that made me famous, at least for a time.

Twenty-Seven

Now, four years later, I didn't feel famous or accomplished. In the morning light, my apartment still smelled of Greenbaum's cigar. I pulled the chair away from the door, lit a nail, and made coffee.

I had my strong suspicions about Carrie/Cynthia's game, but the smoke bomb ensured that my evidence, in the form of letters and diary, was gone. All I had left were two boxes of expensive women's clothing, size small, and her hardcover journal. I had no interest in reading the juvenile fiction of a nineteen-year-old, whatever her pretensions. But I picked it up anyway—the cover read "My Stories," and prepared to make a go of it.

But it wasn't a journal. After the first page, also labeled "My Stories," it opened to reveal a hidden compartment. A black spiral notebook, five inches by three, stared out at me.

I lifted it out and proceeded to read.

———

I spent the next week discreetly interviewing the clients of Summer Tours.

A state senator, Superior Court judge, bank president, city commissioner and other big wigs.

Whether in their offices, over lunch at the Arizona Club, or in more hidden nooks such as the Original Mexican Café on East Adams Street, each confessed to consorting with the college girls provided by Carrie. All were "summer bachelors" because they had the means to send their wives to cooler climes. They happily paid the steep fees for companionship they could have only dreamed of in the past. None seemed capable of killing.

I sewed it up with another trip to Tempe, where Pamela, the auburn-haired smoke-ring blower, admitted she had been one of the dozen girls who stayed for the hot months and made money. She fiercely denied being a roundheels and offered up the justifications of the young and attractive. As I've said, I'm not a moralist. I could not have cared less if murder were not involved. Pamela finally came to realize that she might have been cut up beside the railroad tracks, too.

The problem after all this gab was that I felt no closer to finding Carrie's killer.

Twenty-Eight

Victoria's latest letter was the one I most anticipated: An invitation to Los Angeles. I grabbed it and told the Central Methodist choir director I would be missing some rehearsals.

That night, I boarded the westbound *Sunset Limited* and let the porter show me to my Pullman berth as the lights of Phoenix, then the orchards and farms, slipped away. Afterward, I went to the dining car for a delicious meal served on fine Southern Pacific china as we sped through empty desert.

Later, I went to the lounge-observation car at the end of the train, lit a smoke, and let the bartender fix me a martini. This was definitely a sign that Prohibition was on the way out. As I sipped my drink, I studied the photographs Victoria had sent me from Los Angeles. Her photographs. The majestic Los Angeles Coliseum from the 1932 Olympics. Griffith Park with a sweeping view of the city, where she wrote that an observatory was being planned. Downtown with dense, multistory commercial buildings, movie palaces, and crowds. A massive Union Station under construction. The towering new City Hall. Santa Monica Pier and the Pacific Ocean. Tony Beverly Hills. The HOLLYWOODLAND sign.

She also had an assortment of crime photos taken on scenes with the LAPD.

Phoenix had nothing like this, and I was pleased with the artistry of her photographs. Yet I wondered if she could ever be happy in little Phoenix again. Or happy being with me, a small-town shamus with uncertain prospects.

Should I have proposed to her a long time ago? Would that have made a difference? I never wanted to stand in her way. I hoped to be a part of her future, wherever it was, but the tone of her letters from California was slightly more distant with each one. As for me, I never found how to assemble the truest and best words I knew, to explain how I felt about her. Now I suspected this trip would be goodbye.

I ordered another drink and mulled over the case as the car rocked. A speedometer on the wall said we were racing along at eighty-five miles per hour. My pop had taught me that the farther back from the locomotive, the rougher the ride. Still, the quality of this car was such that most passengers wouldn't notice. Suspect after suspect had been eliminated. Although I had learned much about Carrie Dell and her enterprise, I didn't know the ultimate answer: Who killed her.

After finishing my cocktail, I wandered the train, read in my seat before the porter made my bed, and we rolled into Yuma for a short stop. Soon after leaving, the conductor found me.

"Detective Gene Hammons?"

I showed him my badge. "That's me."

He handed me a telegram from Phoenix.

I opened it. And I finally knew.

Detraining at Indio and catching the next train back to Phoenix seemed the prudent thing to do. I thought about wiring the news to Captain McGrath. But how would I make the many explanations—about pilfering evidence from the murder scene, secretly matching prints with confidential police personnel files at the top of the list? And I badly wanted to see Victoria.

In the rear of the train again, the observation car was nearly empty. The conductor let me open the rear door and step out onto the open observation deck. Beneath and behind me, the *Sunset Limited* sped west, the steel rails polished by a full moon. The train swayed. If anything, we were going faster than eighty-five now. Everything I saw was fleeing behind us, gone, in my past, as we rushed to reach Los Angeles by morning.

Although it was cold, I sat down, zipped my jacket, and let the solitude arrange my thoughts.

The telegram in my pocket was from Don. He had finally matched the prints found on my business card that had been placed in Carrie's purse. They corresponded to the latents taken from the razor that killed Zoogie Boogie, secreted as insurance in Navarre's safe-deposit box, as well as those dusted by the Prescott Police from the murder weapon that slit Ezra Dell's throat. The killer was the same man.

But I wasn't alone for long. I felt a strong hand on my shoulder.

"May I join you?"

For the tiniest moment I was afraid for the first time since the Western Front in 1918. But I tightened my gut. After we flashed past a freight train waiting on a siding, I found my voice.

"Please do."

He sat in the adjacent chair and lit a cigarette. "It was my dearest hope that you wouldn't follow this case so far. Or that I could throw you off, draw the voodoo symbol to point at Navarre as prime suspect."

"But you know me better than that."

"Alas, I do."

"And your dearest hope doesn't jibe with you putting my

card in Carrie Dell's purse. If Don hadn't found it, I would be in Florence right now waiting for the drop."

"Oh, I knew he'd rescue you. The discovery was meant to put you on the trail, and you would find the things that might incriminate me. Which you did and were kind enough to leave on the top of your desk so I could dispose of them."

"Why not investigate it yourself?"

"Oh, too risky. The girls knew me, and it wouldn't do for me to go poking around at the college."

"Her father and Zoogie Boogie?"

"I had to get what they knew. If they knew my name."

"And Jack Hunter in prison?"

"I was lucky enough to intercept that note he sent you at headquarters. I don't know what he wanted to tell you. But why take the chance? I sent word to a stoolie at Florence who owed me."

"You murdered four people. It's hard to believe."

"It's easier to get sucked in and keep killing than I ever realized. First, I had to kill my Baby Girl. That was the hardest. Afterward, covering my tracks was paramount and the killing was easier. Old man Dell, Zoogie, they saw me, knew my face and name. At the least, I'd lose my job and family. At the worst, I'd swing."

"Big Cat."

"That's what she called me."

"But why kill her and do it that way?"

When he silently smoked, I made a try.

"I think you were her protector and then her lover. Older man, young woman, however confident you are, you can't believe how lucky you were to have this goddess in your bed. With the powerful people involved with Summer Tours, you had blackmail material to make you a very wealthy man. But she had the power, and you didn't like it. She bent men to her will. You felt emasculated and yet you couldn't stop wanting her. She was the itch you couldn't scratch. It was a fun summer, but then she was ready to move on. And you couldn't have that. She made threats. You sure as hell couldn't have those. The breaking point was when she told you she was pregnant."

"Keep going."

"Then you killed her with the blackjack. Maybe you didn't even mean to do it. Maybe she hit you first and you hit back, hard. Then your blood was up. You couldn't leave it at that, drop her body in an abandoned mine in the desert. More than your blood was up. Real evil took over. You'd seen so many ways people kill each other. And it got to you, taught you. You dismembered her, dressed her in the fine clothes she favored, displayed her just inside the city limits. After you calmed down, you hoped it would either be written off as a train suicide or brushed under the rug because the city didn't want another sensational crime. Another lust murder, like the University Park Strangler. As the final backup, you put my card in her purse and set it against the tree, in case the cops didn't pursue the killing as a homicide, which they didn't. That way I'd blaze the trail so you could do some cleaning up."

He sighed. "You turned into a hell of a detective."

"And now I have your prints."

After a long silence punctuated by the locomotive whistling ahead, the familiar brogue resumed. "I never figured you'd get that far, lad. But you did, and so you might say this rendezvous between the two of us was inevitable."

Muldoon pointed at a vast shimmering body of water off to the west. "That's the Salton Sea. Sits below sea level. Happened by accident, you know, when a canal broke and the Colorado River poured water in here for two years. It was never meant to happen. But there it is. Surprising but inevitable."

"Here's the piece I don't understand, Turk. The gold pocket watch. How did that end up at an Okie camp east of town?"

"Baby Girl gave it to me as a gift in better times. Later... Well, I knew it was too risky to keep it, so I gave it to a drifter. He looked like he could use some luck, move out of town, and nobody would ever find the watch."

"But I did find it. You taught me well, Liam."

He tossed the nail over the observation car's three-foot-high brass railing and it flew out into the night like a red comet. "I miss those good times, lad, the ones with you and me. Catching the strangler. I'd admit to feeling a bit jealous of what a smart and capable detective you'd turned out to be, and so quickly."

"But why would you kill your child?"

"She wasn't pregnant. That was a ruse to manipulate me."

"She was pregnant. Don had a postmortem carried out." I took a risk and continued. "She made her lovers use rubbers, but you refused. Only you could have been the father."

He stared at me. "Oh, Jesus, Mary, and Joseph..."

Then he came fast, very fast for a big man, and ripped me up from the chair. Next, I was hanging backward over the railing with his hands around my throat.

"Go easy, lad, and at this speed it will be over in no time at all. Only a little pain, then sweet oblivion."

But I wasn't going easy. I brought my knee up and connected with his groin. He let go. I gasped sweet breath and rose to my feet as he threw a haymaker in my direction. But he was off-balance, hurting in his balls, and I easily evaded the punch. I delivered a series of my own sharp jabs to his eyes and gut and kneed him in the groin again for good measure. He was bent nearly to the floor, groaning.

"Stay down. I'm taking you back to Phoenix under arrest."

He moaned, "That will never happen, lad."

In an instant he threw himself past me and was over the brass railing. I don't know if my punches had blinded him or if this was deliberate, suicide. Then he had second thoughts and grasped the railing desperately.

I braced myself and brought my arm toward him. "Reach up, Liam, and take my hand!"

The ties and ballast flew beneath him. His eyes were full of terror.

"No, lad. But thank you for trying."

He let go.

I watched his body tumble hard onto the railbed, roll and roll, arms and legs akimbo, until it was devoured by darkness.

AUTHOR'S NOTE

Barry Goldwater became a Phoenix City Councilman in 1949 at the urging of Harry Rosenzweig, running as a reform candidate. In 1952, he was the surprise winner of a seat in the U.S. Senate. Goldwater's Department Stores was sold in 1963. Barry Goldwater is widely credited with being a pivotal figure in the rise of modern American conservatism. He was the Republican nominee for president in 1964, losing to Lyndon Johnson. Although never officially connected to organized crime, Goldwater enjoyed the company of a fast crowd. When he died in 1998, Barry Goldwater was the most beloved figure in Arizona. He maintained a long friendship with Gus Greenbaum, who attended his funeral.

Gus Greenbaum enjoyed a long career in organized crime, becoming legendary as a turnaround artist for Las Vegas casinos. He was dependable and professional, "master of the skim"— where the mob stole money from casino winnings before it could be recorded and taxed. Greenbaum didn't want to leave Phoenix and repeatedly asked to retire so he and his wife could enjoy their home there. But the Outfit kept calling him back to fix problems at casinos. He was torn between a desire to live full-time in Phoenix

and his love of the Las Vegas excitement—and being a big man in
the town. Greenbaum became an alcoholic and a heroin addict.
The Outfit began to question his reliability. This proved true
when they found the master of the skim was skimming himself,
and too much to be tolerated. In 1958, he and his wife were
assassinated in their Encanto-Palmcroft home in Phoenix. The
crime was never solved.

Sharlot Hall came to Arizona Territory as a child in 1882. In
1906, she was active in efforts to prevent Congress from making
Arizona and New Mexico one state. Her epic poem, "Arizona," was
placed on the desk of every congressman. She served as territorial
historian from 1909 to 1912, when Arizona became a state. When
Calvin Coolidge won the presidency in 1924, Hall was deputized
as the elector to present Arizona's three Electoral College votes in
Washington, D.C. In 1927, she moved her extensive collection of
documents and artifacts to the old territorial Governor's Mansion
in Prescott and opened it as a museum. The Sharlot Hall Museum
continues to operate in downtown Prescott.

Winnie Ruth Judd's death sentence was commuted, and she
was sent to the state insane asylum (Arizona State Hospital). She
escaped six times between 1933 and 1963. After her final escape,
she became the live-in maid for a wealthy San Francisco Bay Area
family using a false name. Once unmasked, she was returned to
Arizona. After a legal fight including famed defense attorney
Melvin Belli, Judd was paroled by **Governor Jack Williams**. A
radio announcer who had gained fame broadcasting coverage
of the original Judd trial, Williams went on to become mayor
of Phoenix and three-term governor of Arizona. Journalist Jana
Bommersbach wrote a book about the Judd case, arguing con-
vincingly that Ruth was railroaded by the Phoenix establishment.

Kemper Marley became the richest man in Arizona thanks
to his liquor business and extensive landholdings, which became

very valuable as Phoenix emerged into a major city and spread out. Marley eventually got a part of the Outfit's gambling-wire business when Greenbaum was called away to Las Vegas. Marley was suspected of orchestrating the bombing death of *Arizona Republic* investigative reporter Don Bolles in 1976, but it was never proved. Most Arizonans today know of him from the Kemper and Ethel Marley Foundation, which has placed his name on institutions around the state.

Father Emmett McLoughlin ministered in some of Phoenix's most destitute areas, becoming a leading advocate of public housing and other assistance for the poor. His efforts at slum clearance brought federal funds to build the Matthew Henson Homes at Seventh Avenue and Buckeye and other projects. He was also named the first chairman of the city's Housing Authority and founded St. Monica's Hospital. He left the priesthood after his superiors accused him of neglecting his pastoral duties and demanded he resign as superintendent of the hospital. For many years, McLoughlin remained Phoenix's foremost advocate of the poor.

Frenchy Navarre continued on as a detective until he shot and killed Phoenix Police Officer David "Star" Johnson in 1944. Johnson was a popular African American patrolman walking a downtown beat. Although Navarre was acquitted, Johnson's partner arrived at police headquarters and confronted Navarre. After a wild gunfight, Frenchy was killed. In life, he was friends with Gus Greenbaum and other mobsters.

Harry Rosenzweig became the founder of the modern Republican Party in Arizona, leading it to dominate a state long run by the Democrats. For decades, he was the political boss of Phoenix. In addition to his jewelry business, Harry and his brother, Newton, developed the high-rise Rosenzweig Center office-hotel complex in Midtown Phoenix. Harry's connections to organized crime were suspected but never proven.

Wing Ong graduated at the top of his class at the University of Arizona law school. In 1946, he was elected to the Arizona House of Representatives, the first Chinese American to reach this milestone in America. He was elected to the state senate in 1966.

Carl Sims succeeded as a gardening and painting contractor. He went on to work for the Highway Department and become a Maricopa County deputy sheriff. In 1950, Sims was one of the first two African Americans elected to the Arizona House of Representatives.

Del Webb became the most successful contractor in the Southwest and a very wealthy man. Webb's projects ranged from the Poston Relocation Center, where Japanese Americans were interned during World War II, to Sun City. He was also a co-owner of the New York Yankees. In 1946, mob boss Bugsy Siegel hired Webb to oversee construction of the Flamingo Hotel and Casino in Las Vegas.

Read on for an excerpt from

THE BOMB SHELTER

another exciting book by Jon Talton.

Chapter One

At 11:10 on the morning of Friday, June 2nd, 1978, Charles Page spun the platen knob of the Smith Corona Classic 12 typewriter on his desk at the Arizona State Capitol pressroom. It advanced a roll of gray newsprint that fed in from the back. He pecked out a short sentence and spun the knob again so the words were visible above the paper holder. They read:

Mark Reid, 11:30 a.m., Clarendon House.

Page slid a reporter's notebook in his back pocket, picked up his briefcase, and walked a block to his car. A mile away at the newspaper building, the presses were about to start their run, putting out his afternoon paper, the *Phoenix Gazette*. He didn't have a story in today's edition. The committee hearing he covered this morning hadn't produced news.

Outside, the temperature was already more than a hundred degrees, headed to a forecast high of 103. After stopping to make small talk with a state senator, he walked quickly across the plaza that separated the two chambers of the Legislature.

Page was a good-looking man, six-foot-two, still as slender at age forty-eight as he had been at twenty. His wavy hair was light brown, styled in an old-fashioned pompadour with more trendy sideburns. He favored leisure suits.

It couldn't have taken him more than five minutes to reach the parking lot, where his nine-year-old red GTO was parked in a space reserved for the press.

His mother and father called him Charlie. But when he flew for the Air Force in Korea, he gained the nickname Buzz. This had less to do with being a pilot of F-86 Saber fighter jets than the fact that his squadron already had two other men named Charlie. One stayed Charlie, the second became Chuck, and he was christened Buzz. Charlie and Chuck were later shot down in dogfights against Russian-piloted MiGs near the Yalu River, both killed. He survived fifty-six combat missions, came home, graduated with a journalism degree from the University of Missouri and, after working at some small papers, found his spot at the *Gazette*.

There he made a name writing stories on land fraud and organized crime. He regularly scooped the bigger morning paper, the *Arizona Republic*. Even though both newspapers were owned by the Pulliam family, each competed fiercely against the other. His success on the land-fraud beat and the other prominent stories he wrote earned him another nickname, "Front Page," from admiring colleagues. In recent years, he delved into RaceCo, a sports concession that ran the state's greyhound dog racing tracks and had connections to organized crime. And in 1975, he produced "Strangers Among Us," a five-day series of stories on the two hundred Mafia figures who had relocated to Phoenix in recent years. He named names, and how some were close to political leaders. It was a finalist for the Pulitzer Prize and enhanced Page's national standing among his peers.

He wore the acclaim lightly. Buzz was unassuming, a good listener who seemed shy outside his circle of friends who knew him for his loud laugh and practical jokes. This caused the targets of his investigations to underestimate him, which was an advantage. But the results he got made him enemies. All the years of going through documents and sitting at a typewriter also cost him his fighter pilot eyesight. As a result, he wore black, horn-rimmed glasses. Women liked him.

Then the bosses suddenly moved him to cover the Legislature. That had been a year ago. The demands of investigative reporting cost him his first marriage. People who didn't know him well believed he was happier to be out of the pressure cooker and the regular threatening phone calls and letters that came with his old beat. He stopped his ritual of putting scotch tape where the GTO's hood met the fender—if the tape was broken, someone might have tampered with the engine, even placed a bomb there. Or that was what he told his friends and colleagues.

In fact, he hated the change. He was mostly bored. Nor did the capitol job keep him out of controversy. When the governor named the wealthy rancher Freeman Burke, Sr., to the state Racing Commission in 1977, Page wrote several stories on Burke's unsavory past and how he had been the biggest contributor to the governor's campaign. The Legislature refused to approve Burke for the board that regulated, among other things, dog racing.

I would learn later that "Front Page" was quietly working on a project that would get him back as the *Gazette*'s top investigative reporter. The week before, he had run into a colleague at a grocery store. He told her he was wrapping up "the story that will bring it all together, blow the lid off this town, finally." Page was not given to bragging or superlatives. I would also learn that he was keeping a sheaf of sensitive material, too hot to keep in his desk at the capitol bureau or in the *Gazette* newsroom, much less unattended in his apartment. He moved it around, to hiding places only he knew.

He was on his way to meet a source at the Clarendon House Hotel in Midtown Phoenix, a couple of blocks north of Park Central shopping center. Buzz Page didn't know what to make of Mark Reid. He was cautious. Reid was an enforcer for his old nemesis, Ned Warren. Page's stories helped put Warren in prison on multiple counts of land fraud and bribery. This after years of well-documented crimes and foot-dragging by the County Attorney. Another red flag was that Reid hung out at the dog tracks. Page was convinced that pressure and threats from RaceCo had forced his bosses to send him to the Siberia of the capitol bureau.

On the other hand, Reid promised Page a piece of information that was critical to his big story. If he never talked to riffraff, he wouldn't have half as many sources.

Their relationship went back two weeks, when a source of Page's at the courts connected him with Reid. They met at The Islands, a bar on Seventh Street in Uptown. Reid said he had evidence that would connect organized crime and RaceCo to prominent local leaders: Congressman Sam Steiger, Senator Barry Goldwater, and Harry Rosenzweig, a long-time Republican boss and businessman. Page was skeptical. Steiger had been a good source on his land-fraud stories. Goldwater had always been friendly.

But his gut told him to see what Reid had to say. That meeting provided little. Reid said he needed time. He would contact the reporter when a man from Los Angeles visited. The mystery man had the details Reid had dangled. More than that, Reid seemed clued in when Page asked vague questions about his current story. Not enough to show his hand, but to elicit more information from Reid than the reporter gave away. The strand seemed promising.

The call came that morning. "Meet me at the Clarendon."

Page probably avoided the straight shot north. That held too many bad memories. Not long before, his girlfriend Cindy had been killed by a train at the railroad crossing west of the six-points of Grand Avenue, Nineteenth Avenue, and McDowell Road. Friends said he stayed away from that intersection as if it were radioactive. They didn't know how he continued to work, he was so grief stricken over her death.

Instead, he went east to downtown, ran a quick errand, and then, back in the car, drove north on Third Avenue. It was a little more than a mile and a half to the Clarendon, through the old residential neighborhoods that were declining—at some point the Papago Freeway was coming through. Midtown, with its new high-rises along Central Avenue and busy Park Central mall, was vibrant, the place to be. Sometimes Page went to the Playboy Club, drank bourbon on the rocks and looked out at the lights of the city. More often, he had lunch at the Phoenix Press Club. Unless it was necessary to meet a source, he tended to stay away from the nearby bars where the mobsters and lawyers drank.

Around 11:30 a.m., Page swung the GTO into the second line of spaces behind the hotel and parked. It was an unshaded surface lot like most of those in Phoenix, no tree to keep the car cool as with his capitol parking spot, but nothing could be done. The asphalt lagoon was empty of people and only about one-third full of cars. No sign of Reid. The lunch crowd had yet to arrive.

Reid wasn't inside, either.

Page waited inside the lobby for fifteen minutes and then heard his name being called from the front desk. He picked up the white courtesy phone and heard Mark Reid's voice.

"The meeting's off for today," Reid said. "The guy from LA chickened out. Maybe I can talk him into it later."

"Well, thanks for calling at least. Let me know if he changes his mind."

Page put the phone down and walked back out into the heat.

There was time to have lunch at the Press Club. He slid into the GTO, started the car, and backed out. The car rolled fifteen feet in reverse when the explosion came. It ripped upward, slightly ahead of the driver's seat, blowing out the glass of the driver's side window.

The sharp sound could be heard a mile away. The explosion shattered all the windows on the Clarendon that faced the parking lot. Hubcaps and other auto parts were strewn across the asphalt, while a blue haze hung over the area. Witnesses recalled the blood, so much blood, a man calling, "Help me, help me!" and a hunk of bloodied flesh the size of a baseball lying twenty feet from the car.

Within ten minutes, fire trucks arrived, then an ambulance. Page was still conscious as they pulled him out and carefully placed him on a stretcher. His body below the waist was a mangle of burns and smashed bones in a soup of blood. His left arm was barely attached to his shoulder. His face was gray with ash and shock. His eyes were wide and unfocused. The EMTs and firefighters applied large trauma dressings and tried to stanch the bleeding.

St. Joseph's Hospital was less than a half-mile away. As they laid him flat, trying to keep his limbs together, he screamed in pain. But words came, too, through clenched teeth. He fought to get every syllable out.

"They finally got me," he gasped. Then louder: "Reid, Mafia, RaceCo! Find Mark Reid…"

Then he passed out. But even unconscious, he twitched and moaned.

Later, a veteran Phoenix detective would say he had never seen a human being who suffered so much.

They finally got me. Reid, Mafia, RaceCo! Find Mark Reid.

Those were the last words he spoke.

ABOUT THE AUTHOR

Fourth-generation Arizonan Jon Talton is the author of thirteen novels and one work of history. These include the David Mapstone Mysteries, the Cincinnati Casebooks, and the thriller *Deadline Man*. Talton is a veteran journalist, having worked in San Diego, Denver, Cincinnati, Charlotte, and now as a columnist for the *Seattle Times*. He also writes the Phoenix-centric blog Rogue Columnist. www.jontalton.com